Murder in an Irish Cottage

CARLENE O'CONNOR

KENSINGTON
PUBLISHING CORP.

www.kensingtonbooks.com

KENSINGTON BOOKS are published by

Kensington Publishing Corp.
119 West 40th Street
New York, NY 10018

All Kensington Titles, Imprints, and Distributed Lines are available at special quantity discounts for bulk purchases for sales promotions, premiums, fund-raising, and educational or institutional use. Special book excerpts or customized printings can also be created to fit specific needs. For details, write or phone the office of the Kensington special sales manager: Kensington Publishing Corp119 West 40th Street, New York, NY 10018, attn: Special Sales Department, Phone: 1-800-221-2647.

The K logo is a trademark of Kensington Publishing Corp.

ISBN-13: 978-1-4967-1908-9
ISBN-10: 1-4967-1908-5
First Kensington Hardcover Edition: March 2020
First Kensington Mass Market Edition: February 2021

ISBN-13: 978-1-4967-1911-9 (ebook)
ISBN-10: 1-4967-1911-5 (ebook)

10 9 8 7 6 5 4 3 2 1

Printed in the United States of America

Chapter 1

Ellen Delaney sunk the last spoke into the soft earth, then worked her way around the tent's circumference, tying off the stakes and giving it a good shake, making every effort to see that it would stand whatever curse might befall a lone soul under the solstice moon. It had been some years since she'd gone camping, but she could still pitch a tent. When it was solid she counted off ten paces to the hawthorn tree. At the height of bloom, its gorgeous white flowers were a stark contradiction to the mythology embedded deeply into the gnarled tree, right down to its tangled roots. Just beyond it, popping out of the grass, like an image in 3-D, one could see a distinct ring, which from above would look like a giant O. *A fairy tree and a fairy ring.*

The ring in the grass was made up of wild mushrooms, yet like the tree, the circle was endowed by some—

mostly the older folks in this village—with mythological properties, and it came with dire warnings. It was the domain of fairies. Cunning, playful, and vindictive creatures who could bestow riches with one hand while striking them down with the other. The tales of their mirth and feisty deeds were as long and dark as the Irish night sky.

Nonsense, of course, and it would soon be put to rest. And it wasn't as if anyone was asking for them to be taken down. Live and let live, leave well enough alone. She and her grown daughter had recently moved to Ballysiogdun, and their stone cottage, visible in the distance, was said to be in the middle of a fairy path. Typical that no one deemed to mention it until *after* they'd moved in. It was true that on the other side of the cottage, if one continued in a straight path, one would soon come upon *another* fairy tree, and another fairy ring, placing her cottage squarely in jeopardy. Structures built in the middle of fairy paths did not bode well. And apparently, the fairies wanted it gone.

Rubbish. If the cottage posed such a danger, then why hadn't the councilman ordered it bulldozed before she and her daughter moved in? This was Aiden Cunningham's fight, not theirs. He was a coward, that's why, already bending from the backlash of the villagers. Perhaps *one* villager in particular.

If the villagers wanted to point the finger at someone, it should be each other. With their lies, and cheats, and schemes. Maybe she should start outing their secrets, let them have a go at each other. If there was one thing Ellen Delaney had learned, it was that a woman her age was often completely overlooked. Perhaps a more delicate type would be hurt by this fact, this surreal invisibility.

But it had served Ellen well. She knew so many dirty little secrets, and she wasn't afraid to expose them. If tonight didn't do the trick, she was going to do exactly that.

Sinners were calling for the destruction of her home, not fairies, or shape-shifters, or piseog, one of the many Irish words that referred to the supernatural. Such tales belonged in the pages of a book. Ellen groaned at the thought of the professor's book. Dylan Kelly. He was also behind this. Riling everyone up with the promise of wild tales. Enough. She didn't want to think about them anymore. Ellen Delaney dove into the tent and rifled through her bag for her bottle of Powers whiskey. This nonsense would end tonight. She had made a bet. In her quieter moments, she called it a "Deal with the Devil," but she would see to it that the terms were honored. As she sipped on the whiskey and looked out over the soft green hills, kissed by the lingering sun, the conversation played in her mind, like background music:

"If you're so sure fairies don't exist, spend the night near the fairy ring."

"I will, so."

"Sundown to sunrise."

"Not a bother."

"Alone."

"If I do, what's in it for me?"

They opened the calendar to study the cycles of the moon. The twenty-first of June, the summer solstice. Ellen's daughter was leaving for a conference in Dublin just at the right time. Ellen had no intention of forcing Jane to camp overnight with her; she wasn't built for it. Legally blind, her daughter startled easily. With Jane gone, it was the perfect weekend to do it. She said as much, and the next thing she knew the date was set. Friday evening, sundown. An official agreement between villagers. The contract had been drawn up, witnessed, notarized, and signed.

Streaks of red and orange in the sky promised a remarkable sunset, and soon a full, honey-colored moon would send sweet light shining down on her. Ellen continued to gaze out over the meadow as she sipped her whiskey. Sixty-four years of age and she never failed to be awestruck by the landscape. One didn't have to profess a belief in fairies to cherish the trees, and the rolling green hills, and the cragged rocks. *Preserve away, just don't get carried away!* Stories had their place, and their place was on the lips of seancaíthe—professional storytellers enthralling folks gathered around a roaring turf fire.

Yes, she respected storytellers, with the exception of Eddie Doolan (don't get her started), who could be seen spouting off everywhere she looked, draped in theatrical garb and stuttering around pretty women. He was giving professional storytellers a bad name, had no right to call himself a seanchaí.

Speaking of fools, in the distance a clump of color soon turned out to be her fellow art students, hiding behind their easels. Annabel's evening painting class. She'd forgotten all about it. Was Mary Madigan among them, Annabel's prize student? They would capture the setting sun, and the full moon, and then be gone. She prayed her tent would go unnoticed, relieved that the brown material blended in with the night and no one would think to look for it. She thought of making a fire but didn't want to draw any unnecessary attention to herself.

When the sun finally dipped below the horizon, the art students packed up and disappeared. The moon did not disappoint—a fat orb pulsing with life. So palpable was its glow, Ellen could almost feel a magnetic pull, igniting the first prickle of fear. *Nonsense.*

She crawled into the tent lest her imagination get the best of her. Moments later she opened the flap and peered out at the hawthorn tree. She had to admit, against the amber sky the gnarled branches were ethereal and downright witchy. She took a last gulp of whiskey, noting with some shock the dent she'd put in it, as the nibbles of worry turned into vicious little bites. Would their deal be honored? How could anyone prove she'd actually spent the night? It dawned on her now, how foolish she'd been not to ask. Was she being watched? Once the thought hit, it took root, digging deep into her psyche. Someone, somewhere, was watching. Maybe several someones.

Let them.

There was a slight chill to the air and she snuggled farther into her sleeping bag. Fairies! Those tales were for fools. What time was it? Had she been here an hour or four?

They put a stray on you. If a fairy put a stray on you, you could be standing in your own yard and nothing would look familiar. What felt like days might only be hours. Was this what was happening to her?

Stop it. Stop it right now. Shame on her, a schoolteacher. She knew where she was. She knew who she was. A right fool. All to prove to an even bigger fool that no fairies meant her harm.

She just needed to fall asleep, that was the key to surviving this night. She'd been forbidden to bring her sleeping tablets. *Cheating.* At least the whiskey went un-challenged. She'd gotten the short stick, she saw that now. What was to stop a person from creeping up on her, pretending to be a fairy? She would not be fooled, or frightened. There was no need to jump at the crack of every little twig. She set her head back in her sleeping bag, pulled it up to her face, and closed her eyes. Outside there was a faint whistling of the wind, and her limbs began to relax as she listened to nature's tunes. How sweet. It sounded like flutes.

Flutes! Someone was playing music nearby, trying to make her think it was fairy music.

She shot up, wishing she had brought a weapon. A knife from the kitchen at the least. She pawed her side for her torch. If anyone tried anything, she could strike them with it, and run. She found it, gripped it, then relaxed again once it was securely by her side. The wind was louder now, more of a roar than a whisper. She attempted to soothe herself by imagining cheerful fairies, dancing around the ring. Nothing to fear as long as you stayed out of their way.

The cottage was in their way. Why else had all the poor souls who lived there before her come to such misfortune? Just say it . . .

They died.

She sat bolt upright, for the voice had sounded real, not in her head, but like someone whispering the words directly into her tent. *They died, they died, they died.* A chorus of whispers now. How could that be? How could anyone know what she was thinking and finish her sentence out loud?

She reached for her torch but felt only the soft ground

underneath the tent. It had been right there, right by her side. She was being tricked. Set up. She pawed the ground on both sides, all around the tent. Her torch was gone!

The sound of giggling, like children, filtered into the tent, making her blood run cold. "Who's there?" She sounded terrified, which infuriated her. Another twig snapped. She sat hunched over inside her tent, eyes squeezed shut, livid at the tricks that were being played on her.

Malevolent.

The word came into her mind, and she felt little pin-pricks all over her body. What if this wasn't a simple prank; what if someone meant her real harm?

Run.

A dark shadow fell over the tent, and she squeezed her eyes and scrunched her body up in a ball, and that's when she felt it. The tip of a bony finger touching her face, trac-ing her jawline. Her hands automatically tried to slap it away and met with nothing but air. Her eyes flew open. She saw nothing but the black of night. And yet someone was there. *A creeper creeping.*

Stories she'd heard over the years settled around her neck and squeezed like a pair of old hands. The farmer whose head was severed while trying to pull a fairy tree out of the ground with his tractor; the woman who had the gift of sight, only to have dozens of black beetles crawl out of her eyes the moment she died; cattle that were seemingly healthy one day struck dead in farmers' fields the next. No one spared. Not even children. Sick-ened in their cribs, their souls snatched and switched. She shivered. She was hallucinating. Hearing things, seeing things, feeling things. Her limbs were tingling. Would they shut off that music? She clasped her hands over her ears as colored lights danced in her mind. Something strange was going on. This wasn't worth it. *They died, died, died.* She had better do something before she was next. *Dead.* She scrambled out of the tent, set her sights on her cottage, and ran.

Chapter 2

Summer had officially arrived in Kilbane, County Cork, Ireland, and the interior of Naomi's Bistro captured the moment like a still-life painting. Sports equipment lay dumped in the hallway, runners littered the stairwell, and sunglasses hastily forgotten by customers stared up from tabletops. Once they opened for brekkie, the front door of the bistro would be in constant opening-slamming motion. Siobhán O'Sullivan loved every bit of it except for the occasional grumpy customer, the weeds that turned the back garden into a jungle if they didn't keep up with it, and picking up after her siblings, and when that got old, nagging them to pick up after themselves. Blessed be thy summer days, but summer had a way of making everyone revolt. Alarms were ignored. Showers took longer. Even the rashers seemed to sizzle slower on the grill. Siobhán had just collected a pile of shoes and sunglasses, and was about to drop them in the lost and found bin, when a familiar knock sounded on the door. Three quick raps, a pause, and two more.

Siobhán dumped the gear and was already smiling when she opened the door. Macdara Flannery stood in front of her, his messy brown hair and smiling blue eyes a welcome sight. Her fiancé. Would she ever get used to that thought? They'd been secretly engaged since the spring, a delicious secret between the two of them. The gorgeous engagement ring he'd given her, an emerald set up high surrounded by diamonds forming a Celtic cross, was upstairs locked away in a keepsake box by her bed.

"Dara," she said, leaning in for a quick kiss, "are you here for brekkie?"

It wasn't until he stepped completely in that she saw his forehead was creased and his eyes weren't as smiley as usual. He leaned against the door frame. "I have to go to Ballysiogdun."

Ballysiogdun was a blink-and-you'll-miss-it type of village in rural County Cork. "Whatever for?" She waved him into the dining room. "Tea? Brown bread?"

"Cappuccino," he said. "To go."

"I like your style." She set about making them both one, humming along to the whir of her favorite espresso machine. He was chewing on something and best let him spit it out for himself. She was on her summer break, an entire ten days off from garda duty. She wished she were going on a proper holiday, sunning in Spain, or even a few days in Dublin with Maria, but finances were stretched and a long list of family and bistro obligations dangled in front of her. How she missed the days when summer equaled freedom. When months were rolled out in front of her like a sun-kissed present. As an adult, it was just another season, hopefully with a bit less rain and an uptick in the temperatures. A time to weed the back garden and go for longer runs.

Macdara glanced around. "Where's your brood?"

"Ann and Ciarán are having a lie-in. James and Elise are driving me mental with their on-again off-again romance and I have no idea where he is—"

The sound of heels clacking down the stairs startled them, followed by a flash of long black hair, a waft of perfume, and then the slam of the front door. Gráinne. Another one to keep an eye on. Siobhán looked out the window in time to see her sister wiggle off to Sheila's Hair Salon. She was dressed in a short skirt, tights, heels, and her leather jacket. Was she getting her hair done this early? Did Sheila even wake up this early?

"Hiya," Eoin called out with a wave as he ambled past Siobhán before disappearing into the kitchen. It took a moment for her to clock what was different about him. He hadn't been wearing his Yankee baseball cap; instead he'd replaced it with a hairnet. Her brother was maturing. Seconds later came the smell and sound of rashers on the grill. Eoin had one more year until his Leaving Certificate, and after that hopefully university. For now, he was the main man running the bistro with their employee Bridie during the day, and working on his graphic novels at night. They starred, of all things, a superhero character based on her, frankly, and he'd made her into a redheaded Amazon lifting sheep over her head with one hand, but she wasn't about to complain and stifle his creativity. On the surface, all was well with her brood. If only that meant peace of mind.

Siobhán found she worried even more when things were going well. She didn't want to be a when-was-the-other-shoe-going-to-drop type lass, but with six of them, even if a shoe didn't fall, there was at least always an untied lace to trip over. She was a proactive worrier.

She placed Dara's cappuccino in a takeaway cup and handed it to him. "Brown bread?" She'd already made three batches this morning and was dying to dig in.

"I'm not hungry."

She raised an eyebrow. Rare were the days when Macdara turned down any food let alone her brown bread. Enough stalling, he needed a push. "What's the story?"

"My cousin Jane called. Aunt Ellen is in some kind of trouble."

Siobhán knew that his mother had a sister and Macdara had one grown cousin, but she'd never met either of them. "What kind of trouble?"

"Jane wouldn't say. It's something bad. I could hear the terror in her voice."

"Terror?" Macdara wasn't a man prone to exaggeration unless he had a cold, and then he behaved as if the Four Horsemen of the Apocalypse were riding straight for him.

"She was on the verge of hysteria. Said she didn't trust her local guards. I told her I would be there straight-away." His eyes flicked to her right hand. Zoomed in on her ring finger. Not this again. He loathed that she wasn't wearing her engagement ring. It was way too dear. There was no way she was going to wear it. Not while cleaning. Or jogging. Or working. Or riding her scooter. Or going out to the shops or pubs. Or baking brown bread. Or eating brown bread. Too risky. Each outing an opportunity to lose it. She'd rather die.

"It's safe," she said. "I'll always keep it safe."

"And secret," Macdara said, sounding none too pleased about it.

"We can't torture people with a long engagement. You know how nosy folks are. They'll hound us nonstop."

"Is that the real reason?"

She frowned. He wasn't playing nice. It's not like he had to wear a giant ring effectively announcing that he was off-limits. She was still the newest member of the guards. Before they revealed their engagement, they were going to have to confess their relationship to their superiors. They could even be assigned to different garda stations. He knew all this. Yet he was pouting. "Why are you meeting your cousin in Ballysiogdun?" Deflection was a trick Detective Sergeant Macdara Flannery knew well, but she was banking on him realizing the futility of grilling her any further.

She had never been to the village, only through it, but she'd heard tales. As "small world rules" would have it, a lad who was in her class at Templemore Garda College worked in that village. Danny MacGregor. He said the folks there had their own way of doing things. Was he one of the guards Macdara's cousin didn't trust? If so, she had the wrong end of the stick. Danny was a good man all around, and in training promised to be an excellent guard.

"It seems they moved there a year ago," Macdara said. "I only get the news from my mam."

Siobhán raised an eyebrow. "How old is your cousin?"

"She's in her thirties. But they have always lived to-gether."

Given that she would live with her siblings forever if she could have her way, Siobhán wasn't going to judge. "You didn't know they moved?"

"Aunt Ellen and Mam had a falling out. Last I knew they were living in Waterford."

Waterford was a lovely place to visit. Why couldn't they still be there? "How can I help?"

He relaxed and a soft smile brightened his handsome face. "I was hoping you'd want to come along."

"Really?" The long list of things she had to do scrolled through her mind.

"You are my secret fiancée, aren't you?"

"I am." She mentally crumpled up her to-do list.

"It's time you met more of my family."

"I agree. However . . ." He arched an eyebrow. "It doesn't sound like this is a good time for happy introductions."

He treated her to a sheepish grin. "I'm not good with hysterical women."

There it was. The real reason he wanted her to go. He wanted a buffer between himself and a hysterical woman. Typical. "And you think I am?"

"You have your moments, don't you?"

She poured her cappuccino into another takeaway cup. She could hardly argue with that. She held up her finger. "Let me have a word with Eoin."

"Grab your Wellies," Dara said. "We're going to need them."

Siobhán gazed out the car window, taking in the soft hills glowing underneath the summer sun, dotted with grazing cows, fat sheep, and rocky hedges. She was happy to let Macdara drive. Better he focus on the road than her naked ring finger. Ballysiogdun was a long enough drive, and if she didn't find a way to keep him occupied, she feared he'd try to return to their earlier argument. One cappuccino hardly sufficed as enough fuel for his grudges. Luckily, she had the perfect excuse—she was dying to know more about this mysterious cousin who had summoned him.

Macdara cleared his throat. "Have you told *anyone* about our engagement?"

Her efforts had been in vain. "I whisper it to the stars at night."

"Do you now? I suppose I should count m'self lucky."

"The Little Dipper approves, but the Big One says the jury is still out." She paused, and when he didn't laugh she figured it was too late to stop now. "I guess that isn't any constellation." She laughed so hard it took her a while to realize she was the only one. Nothing. Not even a smile. Why didn't he understand? Once she started wearing the ring it would become everybody's business. They'd never get this time back. A secret just between them. "It's not that I'm not chuffed to bits."

He gripped the steering wheel, and she gripped her seat as he sped up. "You've changed your mind about the ring?"

"Macdara Flannery, I love that ring nearly as much as I love you."

He frowned, and then laughed. *Finally*. It melted her heart just a little. "Then why?"

"Don't you see? We'll be hounded nonstop. 'When is the wedding? Where is the wedding? Why are you waiting so long?'"

"Maybe we shouldn't."

"Shouldn't what?"

"Wait so long."

They had agreed not to set a wedding date. In her

mind, they could be engaged for five years or more. What
was the rush? Things were going well, and it was an un-
spoken rule that you didn't mess with things when they
were going well. She listened to the sound of the tires on
the pavement, the wind whistling through the open window, and imagined she could hear the soft *thwack* of the
windmills churning in the distance. She focused on the
greenery outside. It was calming. "What is your auntie
like?"

"Are you changing the subject?"

She gently shoved his shoulder. "Marrying a man with
big brains, aren't I?"

He shook his head, but she could tell he was going to
leave it for now. "Well. You've met me mother."

"Yes." She had met Nancy Flannery a few times. *An
image of her downturned mouth and disapproving eyes
came to mind.* It was impossible to imagine her being
thrilled with the news. No one was good enough for her
son.

"She's the pleasant one."

"Your *mam* is the pleasant one?" She hadn't meant it
to sound so harsh. When Macdara laughed again she almost committed to marrying him whenever and wherever
he wanted. His laugh always sounded like home. She would
have to be careful around the subject of his mother. Nancy
Flannery was a good woman. She just didn't seem to approve of Siobhán, and it was nearly impossible to have a
conversation with her about anything but Macdara. The
Irish mammy and her golden boy. Like a boomerang, the
subject always came back to him. Given he was her only
son, and Siobhán happened to agree that he was somewhat wonderful, she could hardly blame Nancy Flannery
for wanting only the best for him. Nancy Flannery's dreams

for her son didn't include a much younger woman and her five siblings, struggling to make a go of it. Siobhán had a feeling Nancy also didn't approve of Siobhán becoming a guard. Life was hard enough without the weight of other people's expectations.

"I wonder whose feathers Aunt Ellen has ruffled this time," Macdara said, drumming his fingers on the steering wheel as they sang along to an old Christy Moore CD. "'I stumbled into a fairy ring and jeezuz I couldn't get out. . . .'"

"She's a feather ruffler is she?"

"Aye. More accurately, she's a feather plucker. Her entire life she's rubbed folks the wrong way. As a schoolteacher, it was rumored she was worse than the worst of the nuns." Siobhán shivered as she always did when school and nuns were mentioned in the same sentence. "I have no idea why they've moved to Ballysiogdun. There must be a story there, but they aren't telling it."

"We'll find out soon enough." Siobhán felt a tingle. Stories. Secrets. How she loved them. As long as they weren't hers.

The rest of the ride passed pleasantly as they sang and chatted. Before she knew it, over an hour had flown by. Up ahead a weathered sign on the side of the road welcomed them to Ballysiogdun. Just beyond it the narrow road ended abruptly. A large tree lay across the roadway, blocking their progress. Macdara pulled to the side and parked in a grassy embankment. "Guess we're here."

"Look." Beyond the tree, a crowd of people were standing in the middle of the road. There must have been twenty or more. Voices rang out, and she swore she heard multiple people say something about a fairy ring. Given they'd just listened to Christy Moore crooning about one, Siobhán couldn't help but shake her head at the parallel.

Siobhán was familiar, of course, with fairy paths, and fairy rings, and fairy forts, and fairy trees. Fairies were a part of Irish folklore, and made for rich stories around the fireplace, mythical tales in books, and of course song lyrics. Some of the fairy forts were stunning archaeological sites and protected under Irish law. Most Irish didn't believe in fairies, but a certain amount of respect was due. Why mess with a fairy ring or a fairy fort or a fairy tree? Wisdom said even if a fairy tree was in the middle of good grazing land and it would be easier if it was cut down, it was better to leave well enough alone. Even some roadways had been altered to go around fairy trees rather than take them out. Too many tales abounded of those who went on to disturb them and came into grave misfortunes, including death. Even bringing the branch of a fairy tree inside your home was considered bad luck by some, but she knew other families who always had hawthorn sticks in their home. There was no one-size-fits-all especially when it came to superstitions.

Siobhán exchanged a look with Macdara. "Did you hear them say something about a fairy ring?"

Macdara nodded. "I was afraid of this."

"You were?"

"This is a small village. Some, according to the rumors, believe in . . . the Little People."

"The Little People?" She'd heard all the terms, of course, the caution that fairies did not wish to be called fairies, and one should respectfully refer to them as the Little People, or the Hill People, or the Good People, or the Good Folk. She just never knew Macdara was in that camp. What else didn't she know about the man she was supposed to marry? "Macdara Flannery. Do you believe in fairies?"

"Of course not." He shifted his baby blues away from her.

"Sounds like it to me." She was thrilled to have something to tease him over. Ammunition for the next time she was tasked to lighten one of his moods. The secret was never to push it too far.

"I believe in leaving well enough alone."

As did she. And why shouldn't they honor the tales of yore? People all over the world did all sorts of superstitious things. They avoided walking under ladders, feared black cats, tossed salt over their shoulders. Who's to say it wasn't doing something to balance your luck?

Macdara stepped out of the car, and Siobhán grabbed the sack she'd brought filled with a platter of brown bread and followed suit. In the crowd, she spotted a hefty woman holding up an even bigger sign: BULLDOZE THE COTTAGE.

"We're just going to leave the car here?"

Macdara glanced at the tree in the road. "Would you prefer I drive into the meadow?" The meadow stretched forever and looked as if it held many hills, and dips, and rocks, and patches of mud.

"Is there another road?"

"The directions are to follow this road a little farther to the cottage. We'll have to hoof it."

"It must have rained hard last night." The meadow glistened and Siobhán could smell the peat and imagine how soft the ground would be beneath their feet. The sun was out now, and just as Siobhán had the thought, she turned and saw it; just behind the largest hill arched a magnificent rainbow. The colors were so bright and clear, it didn't look real. "Dara, look." She pointed. It was such a gorgeous sight in front of her, the craggy hedges, the rolling hills, yellow wildflowers mixed with heather sprouting on the roadside, and the entire postcard-perfect scene topped off with the show-stopping rainbow. A much warmer welcome than the dilapidated wooden sign. She was suddenly sorry she had dismissed this village out of hand. From what little she'd seen, Ballysiogdun was gorgeous.

Macdara gave the rainbow an appreciative nod. "I told you to bring your Wellies, didn't I?"

She wiggled her toes in her Wellies, relieved she had listened to him for once. "Are you sure it's alright to park here?" She winced, hoping she didn't sound like a nag. That wasn't the kind of wife she was going to be, was it?

"No car is getting past this tree. By the time a tow truck makes its way out here we'll be long gone." They approached the crowd. One by one the members of the group noticed them and began to stare back.

"Let's find out what's going on," Dara said.

"Maybe they gathered to see the rainbow."

"Something tells me that isn't the case."

Siobhán agreed, but she held on to the positive thought. "Well, how do we find out?"

"Find the man in the center of the crowd," Dara said.

"Or woman," she called as they climbed over the felled tree and pushed farther into the thick of things.

Chapter 3

Up ahead, they spotted him, the man in the center of the mass. He was tall and slim, dressed in a tan suit (ill chosen for a summer day), with slicked-back hair and thick spectacles that kept sliding down his nose. He stammered as he tried to calm the crowd. "I beg of you. Disperse! We will discuss this at the town meeting." Sweat trickled down his generous nose, causing his glasses to slide once more. "Let's handle this with decorum." He scanned the crowd. Nobody else seemed keen on decorum. "Please," he croaked. "There's nothing to see here." He turned to a hefty man beside him, the only other one in the crowd wearing a suit, only his seemed more suited to a funeral than a protest. "Councilman, do you have anything to add?"

The councilman looked startled to be called upon, then

cleared his throat. "As Professor Kelly stated, we'll take this up at the town meeting."

"We want it bulldozed *now*!" It was the hefty woman with the large sign. "Last night was the last straw." In her other hand she held a large staff wrapped in colorful yarn. She pounded it on the ground causing her gray curls to bounce underneath a floppy yellow hat. "How many more people have to die?"

"Nana, please." The plea came from a younger woman to the left of her, rubbing the end of her chestnut braid as if it were her rosary beads, occasionally stopping to pat the head of the wee child clinging onto her leg. The child began to wail.

"Sorry, luv." Nana reached over and patted the small boy on the head. He buried his face into his mother's hip.

"Die?" Siobhán said. "Did you say die?"

"We should burn it to the ground," another voice rang out.

"Those were the strangest lights I've ever seen in me life," another one crowed.

A dainty woman stepped forward. "My students were here before it all began. We were going to paint the sunset. That tree"—she turned and pointed to the one blocking the road—"fell just after we heard the scream. As God is my witness, there wasn't even a breeze." She lifted her delicate chin as if inviting the sun to set her blond bob aglow for an angelic effect.

"The Good People," someone said. "They're furious."

"And that black dog, did you see him?"

Siobhán stepped forward, mesmerized. "A black dog?" The ghost stories of her childhood were often filled with mysterious black dogs leading lost children home.

"Siobhán," Dara said under his breath. He did not want her to get involved.

"I saw a black dog alright. He was the size of a small horse," a man offered. More voices joined the chorus:

"We warned them, and now look!"

"It's the scream I'll never forget."

"Aye, a banshee."

Several heads nodded at that. Siobhán stared, transfixed. "What's the story?" She nudged her way next to the nana with the staff and repeated her question.

"Did you not hear the ruckus last night?" Nana swung her staff to the hill in the distance. There sat a hawthorn tree bursting with white flowers, its gnarled branches stark against the morning sky.

"I'm afraid we've only just arrived."

"The fairies gathered last night under the solstice moon." The woman pointed once more to the hill. "All of us are here because we heard or saw something last night that we cannot explain."

Siobhán drew closer. "What exactly happened?"

Macdara touched her shoulder, making her jump. "Who's a believer now?" he whispered in her ear. She gently shoved him off as people around them began filling in the tale.

"Fairies," someone else said. "Dancing. We heard the music. Flutes. They were hypnotizing us with it."

"The strangest lights I ever saw. They were blue and glowing."

"I saw white lights. And I think I heard the music. Flutes, so many flutes. It was fairy music alright."

"I saw a flickering light. I thought it was a fire."

"It was hard to separate the glowing lights from the light of the moon."

"Then came the terrible, terrible scream, and soon after, the tree fell on its own accord, blocking the road."

All heads snapped to the road. The woman with the colorful staff shuddered. "Never heard anything so grief-stricken in my life. The scream of a banshee." A banshee, Siobhán knew, was a harbinger of death, often depicted as an old hag shrouded in a dark cloak. Were these supposed events what had Macdara's cousin so spooked? "It's that cottage, don't you know," the woman continued. This time she jabbed her staff in the opposite direction. "Built in the middle of a fairy path."

"Whose cottage?" Macdara asked. "The Delaneys'?"

"How did you know?" Nana pounded her staff into the ground and leaned on it like it was a third limb.

"Ellen Delaney is me aunt," Macdara answered.

"Is she now?" the woman said. "I'm Geraldine Madigan, this is my daughter-in-law, Mary, and the wee one is William."

Siobhán smiled at the boy, who peeked out at the mention of his name, his big blue eyes twinkling.

"Have you seen them today?" Macdara asked.

Several glances were exchanged. The councilman stepped up. "I'm Aiden Cunningham. Welcome to Bally-siogdun. I'm sorry you've caught us in the middle of such high drama." He laughed as if it was nothing, then looked around, his face turning grim when no one else joined in. He gestured to the distance. "The cottage is just over the hill." He pointed again. "Down a ways until you see the gate; it's through it, then to the left." He glanced at their feet. "You have your Wellies. Well done."

Siobhán pointed at the hawthorn tree. "Is there a fairy ring there?"

"Indeed," Geraldine Madigan said. "And on the other

side of the cottage you'll find nearly the same, a fairy tree and a fairy ring. The cottage is in the middle." She moved in on Siobhán. "That's why it needs to come down, so."

Aiden Cunningham approached. "Let's not burden our guests with this conversation." It was clear he didn't want them around. Why was that? Perhaps he didn't want them spreading rumors that many of the folks of Ballysiogdun believed in fairies.

"I wouldn't stay long," Geraldine said. "Either of you."

Siobhán turned to Geraldine. "Earlier someone mentioned someone dying."

Geraldine nodded. "Five past inhabitants of the cottage have met with untimely deaths," she said. "It's proof the Good People aren't happy about the structure."

"Five?" Siobhán said. That sounded grim. "Over what period of time?"

"We should go," Macdara said. He tugged gently on Siobhán's sleeve, and they started on their way.

"The first man took his own life. Hung himself in the cottage."

Siobhán stopped and turned back. "Sadly, that happens." She was a firm believer that they all needed to do whatever they could to bring the rates down. Relentless rain and too much alcohol or drugs never helped a person out of a black mood.

"The second man was killed in a motor accident just two weeks after he moved in."

"Another common tragedy." Siobhán didn't want to dwell on this one as her own parents had been killed in an automobile accident several years ago.

"The third died in his chair by the fire. The official word was he died from smoke inhalation."

"Smoke from the fireplace?"

"It seems so." Siobhán turned to Macdara to see if he was as riveted as she was. Instead, he shook his head. "The fourth was stabbed while traveling in Wales one month after moving in."

"And the fifth?" Siobhán had to hear it out now.

"The fifth dropped dead in the doorway. Heart attack it was." Geraldine leaned in. "Something put the heart in her crossways."

"Over what period of time?" Siobhán repeated.

"Over the span of two decades, but that's not the point." Geraldine stepped forward. "Every single person who has rented it up until now has died. Would you want to live in it?"

Geraldine's words were biting. Siobhán had to remind herself that she had stepped into an ongoing drama that had nothing to do with her personally. "No. I surely wouldn't."

"Last night was the last straw," Geraldine continued. "They have to listen to reason now."

"They?" Macdara said. When no one answered, he filled it in for himself. "My aunt and cousin, you mean."

Professor Kelly stepped forward. "The people of this village are suffering." He edged in closer and lowered his voice. "It doesn't matter what you believe," he said to Siobhán. "It's what they believe." His eyes flicked toward the hill. "And that scream last night. I must admit, it was like someone walked over me grave."

"What about the strange lights?" Siobhán asked.

"Siobhán," Macdara said, now pleading with her.

"I didn't see the lights," he said. "It was the scream that woke me up. Maybe by the time I put my coat on and hurried outside the strange lights had disappeared."

Or maybe they were never there at all.

"And until the deed is done those women should see fit to open the front and back doors of the cottage," another added.

A common belief was that if you couldn't remove a building that was in the middle of a fairy path, you should open the front and back doors allowing the fairies to pass freely through the structures. Fairies, it was said, lived alongside humans, when they weren't underground, and they simply asked that the humans stay out of their way. Back in the day you had to be careful where you emptied your pails of milk, lest you throw it out and drench a passing fairy. She turned to Macdara. "Is this why she called you?"

His face seemed to reflect the same concerns. "If it isn't, I'd hate to see what else is going on."

As they trudged across the soft meadow, feeling the eyes of the villagers on their backs, Siobhán was grateful for her Wellies. It was hard to traverse the meadow and balance the sack, but she had no intention of dropping her brown bread. Macdara offered to carry it, but she trusted his sense of balance even less and waved him off with a look that made him laugh. The farther in they walked the softer the ground became, rendering the trusty boots a must-have. Once they were over the hill, the rusty gate as described by the councilman came into view.

It was swaying despite the lack of a breeze, and Siobhán could hear a gentle squeak. Green paint flaked from the gate, and when it yawned open it revealed a narrow dirt path clogged with brambles and briars. Dark clouds swirled in, and the threat of rain hung heavy. Siobhán had a foreboding feeling. The calm before the storm. Her fingertips tingled. *Fairies.*

They stopped just before entering the path, as if once they stepped through, there would be no return. "Have you ever seen a fairy?" she asked Macdara.

"This again?"

"Never hurts to ask twice."

"I beg to differ. You're giving me a pain." He paused. "Have you?"

"No."

"That's sorted then."

"My grandfather had some good stories though."

"The one who taught you to whittle?" Macdara took the first steps onto the path beyond the gate, and Siobhán followed.

"The very same." He'd taught her his hobby because he thought it would help calm her fiery temper. There was something about the never-ending rugged land that made her want to sit down and whittle the days away.

"I grew up with tales of Cucúlin, and Druids," Macdara said, as he ducked to avoid hitting his head on the branches intertwined above. Tales of Druids and kings. Siobhán smiled, imagining a wee Dara transfixed by it all. "That's as mystical as I get."

Out here Siobhán could almost feel the thin veil that was supposed to separate the human world from the fairy world, and she could not help but wonder, what if? Her grandfather had regaled her with tales of the Tuatha Dé Danann. A supernatural race in Irish mythology, they dwelled in the Otherworld but interacted with humans. The Tuatha Dé eventually became the Aos sí, more commonly referred to as fairies. Siobhán used to lose herself for hours in those captivating tales. She edged closer to

Macdara, chiding herself for the twinges of fear. Her brother Eoin would love it here—so much material for his graphic novels.

The path came to an end, opening up on a stone cottage in the valley to the left and a weathered farmhouse over the hill to the right. They were the only two structures as far as the eye could see.

"The branches get thick through here," Macdara said. "Watch out for nettles."

Siobhán was well aware of the awful sting of nettles and was always on the lookout for the pointy green herb. "We could make a soup." Two minutes in boiling water and a handful of other ingredients could transform biting nettles into a nice healing tea or soup. The juice could even be used to cure the sting of a nettle, although it was handier to find a dock plant. Siobhán was starting to feel itchy and hungry in equal measure. She had brown bread in her pack for Jane and Ellen, and lamented that it would be rude to take a bite out of her offerings.

The ground was uneven, challenging to traverse. "I'm starting to see why Geraldine was carrying a big stick," Siobhán said.

"Too bad she wasn't speaking softly," Macdara quipped.

Straight ahead, behind a bush, she caught a flash of red. She squinted. It was a man, crouched down and peering out from behind the leaves. It was his shirt that caught her eye, a bright red flannel. Probably a farmer. Did he live in the house in the distance? If he was going for stealth he should have reconsidered his wardrobe. Seconds later his head popped out, giving her a glimpse of a black hat pulled low, covering his entire brow. He lifted something up to his eyes. Binoculars. Trained on them. A nosy farmer to boot. She waved at him. He dropped the binoculars, then crouched over and ran toward the farmhouse in the distance.

"How odd," Siobhán said.

"What?" Macdara stopped to kick a rock out of his way.

"There was a farmer hiding behind a tree. Peeping at us through binoculars."

Macdara's head popped up, and he followed Siobhán's fingers, but the farmer had disappeared. Beyond the tree, just ahead of them and to the left, a slip of a woman was tapping a cane left and right, making her way toward them. She wore a flowered summer dress, and large sunglasses covered most of her face. Macdara hadn't mentioned that his cousin was blind. She stopped and lifted her head. She had Macdara's messy brown hair, only hers was longer and falling over her shoulders. "Dara?" Her voice wobbled. "Is that you?"

"It's me, luv. How did you know?"

She attempted a smile, but her lips shook as if it was an impossible task. "You wear the same cologne."

"If it's not broke, don't fix it," Siobhán blurted out. She loved Macdara's cologne. *Intoxicating.*

"You must be Siobhán."

"Yes, hello, so lovely to meet you."

"There's no time for introductions," Jane said, her voice wobbling. "Something horrible has happened." She swung her cane until the tip pointed at the cottage.

Their heads swiveled to the stone building with flaking white paint. Moss crawled up the sides, and the red front door yawned open. A large window to the left of the door was shattered. A suitcase lay discarded next to the door. Colorful flowers spilled onto the front yard and manicured paths could be seen on either side leading to a back garden.

"Were you robbed?" Macdara's voice was in protector mode, a tone Siobhán knew well.

Jane was already shaking her head. "Mam," she said, pointing at the cottage. "I can't." She hung her head. "Mam is in there. She's . . . dead."

Siobhán nearly dropped her sack with the platter of brown bread. She didn't quite know what emergency she was expecting. Illness. Money trouble. Family arguments. Then when entering the town, she assumed the uproar was about the cottage. Why hadn't Jane told Macdara straightaway that her mother had passed? She glanced again at the broken windows. Had someone broken in? Had the guards been called? This wasn't her cousin, so she squeezed the platter of brown bread as tightly as she could as if that might keep her piehole from moving.

Macdara moved in and gently laid his hands on Jane's elbows. "Tell us everything."

"I was in Dublin all weekend for an herbal conference. I returned to find the door open, the window smashed, and Mam . . ." She broke down again. "She's lying on the bed. I couldn't feel a pulse or a breath. So cold. So still." Jane shook her head as if trying to rid herself of her thoughts. "I don't understand what happened. I don't understand."

"Did you call the guards?"

"Yes. I called nine-nine-nine. Then I called you. I've been waiting." In the smaller villages emergency services could be spotty, but this was taking it a bit too far. Siobhán wondered if the felled tree had rerouted them. "I told them she had passed, but I didn't mention the open door or busted window. Perhaps my mother's death isn't an emergency to them."

"Stay here," Macdara added. Jane nodded.

Macdara gave a nod to Siobhán. "Stay behind me. Understand?"

This was no time to quibble. She nodded back. "There's a platter of brown bread here," Siobhán said, setting it down next to the rock where Jane stood. "You probably need to force a little something into you, but believe me, you don't want to faint."

"Hurry," Jane said.

Macdara approached the open door sideways, and Siobhán took up formation behind him. "Garda Flannery," Macdara shouted into the cottage in a booming voice. "If someone is in there, get on the ground and put your hands on top of your head." It was highly unlikely someone was hiding inside, but given the obvious disturbance it was smart protocol.

They waited. Not a sound from the old stone cottage. "We should have booties and gloves," Siobhán said.

"I know," Macdara said. "They'll have to take our footwear impressions if it turns out to be a crime scene. Don't touch a thing." She nodded. Macdara took a step inside. The old floorboards creaked. Once, then twice. To their right was a plain but tidy kitchen, wiped clean of everything but a kettle on the cooker and a stack of papers on the counter. To the left a sagging green sofa and water-marked coffee table were arranged near a wood-burning stove. An oval wool rug lay over the cement floor. Nothing was out of place except for the open door and shards of glass beneath the busted window. There was a slight layer of dust and dirt on the floors, but given the location of the cottage, and the age of the home, it was probably rare that the floors were pristine.

Macdara pointed to the narrow hall leading to the bedrooms and put his finger up to his mouth. A few steps in, a door to a bedroom on the left was flung open. A cross dominated the space on the wall above the bed. Lying beneath it was an older woman. She could have been sleeping except she was situated on top of the covers. The most startling bit was her outfit. She was wearing a fancy red dress, red heels, a white hat, and gloves. Her hands rested on top of her stomach, the right resting atop the left. The image of a woman dying peacefully in her sleep ended there. Her eyes were open and scarred by broken blood vessels. A white feather clung to her cheek, and an inordinate amount of foam pooled at the corner of her bruised mouth. The poor woman was indeed dead, but her passing had been anything but peaceful.

Chapter 4

"Is it your auntie?" Siobhán asked quietly as they stared at the body. She instinctively crossed herself.

"'Tis." Dara hung his head for a moment. He placed his fingers on the lifeless woman's wrist, then neck. It was obvious she was dead, but Siobhán knew he had to check.

Siobhán maneuvered to the other side of the bed. There on the floor was a pillow and an overturned teacup. She motioned for Macdara to join her. They stared down at the items. Neither the foam at her mouth, nor the bruising, was normal for natural death. "Poisoned?" Siobhán's voice was barely a whisper.

"And then smothered," Macdara replied, glancing at the feather clinging to his aunt's cheek. "The poison must not have worked; it simply subdued her."

The killer had finished the job with the pillow. "Why didn't the killer take the teacup? Or return the pillow to the bed?"

Macdara took a moment to mull over her question. "Perhaps the killer thought no one would bother to investigate thoroughly."

"Or they were interrupted and had to flee." Siobhán supposed that in this village anything was possible, even the improbable. She noted the one window in the room looked directly onto the bed. Pale curtains stretched open. She pointed. "Wouldn't she have closed them?"

Macdara turned his back on the body and studied the window. "I dunno. Isn't that the point of living out in the middle of nowhere? There's not supposed to be anyone peeking in windows. Let alone . . ." He dropped the thought.

Was he browned off with her? She'd gone straight into investigative mode, had forgotten that this was his auntie. "I'm so sorry." It was a strange feeling having to comfort him at a crime scene. "Do you think one of the townspeople did this because of . . . the Little People?"

"I have no idea what to think."

Of course he didn't, but posting the question was a standard back-and-forth for guards. He was too close to the victim to participate. She reached him and laid her hand on his arm. He moved away. "Why don't you wait outside?" she said.

"We both need to wait outside." He turned to her. "How am I going to tell my mam?"

His mam. Someone else she'd forgotten. It was necessary when investigating not to allow your emotions to in-

terfere. But this wouldn't be their case. He needed his fiancée right now, not a guard. "I'm so sorry, Dara."

He removed his mobile phone, held it up, and snapped
pictures of the scene. This would probably be their only
chance. Siobhán grabbed her mobile and did the same.
Just like the front room, the bedroom was neat. There was
a standing wardrobe in the corner and the door was
thrown open. A suitcase was visible on the bottom shelf.
They would have to exit and call the guards, but they'd
already intruded, so they might as well take as many photos as they could. As Siobhán headed near the door, she
glanced back and spotted something glittering from
under the bed. "Dara," she said. "Look."

Macdara came to her side and stared at the gold object
resting underneath the bed. "What is that?"

"It looks like . . . a gold coin. . . ."

He tilted his head. "If you say anything about a lep-
rechaun missing his pot the wedding is off."

"Wasn't even thinking it." Although she was now.
First the rainbow, now this . . . all this talk of fairies was
clouding her head.

He sighed. "I wish we could touch it."

"Me too." She was dying to see what it was.

"Every second we're in here we're contaminating the
scene."

"Let's go."

Back in the hall they briefly explored the remainder of
the cottage. A second bedroom, presumably Jane's, sat directly across from Ellen's. The inside was sparse, a neatly
made twin bed, side tables without debris, and a
wardrobe. Like Ellen's there were no decorations. Siobhán thought the room looked lonely, but nothing seemed

amiss. A bathroom was to the right and a back door led out to the garden. Near it, Wellies were propped up in a row, and a basket held multiple gardening gloves. The washroom was tidy, the shower curtain closed. But a single towel was draped lazily over the tub. Siobhán snapped a photo, as it seemed out of kilter. She turned her gaze across the hall and back to the woman on the bed. "She's been arranged." Posed. There was something sinister in the peaceful way they'd folded her hands after what they'd done to her. This village contained something more evil than fairies. *Someone.* "Someone arranged the body, and yet they left the pillow and teacup on the floor." Her thoughts circled back to the open door and the broken window. It was a mystery of this profession that the same clues could either point to a killer who was careless, or cunning. *Like a fairy. Stop it, Siobhán. Get a grip.* "Do you think she had a date?"

"A date?" Macdara sounded horrified.

Why else would she be wearing a red dress on a Friday evening? "She's a single woman, isn't she?"

"She was my auntie."

He was definitely too close to the victim to investigate this case. "We should check if she's been on any Internet dating sites."

"You're joking me."

"You're personally involved. It's already affecting you."

"Look around. Does it look like they have Internet? There isn't even telly."

"But there is a laptop." Siobhán pointed to a vanity dresser she'd just now noticed, squeezed next to the wardrobe. On it sat a silver laptop.

Macdara stared at it. "It's probably Jane's." He started for it.

"You can't." She blocked him with her arm. They knew the correct thing to do was get out of the cottage immediately. But it was torture not to start touching things. "The guards will want to take a look at it."

"For dating sites?" The outrage was still in his voice.

"Yes, and e-mails, and sites she visited, or chat rooms, or anything else they can learn." She scanned the room once more. "There should be a handbag and mobile phone somewhere around here." The guards would have to search for them. It was maddening to have their hands tied.

"Chat rooms?" Macdara looked as if he'd choked on his tongue. "I've never heard of her doing any of those things in me life."

"You said you hadn't seen your auntie in years."

His mouth set in a hard line. "I thought we'd have time," he said softly. "Had I known . . ."

"Of course." They quickly exited and stood just outside the front door, examining the glass. Shattered bits were on either side of the window. Investigators would have to determine if it was smashed from the outside or within. Jane sat on the rock in front of them, her head bowed. Siobhán lowered her voice to a whisper as Macdara stared at his mobile.

"What of your aunt's husband? Did he pass?"

"Yes, ages ago." He glanced at Jane, pain stamped on his face. "It's not going to be our case."

"I know."

The local guards would probably work in conjunction with Cork City, even Dublin. They would assign a detective sergeant and send their forensic team. A village this small wouldn't be left to handle a murder probe on their own. Siobhán and Macdara would be expected to step back. She turned to Macdara and kept her voice low. "Is that going to stop us?" she asked.

"If you believe that," Macdara answered, "you might as well believe in fairies."

Chapter 5

Jane Delaney hadn't touched the brown bread. Some people welcomed food in times of stress, others shunned it. Starving one's grief only led to more trouble, but Jane was in the early stages of shock and it wasn't Siobhán's place to lecture or mother her. It was bad enough they had yet to make it known that the clues pointed to murder. Siobhán wanted to say it straightaway but she was taking her cues off Macdara, who was currently staring at the road in the distance as if trying to summon the guards with his mind. "Are they walking from Cork City?" He jabbed at his mobile phone. "I can't get a signal."

Jane pointed to the road. "Try standing farther out, luv. The village cretins cut off our access."

"Who cut off your access?" Uh-oh. Macdara was revved up and ready to race. Siobhán sort of wanted to watch, but not from the passenger seat.

"The village," Jane replied, spitting out the word. "Which always means the councilman. Aiden Cunningham."

"We met him on our way in," Siobhán said.

"He failed to mention he cut off your access," Macdara seethed.

Jane's tone softened as if sensing it may not have been the best idea to get her cousin worked up. "That was Mam's theory. When we first moved in, we could get reception near the cottage. After we refused to leave, we couldn't. I can't prove it was on purpose." She threw open her arms. "We are out in the middle of nowhere."

Macdara held his phone higher, searching for a signal. "But you had access, and then Aiden Cunningham threatened to remove it, and then you didn't have access?"

"We had access and then we didn't, and that's when Mam accused the village of messing with us."

That's when Mam accused . . . Siobhán made a mental note that Jane was leaving room for the possibility that her mother had lied, but she didn't interrupt Macdara to throw this in. Never touch a hot cooker, her mam always said, and Macdara was boiling.

"When was this?" he demanded.

"A fortnight ago. Shortly after the village held one of their town meetings. After which several of the villagers stormed over here to demand we leave, which, as you can see, we refused." Her face took on a pained look, as if she had just now realized the price they'd paid for their mistake.

"I can't imagine Aunt Ellen taking that well," Macdara said.

Jane laughed. "You're correct. She said she'd have it

sorted this weekend. She was confident she'd reached some kind of a deal."

Siobhán's ears perked up. "What kind of a deal?"

"I dunno. She wouldn't tell me." Jane chewed on her bottom lip. "Doesn't matter now. They got their wish."

"Who showed up that day and demanded you leave?" Siobhán knelt next to Jane.

Jane held her hands up near Siobhán's face. "May I?"

"Of course." Jane's hand quickly traveled over Siobhán's face, and then stroked her hair.

"I hear it's the color of fire."

"Maybe when the sun hits it," Siobhán said. "Otherwise it's auburn." The exact color of Siobhán's hair was often debated, and it did change with the sun. She referred to it as auburn, but most folks settled on red.

"I've heard so much about you," Jane said, dropping her hand. "I'm sorry we have to meet at such a terrible, terrible time."

"So am I, pet. You were telling me about the people who showed up and demanded you leave?"

Jane nodded. "Geraldine Madigan was leading that bandwagon, but plenty of others hitched their horses to it." She tapped her lip with her index finger. "I'm trying to remember all the voices. There was Geraldine, and Aiden Cunningham, and Professor Kelly. I heard children too; could have been Geraldine's grandchildren."

"What about this Aiden Cunningham?" Macdara asked.

"That blubbering councilman? I told Mam he was going to side with whoever made his life the most miserable."

Or perhaps whoever sweetened the pot.

Macdara began to pace, perfecting the look of a man

who wanted to punch another man in the face. "Why didn't you call me earlier?"

"Are you joking me? Mam was having the time of her life. She loved a good fight."

"There is a laptop in her room," Siobhán said. "But we didn't see a handbag or mobile phone."

"You didn't?"

"Not out in the open."

"Do you think it was a robbery?" Jane's fists clenched.

"It's quite possible," Siobhán answered honestly. It seemed ludicrous, to rob this cottage, but desperate people didn't always think straight.

"Does that mean—did someone hurt her?"

"We don't know, luv," Siobhán said. "But it's an open question."

"Don't sugarcoat it. I'm blind, not stupid." Jane stood abruptly, nearly knocking a startled Siobhán over. Siobhán hauled herself to her feet as Jane's hand flew up to her mouth. "I'm sorry. My nerves."

"I understand." And she did. Trauma could turn a person inside out.

"Tell me everything you saw in there," Jane demanded.

It was a fair request. As a sighted person she would have seen everything. Jane deserved equal access. "I will describe every detail, I promise. First, may I ask a few questions while they're fresh in my mind?"

"Go on then."

"Her laptop. Did she use it often?" Why would a robber take the handbag and phone and not the laptop?

Jane nodded. "She was one for research."

"Didn't you say they cut off your Internet access?"

"She'd take her laptop to Molly's in town."

"Molly's?"

"It's a wee Internet café. The village is mad over it, as if it rivals us with Cork City, or Limerick, or Dublin. We aren't even Killarney." She wrapped her arms in a self-hug, nearly breaking every vessel in Siobhán's heart. "We never should have stayed."

Siobhán was dying to have a thorough look at that laptop. She only used computers for work e-mails, work-related searches, and typing up mindless reports. She loathed being on it for too long. Her eyes always glossed over, and if she ever got into online shopping or social madness, she was afraid of the money and brain cells she would expend. It wasn't advisable to give criminals too much information about your private life, and as for shopping, best cut yourself off from temptation. "What was she researching?"

"Fairies, I assume," Jane said. "Fairy forts, and fairy rings, and fairy paths. She was the type to equate knowledge with power."

Had she found something to help in that fight? Had it led to her demise? Siobhán gazed out in the distance. "The fairy ring straight ahead." Siobhán had to stop herself from pointing. "Whose property is it on?"

"Joe and Mary Madigan live in the farmhouse in front of us. I believe his mother Geraldine owns the property behind us."

"When we came in, the villagers were on about strange lights, and music last night and . . . the wail of a banshee."

"I wasn't here," Jane said. "But it doesn't surprise me. They've been wanting to get rid of this cottage for so long. They did this."

"Threats, cutting off your access to the village power. That's clearly against the law." Macdara had returned to their orbit, and he was taking names.

"This village plays by their own rules." Jane gripped her cane as if guarding herself from them. "I've waited long enough. Tell me everything you saw." She took a deep breath and grabbed Siobhán's hand as if bracing herself.

Macdara cleared his throat. "From a glance, we're worried she may have met with foul play."

"Because of the window?" Siobhán forgot that Jane was holding her hand until she squeezed it. Hard. It was a good thing she wasn't wearing her engagement ring. She counted to ten before pulling her hand away. "What else?"

When Macdara didn't speak up, Siobhán did. "We saw foam coming out of her mouth, an overturned teacup and pillow on the floor—"

"Foam?" Jane said.

"It's possibly an indicator of poisoning."

"No. No."

"There was bruising near her mouth and a white feather—possibly from a pillow—sticking to her cheek."

Macdara winced but Jane remained stoic. Jane looked up. The sun was back out and glinting off her glasses. "Are you suggesting her tea was poisoned?"

"I'm only reciting the facts."

"She made her own herbal tea. From our back garden."

"Is there any way your mother may have ingested the toxin on purpose?"

"No! Of course not."

Siobhán didn't think so but she had to rule out the possibilities. "The white feather suggests—"

"Siobhán." Macdara's tone was harsh. "Let's leave the conclusions to the state pathologist, shall we?"

"It suggests she was smothered with a pillow," Jane said. "Suffocated."

"Yes." Siobhán turned to Macdara. "I know this is hard. I'm sorry." He bowed his head.

"Go on," Jane said. "Please."

"She was wearing a red dress, and red heels, along with a white hat and white gloves."

Jane tipped her head as if listening to something in the distance. "Did the killer dress her?"

Siobhán started. She hadn't thought of that. "I don't know. We have reason to believe someone posed her. . . . Her hands were folded across her chest."

Jane cried out. "Who would do such a thing?"

"It's difficult to say if someone else dressed her. Perhaps your mother was going somewhere."

"Behind my back." It was an odd comment. Siobhán would have to keep in mind that Jane was also a suspect; she doubted Macdara would be able to do the same. "Someone in town did this. To prove their nasty point."

"Does Aunt Ellen collect coins?" Macdara asked.

Jane laughed. "Mam? A collector? No." She stopped. "Why?"

"We couldn't touch it, but there was something gold underneath the bed," Siobhán said. "It looked like a gold coin."

"That's odd. . . . You didn't pick it up?"

"We can't touch anything," Siobhán said. "It doesn't ring any bells?"

Jane let out a half laugh. "Do you think we'd be living

here if we had even one gold coin?" She sounded bitter. "I have no idea what it is."

"It will be thoroughly investigated," Macdara said.

"Is there any way you could go in and retrieve it now? I can let you know if I hear the guards approaching."

"No," Siobhán said, gently but firmly. "We've already intruded on the crime scene once. We won't do it again."

"Why is it you ask?" Macdara said.

"If there's a gold coin in the cottage I don't want them to steal it."

"We're the Guardians of the Peace," Siobhán said. "We take our oaths seriously. They won't steal it." She wasn't sure of it all. Not all guards were honest, they were human, but hopefully it sounded reassuring.

"We'll make sure of it," Macdara added.

Jane took a few steps away from the cottage. "It's my fault. I shouldn't have left her all alone."

A soft breeze came through, bringing with it the scent of heather and damp earth. What a mercurial weather display. Mother Nature was the boss here, and she wanted you to know it. Jane's head suddenly snapped up. "What about Mam's truck?"

Truck? There wasn't a vehicle in sight. Macdara and Siobhán simultaneously swiveled their heads. "Where would it be?" Macdara prodded.

"Parked anywhere near the cottage."

"There's nothing."

"It's a red pickup."

"There's no truck, luv," Siobhán said. She studied the terrain. "There's no driveway or road either."

"Mam usually drove straight through the meadow."

Macdara walked a few paces and stared at the ground. Siobhán followed. There was a definite path in the grass where tires had churned up grass and dirt. "The grass is flat here, and fresh dirt has been kicked up. I'd say someone drove through here recently."

"The killer took off in her truck then," Jane said.

Siobhán vowed to never forget her trusty notebook again as she pondered the missing truck. Macdara grabbed his mobile.

Of course, what an eejit. Siobhán could take notes on her mobile phone. She pulled it out, pulled up the Notes app, and began to tap her observations out as fast as she could. *Welcome to the present day, O'Sullivan.* Part of her hated it.

"What's the number plate?" Macdara asked.

"I have no idea," Jane said. "I'm sorry. But everyone here knows Mam's beat-up red lorry."

Macdara nodded. "I'm calling the guards back. I'll let them know to be on the lookout for it." He headed away to place the call.

"This is my fault," Jane said. "I left her with these cretins."

"Don't think like that. If you had stayed with her, you may have come to the same fate."

"Foam at her mouth," Jane said. "An overturned teacup, and a gold coin."

"Did she take her tea in the bedroom?" Siobhán asked.

"Before bed. Yes. Once in a while." Jane began to pace. "If the tea was poisoned, the killer had to be someone she knew and trusted."

"I was thinking the same," Siobhán said.

"But if she had company—wouldn't there be two teacups?"

"It's all conjecture," Siobhán said softly. "The state

pathologist will have to make a conclusive determination about poison, and the cause of death."

"That sounds like a lot of waiting."

"Where were you this weekend?" Siobhán asked, purposefully keeping her voice free of accusation.

"Why, Siobhán O'Sullivan," Jane Delaney said. "Are you asking for my alibi?"

Chapter 6

"I am asking for your alibi," Siobhán answered honestly. "Where were you last night?"

"I was at an herbalist conference in Dublin. I'm studying to be an apothecary."

She would know all about poisonous herbs. That explained the lush garden out back. Ellen Delaney could have poisoned herself, as improbable as that sounded, but she couldn't have smothered herself, posed herself, or driven off in her truck.

"Do you have a program from the conference?" Siobhán asked.

"A program? Do you think I killed my own mother?" Her tone was one of defiance.

Careful. She's family. "Of course not," Macdara said, cutting Siobhán off with his return. He shot her a disapproving look.

"It's a good idea to get your alibi on record." She would not be deterred, not even by Dara. "The name and location of your conference, the hotel where you stayed. Your train ticket. The car you took from the station back to the cottage. The sooner we have it all collected the better."

"We?" Macdara asked.

"The guards," Siobhán corrected.

Jane lifted her chin. "Of course." She made no move toward her suitcase, which was still sitting by the door. Siobhán thought of the suitcase in the wardrobe. She mentioned it to Jane. "It's normally tucked away on the top shelf," Jane said. "Mam always said: a place for everything and everything in its place."

"Could she have been planning a trip of her own?" That would explain the outfit and the suitcase.

"If she was, she was keeping it from me." There it was again, a jealous tone.

"It's not our case," Macdara said. "I'm sure the local guards are capable of handling this."

"You are?" Siobhán said. That didn't sound like Macdara and minutes earlier he had stated the exact opposite.

"I wish I had your confidence," Jane said. "You watch. They're going to blame it on the fairies."

"The guards won't pay attention to such nonsense." Macdara sounded as if he was trying to convince himself.

"You're a fool if you think that. The councilman will cave to the villagers. We're outsiders." The last word was spoken with venom.

"A friend of mine from Templemore is a new guard here," Siobhán said. "Danny MacGregor. He will do everything by the book."

Jane raised an eyebrow. "Garda MacGregor. The handsome one." She lifted her face and smiled. "He has excellent cheekbones."

Siobhán was distracted for a moment by the thought of Jane fondling her ex-classmate's cheekbones. She was right though. Danny MacGregor was a looker.

"Handsome, is he?" Macdara said with a pointed look to Siobhán.

"The green-eyed monster courts me cousin," Jane said with an exaggerated lilt. She turned to Siobhán, a smirk on her face. "Jealousy can be good for knocking boots."

"One of the protesters said that multiple residents of this cottage had died?" Siobhán was desperate to change the subject; her intimate life with Macdara was no business of his cousin.

If Jane heard the question she didn't address it. "I need to walk. I have all this useless energy." She turned her head toward them. "You mentioned you saw the fairy tree on the hill?"

"We did," Siobhán said. "It's quite striking."

"Shall I show you the other fairy tree and fairy ring?"

Macdara's eyes flicked toward the road. "I told the guards I'd meet them here."

"I'd love to see it," Siobhán said. Perhaps they could walk in the direction where the Peeping-Tom-of-a-Farmer had crouched with his binoculars. Siobhán wrestled with whether or not to bring it up. Perhaps there had been enough upsets for the day. She would make sure and tell the guards, and Macdara could break it to Jane another time. The peeper could be the killer and there was no point frightening Jane any more than she already was.

Jane started them off at a fast clip, her cane moving expertly side to side. "Follow me." Jane knew the path well, every dip of the terrain. She seamlessly maneuvered around the trickiest spots, where rocks took over the path and small holes waited to trip an unsuspecting foot. It was apparent she'd walked it many times. "My mother is the sixth," Jane said out of nowhere.

"The sixth?"

"Resident of the cottage to die while living here."

Just like the protesters they met in the road had mentioned. "When was the last death?"

"From my understanding, the cottage has stood empty for two years. The villagers have been arguing about whether or not to tear it down. The councilman rented it to Mam."

Him again. "Aiden Cunningham?"

"That would be him." Siobhán would make it a priority to speak with him. She could only imagine how unpopular the decision had been. "Who owns the cottage?"

"Heavens, I'm not sure. I think Mam said something about the real owners abandoning the cottage and fleeing to Spain. I think the village took over ownership after the taxes went unpaid. This will be their final excuse to tear it down."

"Why do you think Aiden Cunningham rented it to you if the village wanted it torn down?"

"Why indeed. Money?"

The usual motive. But Siobhán couldn't imagine the rent was that dear. Was there another reason?

"We're here," Jane said suddenly, stopping and pointing.

Siobhán felt a tingle as she gazed at the hawthorn trees in the distance. There were six of them in close proximity, huddled in a circle, branches stretched out like children holding hands. Fairy rings could be made of wild mushrooms, or stones, or in this case a circle of trees. It was enchanting. She lost herself in it for a moment before turning back to Jane. "Did your mother have any specific quarrels with any of the villagers—other than the cottage?"

Jane stared into the distance. She seemed to be pondering her answer. "We should get back," she said. "I'm not sure we're wanted here."

Siobhán wasn't sure if she meant here as in Ballysiogdun, or here as in close to the fairy trees. She stopped to see if she could feel anything mystical happening, or hear flutes in the wind, or see Little People dancing. But no. She only smelled the heather and the damp earth, and the fresh grass of the meadow.

When Siobhán looked out at the meadow, and hills, and trees, and craggy rocks, she felt a profound connection to this land. The myths added a certain allure, a depth and appreciation to the beauty. Tales handed down by the people who had lived on this land for hundreds of years and would continue to do so. Respect. She understood that. It was to be admired. But a fairy did not kill Ellen Delaney. A human being did. If the fairies wanted revenge on anyone, it should be on the murderer who was trying to throw the blame on them.

By the time they made it back to the cottage, the guards still hadn't arrived and Macdara looked as if he wanted someone's head over it. This did not bode well for a thorough investigation. Macdara seemed eager to leave. He took Jane's elbow. "You'll be returning to Kilbane with us."

For the briefest moment, Jane looked panicked. Her mouth tightened and she gripped her cane tighter. Then she nodded. "Thank you." Jane moved closer to Macdara, and as they began to chat, Siobhán sensed this was her opportunity to slip away. She stretched and ambled in the direction of where she'd seen the farmer with the binoculars. She reached the bushes where he had hidden and found them tucked just under the bush. His hiding place. Which meant he came often to this exact spot to spy on them. She assumed the same position and lifted the binoculars. The front of the cottage was in full view. From here she could even see the side and a portion of the backyard. She maneuvered the binoculars around to the side of the cottage. There wasn't much to see: the side wall of the cottage, grass, and dirt. She was about to swivel to the backyard when she did notice a little thing. One patch of dirt at the base of the wall rose up, forming a little hill, whereas the rest of it was level. Was that important? Had someone tried to bury something there?

She rotated the binoculars to the garden where lush green leaves and colorful flowers filled the lens, then several small signs popped into view: Painted in vibrant blues and greens against old driftwood, they marked the sections of the garden. MINT, BASIL, THYME... She continued along hoping something a little more sinister would come into view. A skull and a crossbones painted in black, perhaps. Or red letters slashing out the word "poison." Instead, she saw a blooming garden with careening butterflies landing on fat green leaves and spreading their colorful wings. It was a little spot of Eden, and it couldn't have been more enchanting if the fairies themselves had blessed it with magic dust.

* * *

When Siobhán returned, she did not mention the binoculars. Jane needed to be considered a suspect until her alibi checked out. The less information Siobhán fed her, the better. Why hadn't she shown them a train or bus ticket to Dublin? Her suitcase was right there, and she had a handbag on her. It would have been easy enough to do. Siobhán would settle for a receipt from a shop in Dublin. Why wasn't Macdara insisting as well? She would mention the binoculars and the mound of dirt alongside the house when she and Macdara were alone.

"I need a cup of tea," Jane said.

Macdara stepped forward. "Of course you do." He turned to Siobhán. "Why don't the two of you go into the village?"

Siobhán would rather be the one waiting for the guards, but this was Macdara's family and she was going to have to let him take the reins. "A mug of tea sounds lovely."

He threw her a grateful look, took her hand, and squeezed it. "I'll fill you in on everything they say and do," Macdara said. "I promise."

Siobhán turned to Jane. "What do you think? Shall we get our legs under us?"

"What day is today?" Jane asked.

"It's Saturday, luv."

Jane nodded. "The farmers' market is today. You can buy one of Geraldine's walking sticks. You'll need one if you're going to be doing any more exploring around here. And I have a feeling you will."

She had a point there. Siobhán adored farmers' markets. And, she suspected, so did the rest of this village. It was the perfect opportunity to get a glimpse of their suspects. By now, the rumor mill would be churning.

"I would normally be working the market at the herbal stand," Jane said with a touch of self-pity. She had yet to cry, and Siobhán, wondering if this would be the trigger, gave her arm a light squeeze. Jane took a deep breath and stood straight. If she had been on the verge of tears, they were gone now. "To the market."

Chapter 7

Downtown Ballysiogdun consisted of a church, a pub, one gift shop, one fruit-and-veg shop, a butcher's, Molly's Café, and a French restaurant. Everything else was meadow and stone and trees. The farmers' market was set up at the end of the main street. It was six rows deep and in full swing when they arrived. Table after table were piled with crates of fruits and vegetables, cheese, milk, eggs, meat, and crafts. The sound of fiddles filtered through the air along with the smells of fresh baked pies. There was nothing lovelier to Siobhán than a good summer farmers' market. If she were going back to Kilbane she'd be buying fresh flowers and food for the week. She felt a squeeze of guilt. She wished her siblings were here to enjoy the market and help her pick out goodies. Siobhán imagined selling her brown bread here; some healthy competition was always good for a marketplace. A large man with stringy brown hair and draped in a tattered cloak weaved his way through the crowds. Truth be told he looked and smelled like he needed a good wash. "C'm'ere to me," he called as they passed. "Do you want to hear a tale of yore?"

"We do not," Jane said as she clicked past with her cane.

"A seanchaí?" Siobhán had to run to keep up with Jane.

"He wishes," Jane shot back.

Behind them, the storyteller began to mumble to himself, then switched to humming a children's lullaby.

It made Siobhán smile. "He seems like a character."

"Eddie?" Jane said. "He's a nuisance. Blew into town recently. Always looking for a handout."

That explained the odor. He was probably homeless, trying to make a bob telling stories. Jane seemed to have a hard disposition, with little room for empathy. As they made their way through the stands to Geraldine's walking sticks, Siobhán noticed Professor Kelly loitering in front of a table hoisting up a carton of eggs, lifting each one out of the carton and offering them to the light. Siobhán put her hand on Jane's shoulder. When they encountered him on the road he had been urging the crowd to go home. Was he a peacekeeper? Or had he been putting on an act?

Jane leaned in. "Something has stolen your attention. What is it?"

"It's a who," Siobhán said. "Professor Kelly."

"Dylan Kelly," Jane repeated with a nod. "What's the story?"

"He's fondling eggs," Siobhán said. "Holding every one up to the sun."

Jane laughed. "Joe Madigan is right. No one here trusts anyone."

"Pardon?"

"My neighbor Joe Madigan has a reputation of sneaking in cracked eggs." As they passed, Dylan Kelly spotted Jane and turned. His glasses slipped down his nose and he nearly dropped his egg as he pushed them back up with his index finger.

"Careful. You drop it you buy it," a gruff voice said. Siobhán's head snapped up. There was no doubt, it was the farmer she'd witnessed spying on them through binoculars. He had changed his red shirt and was wearing a muted green one, but the dark hat pulled low was the same. He was younger than she first assumed, in his thirties, and handsome except for the scowl. His expression softened when he noticed Jane. Maybe Siobhán should have come clean to her about him being a Peeping Tom. He did not make eye contact with her. Dare she say, he was *refusing* to make eye contact with her? Dylan Kelly set the carton of eggs back on the table.

"You fondle me eggs, you pay," Joe said.

Dylan Kelly shook his head, but removed a wallet from the inside pocket of his blazer and completed his transaction. Joe thrust the carton of eggs at him and Dylan tucked them underneath his arm before heading for Jane. Once he was standing in front of them, he too barely glanced at Siobhán. Maybe they were all under a fairy spell, one that rendered them incapable of noticing anyone who didn't live in their village.

"Miss Delaney, it's Professor Kelly," he said loudly.

"Hello, Dylan," Jane said. "This is Garda Siobhán O'Sullivan."

Dylan Kelly removed his hat with his left hand and placed it on his chest. His head was mostly bald with a few side pieces blowing in the wind. "I am horribly shocked and sorry to hear of your mother's passing," he shouted.

"She's not deaf," Siobhán said. She couldn't help it. He was acting like a fool and nearly pierced her eardrum. "How did you hear?"

Dylan Kelly glanced at Siobhán but did not answer. The phone call Macdara had made to the guards—that was the only way he could have heard. Unless, of course, he was the killer. In that case, it was foolish of him to admit to knowing something that was still under wraps. Somehow the information from Macdara's phone call had already spread to the village. Typical.

"Murder," Jane said, raising the volume of her voice to match his. Several heads turned. "My mother was murdered." She leaned into Siobhán. "Are they looking?"

"Nearly every one of them," Siobhán whispered back.

"Let me know if any make a run for it."

Siobhán's head popped up as if expecting to see someone bolt from the scene. Dylan Kelly's eyes flicked once more to Siobhán. "Garda," he said with a nod.

"Mr. Kelly," Siobhán replied, trying to sound equally formal. "Or should I say Professor?"

He arched his eyebrow. "Retired," he said. "I'm an author now, with my first book soon to be published." He looked as if he wanted to pat himself on the back. He grinned and turned back to Jane. "Murder?" his voice softened. "Are you sure?"

"The state pathologist will conduct a thorough investigation." Siobhán should have warned Jane not to jabber about the case. It never occurred to her that Jane would do so. "What kind of book are you writing?"

"Poisoned and smothered," Jane said, stepping forward.

No, no, no. What was she doing? "It's best not to give away too much information," Siobhán said. "We need to protect the investigation."

"They need to hear this." Jane pushed Siobhán aside. "The Little People did not kill my mother. Someone amongst us did. They poisoned her, and then smothered her!"

This was a disaster, a setback for the investigators. If social decorum didn't dictate otherwise, Siobhán would have thrown herself to the ground to pummel it.

Gasps and murmurs rippled through the crowd. Geraldine Madigan, wielding her colorful staff, barreled toward them with surprising speed, jostling townsfolk out of her way with her elbows. She planted herself in front of Jane, her bosom still heaving long after she stopped. She held a finger up to Jane's face. "Shame on you for not listening to our warnings."

"Geraldine," Jane said. "I should have known there wouldn't be an ounce of sympathy in your old bones."

Siobhán's mouth dropped open. Jane Delaney was combative. There was definitely boiling water under this bridge.

"That cottage is cursed," Geraldine said, spit flying from her mouth. "If it had been bulldozed as we told you, *repeatedly*, your mam would still be alive."

"And here we were going to buy one of your walking sticks."

"You can have as many as you want on your way out of this village," Geraldine said.

Siobhán gasped. It was all she could take. "Have you no decency? She just lost her mam."

Geraldine's eyes seemed to dance with excitement.

"We warned them," she said, stomping her staff. "Over and over and over again."

"What do you think of our lovely neighbors, Siobhán?" Jane said. "Are you listening to your mother?" Jane pointed at Joe with her cane. He jumped and dropped a carton of eggs. They splattered on the ground, yellow goo forming a puddle.

"Confound it!" He stared at the eggs as if weighing his options. Was he going to force a blind woman whose mother was just murdered to pay for the dropped eggs? "Jane, I'm very sorry for your loss." *Good choice.* He turned to Geraldine. "Mother, please. Not here."

Geraldine Madigan set her mouth in a straight line and nodded. "May she rest in peace." She crossed herself.

"You old witch!" Jane lunged toward Geraldine. "If a fairy did this, it's you they should have killed!"

"Enough." Siobhán took Jane by the elbow and literally held her back. "Where is your parish priest?"

This seemed to stop all the chatter. "He divides his time between villages," Geraldine finally said. "If he's not at the church, he may be at the other village. Why?"

"Because I swear you all need to go to mass in the morning. I've never seen such a shameful display in me life!"

"Putting the fear of God into them," Jane leaned in and whispered. "I can see why my cousin is taken with you." Siobhán felt her face flush. It wasn't like her to hold mass over anyone's head, but if anyone needed it, it was this lot. Jane turned back to the crowd. "Joe Madigan," she said, "I assume now that Mam is dead at least we won't have to live with you peeping at us with those binoculars of yours."

She knew? Yet another surprise from Macdara's cousin. She'd meant it when she said her other skills were sharpened. As sharp as knives. There was also a playful tone to Jane's reprimand that Siobhán found jarring. Ellen Delaney must have known about his peeping as well and reported it to her daughter. Why had they let him continue doing it? At least Joe had the decency to turn bright red.

Geraldine pounded her stick. "What are they on about?" She glared at her son.

"My bird-watching," he stammered. "Ellen accused me of spying. I'm a bird-watcher!"

"My son is a bird-watcher!" Geraldine repeated with twice the enthusiasm but half the conviction.

"Tweet, tweet," Jane deadpanned.

"Don't you dare start spreading rumors about me son being a pervert," Geraldine said.

"Leave her be, Mam, she's only joking." His shoulders hunched. He leaned into her. "And please don't use that word."

"I saw you this morning with your binoculars," Siobhán said. "You seemed to be looking at me."

"Birds," Geraldine insisted.

"Birds can be a euphemism for women, can't they?" Jane sounded thrilled with it. Siobhán imagined her wedding. The reception. The seating chart. Jane Delaney was going way in the back.

Joe looked at Siobhán then, quite openly. His handsome jaw was set. "Who are you exactly?"

"This is Garda O'Sullivan from Kilbane, County Cork." Jane stated it proudly. Joe Madigan swallowed, his Adam's apple bobbed noticeably. Interesting. Guards made him nervous. Guilty conscience? The young mother with the chestnut braid they'd met earlier appeared behind Joe Madigan, this time toting two children, a boy and a girl. "This is me wife, Mary Madigan," Joe said. "This is Garda O'Sullivan."

William had his hand wrapped around his mother's legs, just like he'd been clinging to her in the road when they arrived. The girl looked to be around six years of age and she stood by with her big eyes glued to the visitors. "We are so sorry about your mother," Mary Madigan said to Jane. She turned to her daughter, now jumping up and down. "Lilly. Don't make me count to three. One . . ."

The little girl stuck her lip out in a perfect pout but stopped jumping. "Hello, Mary," Jane said. They exchanged pleasantries, but their voices were sour, as if they could barely force niceties out of their mouths. "Did you see my mother this weekend?" Jane asked.

"Me?" Mary said. She glanced at her husband and began to blink.

"Aren't you in her painting class?"

Her shoulders relaxed slightly. "The class was moved to Friday night so we could capture the solstice moon. Ellen was not present."

"Are you sure?"

"Quite sure."

"I wonder why she missed it," Jane said. She turned to Siobhán. "You must speak with Annabel."

"Annabel?" Siobhán asked.

"She's our teacher," Mary said. "She's very encouraging."

"We have to find out if my mam gave her a reason for canceling," Jane said. Siobhán didn't like her use of "we," and the number of times she was being forced to bite her tongue was taking a toll. Jane was right about one thing; she did wish to speak to Annabel. Jane turned back to Mary and Joe. "Did any of you see my mam this weekend?"

Glances were exchanged in the crowd, and folks began to move closer.

"Several have been wondering if . . . somehow . . . she had something to do with the strange events of Friday night," Joe said at last.

"Why in heavens do you think that?" Jane sounded defensive.

Joe cleared his throat. "A woman was seen running through the meadow toward the cottage. Right after that awful scream."

"You saw this yourself?" Jane asked.

"Me?" Joe stammered. "No. I'm only telling you what I've been hearing."

"Joe was out of town," Mary said. She turned to her husband. "Isn't that right, dear?"

"Yes," Joe said. "I was gone from Thursday day to Saturday morning." It sounded stilted, as if he'd rehearsed it, yet his wife gave a satisfying nod.

"What about you then?" Jane asked the farmer's wife.

"What about me?" Mary's tone was clipped.

"You must have seen me mother?"

Mary shook her head. "No. But Geraldine saw her."

All eyes turned to Geraldine. She nodded. "Right after the scream. Running past the fairy ring toward the cottage."

"Are you sure it was Ellen Delaney?" Siobhán asked.

"Who else could it have been?" Geraldine sounded outraged at the question.

"She was only asking if you were sure," Jane persisted. "Answer the question."

"I don't know," Geraldine admitted. "The figure was dressed in dark clothing. But she . . . or he . . . was running toward the cottage. No one else goes near the place if they don't have to, especially at night." She visibly shuddered. "The things I saw that night. The moon. The strange lights. That scream. That horrible, horrible scream." She lowered her head. "Something was going on."

"Every one of you will need to give your account of that evening to the guards," Siobhán said. If Ellen Delaney had been seen running *to* the cottage, where had she been running from?

"Sounds like everyone is being overly dramatic," Jane said. "Or they're protecting a killer."

"How convenient that *you* weren't here to witness any of it," Geraldine said.

Jane's jaw clenched. "What is that supposed to mean?"

Geraldine edged closer, her staff pounding the ground. "Where were you?"

"I was at a conference in Dublin." She pointed to Siobhán. "Ask her."

Siobhán was floored. Not only did she have no proof that Jane had been in Dublin, she'd been the one begging for it. "The guards will get to the bottom of this," Siobhán said. "Alibis will be collected from everyone. Here and now is not the time."

In the distance, she could make out Aiden Cunningham huddled with Professor Kelly. From the pointing each one of them was doing, it seemed they were in a heated conversation. Siobhán didn't realize she was staring until Aiden's head whipped around as if he sensed her. He then turned and propelled himself away from the professor. *How odd.* What had they been talking about so intensely, and why had he reacted that way to her spotting them?

"I can't bear to be around these people another second," Jane said. "I'm so tired."

So much for a nice day at the market. Siobhán touched Jane's arm. "Why don't we go and get that cup of tea?"

Chapter 8

The walls of Molly's Café were painted a vibrant lavender, making the tiny café burst with cheer. Paintings covered the walls on both sides. Molly's was a fraction of the size of Naomi's, but Siobhán was impressed with its welcoming feel. That was half the battle. It was a relief to finally sit down to a mug of tea, and although Jane didn't want anything to eat, Siobhán slipped in a small scone. Jane excused herself to the restroom. Siobhán stepped up to see the paintings. Most of them were renderings of rolling hills and rocky hedges with cows and sheep grazing. Several were of the fairy tree, and a few were of fairies themselves, depicted as short with bright smiles in some, sinister and dark in others. And beautiful women could be summed up as the description in the third category. Siobhán scanned them for signatures. They were all done by different artists and soon she came to the plaque:

ANNABEL'S PAINTERS. This must be the art class that she'd heard about. What did Mary Madigan say? They'd gathered on Friday night to paint the solstice moon but Ellen Delaney had not been with them. Yet later, someone had seen a figure they assumed to be Ellen running toward the cottage. The guards, or herself, were definitely going to have to speak to these student painters.

"What do you tink?"

Siobhán jumped at the voice and turned to find a tiny woman beside her. In her fifties with soft brown hair and big round spectacles, she looked like someone whose spirit animal would be a sweet, wise owl.

"You must be Molly," Siobhán said.

A bright laugh filled the room. "Guilty as charged."

"They're lovely," Siobhán said.

"I rotate them every two weeks," Molly answered with pride. "I love supporting the arts."

"Do you have any by Ellen Delaney?"

Molly's face changed from friendly to guarded. "Why would you be asking?"

"I'm here with her daughter. I was just wondering." As if summoned by the mention of her name, Jane returned, saying hello to Molly as she passed by.

"Her other senses are so sharp," Molly said as if in awe, before hurrying back to her station behind the counter.

Siobhán scoured each painting again, but learned nothing new. Either Ellen's paintings weren't here, or her signature wasn't legible. Underneath Annabel's plaque sat a placeholder stuffed with calling cards. Siobhán slipped one into her pocket, then returned to the table. "I was just looking at the paintings on the wall. I didn't see any by your mother."

Jane shook her head. "Neither did I."

"Pardon?"

Jane threw her head back and laughed. "Sorry, but if anyone is allowed to make jokes about being blind, it's me."

"Oh," Siobhán said. "Of course." But she couldn't bring herself to laugh. It must be difficult dealing with everyone's pity and ignorance day after day.

Jane didn't seem fazed and moved on. "Mam went mental the one time I tried to get her to show her work."

"She did?"

Jane nodded. "One of her paintings used to hang in the cottage. Annabel arrived on one day, looking for pieces for this café. Mam wasn't around, so I gave it to her. I thought she would be pleased. I've never seen her so livid."

"When was this?"

Jane pondered the question. "Approximately one month ago."

"Did she say why she didn't want to show her work?"

"She's always been private."

"What was the subject of the painting?"

"I'm sure I asked her, but I don't remember."

"What happened to that painting?" Siobhán hadn't seen any paintings hanging in the cottage.

"That's another funny bit. I don't know. She never brought it back. When I asked her she said 'Don't you worry about it.'"

Ellen Delaney sounded like she'd been a prickly woman. But Siobhán also knew that not all artists wanted to share their work with the world. Her grandfather, who had been a master craftsman, never had any interest in displaying his carvings. He may have become a famous artist if not for that crippling modesty. Maybe Ellen Delaney had suffered from that same shyness. But from everything Siobhán had heard, she wasn't the cuddly type. And what had she done with the painting? Did it matter? *Don't you worry about it.* Prickly, indeed. Siobhán was lucky to have had a warm and loving mother. She wished Ciarán would have had more time to experience Naomi O'Sullivan's charm. She'd done her best to fill in, but it wasn't the same. Siobhán gave them a moment to enjoy their tea, before she started in again. "I'm sorry if this is difficult, but can you tell me about the last time you saw your mother?"

Jane bowed her head, and then lifted it. "Dara says you're a good detective. Are you going to help find my mother's killer?"

"Yes," Siobhán said. "We both are." It was the truth. Jurisdiction or not, they wouldn't be able to stay away.

"Then I will tell you everything." She placed her hands on the tablecloth as if preparing herself. "I left for Dublin on Thursday morning after breakfast. We had a soft-boiled egg, toast, and tea together as usual. I talked about the conference. I go every year and was excited to be returning. I don't think my mam got two words in." She took a deep breath. "I asked her what her plans were for the weekend, and she said she'd be doing her usual. Normally she took a watercolor class on Saturday mornings, then the farmers' market, and goes to Sunday mass."

"Wait," Siobhán said. "Did she specifically say the class would be on Saturday?"

Jane tilted her head. "No, she said 'her usual.' I was filling in the gaps. Mary Madigan said the class was moved to Friday evening for the solstice moon and that my mother did not attend."

"Would you have expected your mother to shift to the evening class with the rest of the group?"

"That's a good question. I don't know. She didn't like to waste money, and she had to pay in advance for the classes, but she could be stubborn. If a class is on a Saturday, it's on a Saturday. That type of thing. In the end, I say she would have gone unless she had other plans."

"But she didn't mention any other plans. Nothing out of the ordinary?"

Jane shook her head. "I wish I'd been paying better attention."

"You couldn't have known. Let's stick to what you recall."

"I can only say what she does every Saturday when I am here. She does her painting class, she attends the farmers' market and does her messages, takes walks, works in the garden, and sometimes comes here for a spot of lunch and laptop time." It certainly sounded like she kept busy.

"Do you know where she stores her paintings?" She needed to learn everything she could about Ellen Delaney as quickly as possible.

"I assume she kept them at Annabel's workshop. She didn't paint at the cottage."

"Did she describe what she paints? Not just the one painting you accidentally handed over, but *any* of them?" Siobhán took in the paintings around the café once more. She narrated them to Jane. "I wonder if any are hers."

Jane cocked her head. "Do you think it's important?"

"You never know." Jane sipped her tea and waited. "In an investigation you have to pull every string."

"Or risk getting tied up in them?"

"Astute observation," Siobhán said.

Jane gave a smile and set her cup down. "I know one assignment was a still-life project, and they were supposed to pick an object that instilled a negative emotion in them. Mam found that objectionable; I think she almost quit over it."

"Interesting." Siobhán was dying to meet this Annabel. "Did she tell you what object she picked?"

Jane shook her head. "If she did, I don't recall."

"Anything else?"

Jane turned her head in the direction of the paintings. "I think she was painting the cottage."

"Oh?"

"Apparently, she did it to rattle the class." Jane gasped. "My word. You're right. It *could* be important." Jane pushed back her chair with a screech and stood. "I need to get back to the cottage. Do you think the guards have found anything?"

"There's only one way to find out." Siobhán left a small tip, then followed Jane outside. They were quiet on the walk back to the cottage, each caught up in her own thoughts. Now that Siobhán had Annabel's calling card, she would be able to pay Annabel's art studio a visit. Siobhán couldn't help but want to see Ellen's paintings. But Jane was slippery; she'd managed to change the conversation away from *her* weekend once again. Siobhán had already decided that it was best not to push Jane on the subject of Dublin and proving her attendance at this conference. She would leave that to Dara. As they walked, passersby gave Jane a wide berth, as if her blindness was contagious. Siobhán wondered if Jane could feel their reactions, and once again realized how exhausting that must be.

Siobhán was relieved when they were away from the main street and traipsing next to green fields. "Let's go over your return from Dublin. From the moment you arrived home."

Jane took the lead, her cane tapping rhythmically as she spoke. "Mam wasn't there to pick me up at the bus stop. That's when I feared something was wrong. She's the type who would have been there an hour early. If something came up—and I can't imagine what that something would have been—she would have sent someone and insisted they be there an hour early. When I realized she wasn't there, it was like someone walked over my grave."

"I'm sorry if this sounds ignorant, but how do you use a mobile phone?" Why was she so uninformed? She would have to do better.

Jane laughed. "It's okay, most people are ignorant. It has special features that concentrate more on sound, as well as other functions that help. Why do you ask?"

"Did you call her when she wasn't there? Did you speak on the phone at all since you left Thursday?"

Jane came to an abrupt stop, and Siobhán had to step into the meadow not to mow her down. When Jane turned, Siobhán couldn't tell if the stricken look on her face was that of a liar caught in a lie, or if she was concentrating on the question. "I know it seems as if we must have been close." She gave a self-conscious laugh. "And we were. We lived together. But I didn't intend to spend my precious alone time on the phone with my mother, and I'm sure she felt the same." Jane lifted her chin to the skies, which had been sunny since the farmers' market. They began to walk again, once more Jane tapping out a fast clip.

"That is understandable. But what about when she didn't show?"

"I called her, of course. Her phone went straight to voice mail."

"Was that unusual?"

"Not at all. Mam only brought that phone with her if we were apart, and she often forgot to turn it on let alone charge it."

"I thought she was a very organized person."

"Not when it came to that phone." Jane frowned. "It bothers me that you didn't see it in the cottage."

"Honestly, we were in and out. Hopefully the guards will find it."

"They're probably in there right now, touching all of her things. She would *hate* that." There were probably other things she would hate more, such as the fact that someone had murdered her, but Siobhán was hardly going to point this out.

"What about the way she was dressed?"

Jane shook her head. "I have never heard Mam describe an outfit like that. The only time she ever dressed up was for weddings and funerals."

"And you had no inkling or suspicion that she may have been romantically involved with someone?"

"It's not the kind of thing she would have shared with me. In fact, she would have relished keeping a secret like that from me." Jane stopped again and turned. "Do you think she would still be alive if I had called the guards the minute I saw she wasn't at the bus stop?"

A butterfly zipped past them and landed on a patch of heather. She wished Jane could see the beauty around them. But that probably wasn't a helpful thought; perhaps it was better to focus on the positive. "I don't think so, luv. The pathologist will give us the exact time of death, but in my opinion a few hours wouldn't have made any difference."

"I've been thinking and thinking about this." She sped up. "Someone is trying to frame me for her murder."

"Why do you think that?"

"They *poisoned* her. Most likely with something taken out of our own garden."

"But you were in Dublin all weekend. As soon as you give the guards your train ticket, hotel information, and the info on the conference, they'll drop you as a suspect."

"I shouldn't have gone at all. She'd still be alive."

"You can't blame yourself." *Unless you're the killer.* Every instinct in Siobhán warned her that Jane was lying about her weekend away. If she wasn't in Dublin, where had she been? Had it all been a cover to give herself an alibi for murder? If so, did she really think she wouldn't be asked to prove it? "How did you get back to the cottage?"

"The same way we're getting around now. I walked." Siobhán felt like an idiot. Again. "It was more for the ceremony of it that Mam liked to pick me up. I have some sight."

"You do?"

"Yes." Jane stopped. She pointed to the heather. "I can see the shade is somewhat darker here, than the rest of the meadow." She turned to the road. "And even darker there." She looked above them. "Of course I can tell when the sun is out, but even if it weren't for the lighter shade, I can feel it, of course. It can be difficult to determine when I'm relying on sight alone and when my other senses are filling in. You don't have to see pitch black to be considered legally blind. I can make out shapes, and certain shades, just not *features*. Between that and my cane, I get along well enough." As if to demonstrate, she started moving again, at the fastest clip yet.

Even with a bit of sight it would be difficult to navigate the rugged terrain of this village. "What happened when you arrived at the cottage?"

"I discovered the door was ajar. I didn't realize the window had been broken until after I stepped in." Even though Siobhán was walking behind her, she could see Jane shudder. "I thought she was sleeping at first. But she was too cold. Too still. I didn't want to disturb the scene, but I felt a breeze as I was leaving, coming from the window. I discovered the smashed panes of glass with my cane." Siobhán heard a sniffle, and when she caught up to Jane's side, she saw tears rolled down her cheeks. Siobhán wished she had a tissue to hand her, but she was more than a little relieved to see Jane finally shed some tears. "Wait a minute," Jane said, wiping her tears and stopping yet again. "There's something else. A smell . . ."

"Go on."

"At first I thought it was cologne."

"Cologne? Not perfume?"

"Mam didn't wear perfume."

"She was dressed up. Maybe for a special occasion."

"A date?" Jane's lips pursed.

"Yes."

Jane shook her head. "If so, she picked a terrible scent." She placed her index finger on her lips and tapped. "Some kind of furniture polish? Shoe polish? Something between cologne and . . . leather?"

Siobhán whipped her mobile from her pocket and tapped the revelation into her notes. The method was growing on her. "Anything else? Anything at all? More smells. Or sounds?"

"I could hear there was a crowd gathered down the street. I had no idea what people were doing, gathered in the road."

"A tree had fallen across it, and they were chattering about the strange events last night."

Jane nodded. "I thought they knew about Mam. It's one of the reasons I called Dara. Nobody in this village liked us, not even the guards. Now I'm supposed to trust them to investigate thoroughly? You saw yourself, they're taking ages to get to the crime scene."

"It does complicate things," Siobhán agreed. She stopped talking to focus on her breath. She'd done more walking so far today than she did in a few days in Kilbane, counting her morning runs. Say what you want about the smaller villages, but this was some serious cardio.

"The things they were saying . . . a full moon, strange noises, a scream, the figure running toward the cottage . . ." Jane reached out and put her hands on Siobhán's shoulders. "Do you think . . . that was my mother screaming?"

It had certainly crossed Siobhán's mind. Had the killer pursued her home? "Could you think of any reason she'd be out at night?"

Jane shook her head. "Not one. We sometimes went out at night together, for a walk. It's lovely on a summer night. But my mother running across meadows and screaming?" She stopped and stared as if she was imagining the events unfolding before her eyes. "Ask Dara. Mam didn't scare easily. She was usually the one scaring others."

Just ahead several guard cars were parked alongside a gravel path. Siobhán described it. "Finally," Jane said.

They had almost reached the turn-in when Jane grabbed Siobhán's arm, then shoved her into the meadow with both hands. Siobhán let out a yelp of surprise as Jane hurled down the hill after her. Seconds later a blur of a car zoomed past, tires screeching, dirt flying from its wheels.

Siobhán scrambled to her feet as the car disappeared down the road in a cloud of dust. She struggled to process what just happened. There seemed to be only one conclusion. The car had been gunning for them, and Jane Delaney had just saved her life.

Chapter 9

They stood by the rusty gate now marked with white and blue crime scene tape. Moments later, a familiar voice filtered through the air as Macdara made his way toward them. After their close call Siobhán had to hold herself back from hurling herself into his arms. It was terrifying how fragile life was. Behind him on the path was Danny MacGregor, or should she say Garda MacGregor. It had been a while since their days at Templemore Garda College, but she could see straightaway that it was the same jovial Danny. He wasn't overly tall, shorter than Macdara, but he was strong and handsome. His blond hair was cropped closely, and his hazel eyes had the usual playful glint as he grinned at her. She may not have made it through training without Danny's encouragement. "O'Sullivan!" he called out from several feet away. Macdara frowned.

"Danny!" He broke into a jog, then embraced her, lifting her off her feet and whirling her around in a circle. The ground was still spinning after he set her down. "You look a mess, O'Sullivan," Danny said, plucking a leaf out of her hair and roaring with laughter.

"Right, you two know each other," Jane said. "What a happy reunion."

Siobhán brushed dirt off herself. "We were nearly run over."

"What did you just say?" There was Macdara, at her side, his voice filled with concern.

"A car nearly plowed into us. Jane saved us."

"Eejits are always speeding on that road." Danny shook his head in disgust.

"No," Siobhán said. "I mean yes, they were speeding, but . . . I'm telling you . . . it was aiming for us."

"Up there?" Macdara pointed to the road.

Siobhán nodded. "I didn't see any tire tracks."

"We'll check it out," Danny said. "I'm glad you're alright."

"Such a small world," Jane said, her face turning toward Macdara.

"This woman was the star of our class at Templemore." Danny pulled Siobhán in with an easy arm around her shoulders. "I worshipped her."

"Did you now?" Macdara's tone was clipped.

"Don't listen to a word of it," Siobhán said lightly. "Danny was the one everyone worshipped." She leaned in as Danny laughed. "He broke the record for the tires every time."

"The tires?" Jane said.

"We had to carry them while running through an obstacle course," Siobhán said. "Everyone always dreaded it. Except for Danny here."

"It was only to best you," Danny said with a wink.

"That settles it," Macdara said. "He'll be grand on the case. As long as the solution depends on him running fast whilst carrying tires."

Danny laughed again, but Siobhán was simmering. Jealousy wasn't Macdara's best color. Siobhán went to introduce Danny to Jane. "It's a small village," Jane said, cutting her off. "We know each other."

"Six months into the job and I have my own murder probe," Danny said. Excitement danced in his eyes.

"How lucky for you," Jane said. Siobhán could tell the family resemblance from their sarcasm.

All color drained from Danny's face. He was on the pale side of Irish pale, which was saying something, and now his face was nearly translucent. He stammered apologies to Jane.

"The forensic team is here; don't you worry, everyone is focused on finding the killer."

Jane nodded. "As you should be."

Macdara moved to Siobhán's side. Just then another guard rounded the bend. He was in his sixties and weathered, as if years of rain and wind had sculpted his face. "Jane," he called, "is that you?"

Jane smiled at the sound of the voice. "Yes, Sergeant Eegan. Danny was just telling us how thrilled he is that me mother was murdered," Jane said. "Apparently, it will be good for his career."

"What's that now?" Sergeant Eegan said, settling on Danny with a glare.

Danny's face flamed red. "A misstatement is all; apologies again."

A smile played at the corner of Jane's mouth. She was enjoying taking him down a peg. Interesting. Siobhán was going to have to find an artful way to grill Macdara about his porcupine of a cousin.

Macdara introduced Siobhán and Detective Sergeant Eegan, and then talk turned back to the subject of murder.

"We haven't concluded it was murder," Sergeant Eegan declared, looking around as if performing for an invisible audience. "Is there any chance your mother took too many sleeping tablets?"

"Not unless you count a nip of whiskey," Jane said. "It was her cure for everything."

"Maybe she took too many nips?" Eegan asked hopefully. He searched their faces for agreement.

"Unlikely," Macdara said. "Unless you've ever encountered a whiskey that causes one to foam at the mouth."

"And there's an overturned teacup at the scene but no whiskey bottle," Siobhán pointed out.

"And the fact that the door was ajar and the main window broken," Macdara finished.

Eegan frowned, then shifted his weight to the other foot as if one was better than the other for contemplating the matter.

"It certainly looked like foul play to me, Sergeant," Danny said. He glanced at Jane as if bracing himself for another snide remark. "The foam and bruising around her mouth."

"Exactly," Siobhán said. "And her hands neatly posed." She was eager for him to lay out his plan of action. They had to wait for the arrival of the state pathologist, but they could begin questioning the townsfolk.

Something wild went on Friday night and by Saturday morning Ellen Delaney was dead.

"Settled?" Sergeant Eegan said. "Because this green lad says so?" He jerked his thumb to Danny. "Better be careful who you believe around here, little lassie."

Siobhán stuck out her hand, which was very adult of her given she wanted to use it to punch Garda Eegan in the face. "I no longer go by 'little lassie,'" she said with a smile. "You can call me Garda O'Sullivan."

"Would you look at that," Garda Eegan said, turning to Macdara. "Ye are coming out of the woodwork. Well, don't you worry, we've got it covered with Cork City. We'll know as soon as the toxicology report comes back. In the meantime this is my crime scene and you'll have to stay out of it."

"I need to fetch my luggage bag," Jane said.

"Not possible," Garda Eegan said. "It's evidence now."

"It arrived with me. *After* me mam was already dead. It can't be evidence."

"It's in my crime scene and my crime scene will not be contaminated," Garda Eegan said.

Siobhán placed her hand on Jane's arm. "We'll sort you out in Kilbane. I've two sisters. Between the three of us you'll be grand. We can even do a bit of shopping if you'd like."

"I'd like to get my bag." If Siobhán wasn't mistaken, a look of panic rippled across Jane's face. Was there something particular in the suitcase she was worried about?

"Why don't you mark the bag as an exhibit to go through quickly," Macdara suggested. "Perhaps it could then be returned."

"No," Garda Eegan said. "I will not be rushed or have anyone interfering. Either of you."

"Well, what are you waiting for?" Jane said. "Get detecting."

"They'll be waiting for the pathologist to arrive," Siobhán explained. "That may delay matters."

Garda Eegan folded his arms. "We've been given permission to move the body to Cork University Hospital. The pathologist will meet us there to do her postmortem. I'll be sure to mention the sleeping tablets."

Siobhán was getting tired of smiling, which was her signature move when dealing with men who didn't want to listen to a woman. If that failed, she usually paired it with a dose of heavy sarcasm. "With your theory, Ellen Delaney must have busted her own window, ingested a deadly toxin, smothered herself with a pillow, then peacefully folded her hands over her dying body." She stopped for a breath. "And I suppose her truck drove off on its own with her handbag and mobile?"

Eegan's eyes scanned her, from head to toe, and back up again. His eyes flicked to Dara, as if searching for backup. Macdara simply stared back. Eegan shifted his weight, removed his cap, put it back on. "I've heard some of them tablets can make you do things in your sleep. Order items off the Internet."

"This village cut off our Internet," Jane said.

"You're welcome," Eegan replied. "I bet she would have been ordering all kinds of things and you'd be stuck with the bill."

"We can help," Siobhán said, mostly to Danny, who had gone so silent she'd almost forgotten he was here.

"How can you help?" Garda Eegan asked before Danny could utter a word. Not only had the poor lad been sent to this village, he wasn't even allowed to flex his considerable skills. Why on earth did he stay? If Siob-hán's memory served, his girlfriend was from this small village and she had no desire to relocate.

"I'm sorry for your loss," Garda Eegan said. "Go home. We'll take over from here."

He was certainly in a hurry for them to leave. "Have you ever had a murder in Ballysiogdun?" Siobhán asked.

"This would be the first," Danny said. The other guard cut his smile with a look. "Not that we're happy about it. Not in the least. 'Tis terrible." Poor Danny. They all kept staring, and he kept talking.

"My cousin is an excellent detective," Jane said. "So is Siobhán O'Sullivan."

"I won't be reading my CV to either of you," Garda Eegan said. "If you'll excuse us, we have work to do."

"Did you find Ellen's handbag or mobile phone in the cottage?" Siobhán asked. "Do you have an eye out for her truck?"

"Her truck is key," Macdara said. "Unless you think a fairy drove off in it?"

"Good day." Garda Eegan whirled around and strode away. With a last look and a shrug, Danny followed.

"The victim is my aunt," Macdara called after them. "We'll steer clear of your official inquiries, but I will be staying until we're good and ready to leave and I expect regular updates on the investigation."

Siobhán placed her hand on Dara's arm and gave it a squeeze. "Do *you* know if they found her handbag or mobile phone?"

"They asked me to stay back. I don't think so, but I wasn't privy to everything. Nothing has been removed yet though."

"You're sure you didn't see it?" Jane was starting to sound desperate.

"Other than the papers on the counter, and the items we mentioned in the bedroom, the cottage was sparse."

"Papers?" Jane's alarm was obvious. "What papers?"

"A stack of papers on the kitchen counter," Macdara said. "Maybe from her teaching days?"

"Don't be ridiculous," Jane said. "She didn't keep anything like that. The only thing she ever kept on the counter was her bottle of Powers. Good luck if you ever stole *dat*."

"I'm only guessing as to the contents of the papers," Macdara said. "We didn't look."

"How could you not look?"

Now Jane was needling at Macdara. Siobhán's patience was stretching. She told herself she would not snap. Siobhán felt a presence, and looked up to find Danny, half hidden near the tunnel of trees, trying to catch her eye. She made her way over to him. "Did you get a look at the sink?" His voice was low.

She shook her head. "Why?"

"Text me when you're alone."

She glanced over her shoulder where Macdara was watching them. "Alone?"

Danny's eyes flicked to Dara, then looked away. "His aunt is the victim."

Siobhán nodded. She didn't want to keep secrets from Macdara, but Danny was right, Macdara was too close to the victim. And she wanted to know what was in the sink. She would tell him all about it later. Catching a killer was the priority. Wouldn't Macdara do the same if he was in her position?

"These guards will clear out in a few hours," Danny continued. "Text me then." He turned and disappeared.

"What was that all about?" Macdara sounded suspicious.

"He was just confirming that they would be on the lookout for the car that almost ran us down."

"I see." He didn't believe her, but he didn't want to start an argument in front of his cousin. Siobhán shifted her gaze to the farmhouse in the distance. Squeals of children playing rang out from their front yard. The handsome, peeping farmer was high on her list. "While they're doing all this waiting, what do you say we pay your closest neighbors a visit?"

"Those teetotalers?" Jane sneered. "Good luck. The Madigan women are to blame for all of this. They led the crusade against the cottage."

"They're the closest to the crime scene as well," Macdara said.

"Our neighbors, the killers," Jane deadpanned. "Guess there goes borrowing a cup of sugar."

"Maybe you should check into your local inn for a few hours, get some rest," Siobhán said. Jane had been through a lot; she was wound up.

"Don't be ridiculous. You need me to get in the door."

"Besides," Macdara said, "I'd feel better if we stuck together." He gave Siobhán a look. "At all times." Was he trying to warn her not to meet Danny? He'd asked for her help. He had to let her do it her way. If she told him what Danny said, would Macdara agree to step back and have her meet Danny alone? Normally, but he was jealous when it came to Danny. Those were the facts. Too close to the victim, and clouded by jealousy. She had to get a look at that sink, and Danny wanted her to come alone. She trusted Danny, and to him, Macdara was a stranger. Siobhán was going to have to walk a tightrope with this one, and she already feared she was getting too high up without a net.

Chapter 10

Joe and Mary Madigan's farmhouse had the feel of a wooly jumper way past its prime, but too comfy to throw out. It wouldn't have won any awards for upkeep, but something about it said home. Mary Madigan stood on the porch with William clinging to her leg. Toys were scattered in the front yard, and in the distance a tractor plowed the fields. Beyond that cows and sheep grazed on the hilltop. In the yard, Lilly Madigan gripped a pair of dolls by their necks, banging their heads together. Mary Madigan fanned herself with a paperback novel. Her hair hung in waves around her pleasant face. Her bright eyes were inquisitive but guarded as Siobhán, Macdara, and Jane approached. "Is it eggs you're after?" she called when they were a few feet away.

"My mother is murdered, my home is a crime scene,

and this one thinks I want eggs," Jane said under her breath. "Typical."

No love between neighbors, Siobhán noted as her stomach grumbled at the second mention of eggs. It was really a murderer they were after, but there was no law against multitasking. They'd planned on having a meal as soon as they'd arrived and of course that was out the window.

"Garda Flannery and Garda O'Sullivan here," Macdara called. "I'm Ellen Delaney's nephew."

Although the smile didn't quite leave Mary's face, it did seem to freeze in place as if it was taking great pain to keep it there. Her eyes flicked to Siobhán. "We've already met."

"We have?" Macdara's eyebrow went up.

Siobhán filled him in. "First in the road. Then Jane and I met her at the market." Siobhán turned back to Mary. "This is my fiancé," she said. She bumped Macdara's arm with her fist in case he had any doubt she was talking about him.

"Really?" Macdara said, giving her boot a light tap with his. "Total strangers?"

"I'm giving it a practice run," Siobhán shot back. "Happy?"

"No," he said.

"Sorry to meet under such tragic circumstances," Mary said. "Would you like a cup of tea?"

"Love one," Macdara said. "Is your husband home?"

"Joseph," she yelled. Seconds later his head popped out of the barn. The muscles in his arms flexed as he tossed a bale of hay into the pen next to him.

"What is it?" If that was the tone he normally reserved for his wife, Siobhán felt sorry for her.

"We've got visitors." She made "visitors" sound like "assassins."

He leaned a shovel against the wall of the barn and headed for them with a wave. "How ye." A moment later a cow ambled out, following close behind. "Jane, we're very sorry about your mother. What a shock." The words came out rehearsed, and void of true feeling.

"Terrible shock," Mary repeated. If a UFO descended on the front yard and aliens stood on the ship applauding these stiff actors, Siobhán wouldn't have been surprised. She wanted to shake this husband and wife and see if any real emotions accidentally tumbled out of them. Maybe they'd been taken over by fairies. Mary Madigan's eyes flicked in the direction of the cottage. The cow mooed, her big watery eyes pinned on Macdara.

"You've got an admirer." Siobhán nudged Macdara, and he looked up to find the cow tracking his every move. Dara frowned, looked away, then glanced back at his bovine fan.

"I saw the bad people," Lilly sang from the yard. "And a bad, bad witch."

Siobhán took a step toward the girl. "You did?" Lilly looked up, her eyes nearly as big as the cow's.

She nodded, then pointed toward the cottage. "They were dancing."

"Dancing?" Siobhán said. "Who was dancing?"

"The people. And they made a pretty light." Her hands fanned out as she described the light. What a wee dolt. Siobhán wanted to give her a good squeeze. Her brood was all grown up. She missed having wee ones around.

"When was this?"

Mary Madigan stepped in front of Siobhán, blocking her view of the girl. "Please don't encourage her. Her nana has been telling stories of the fairies. I wish she'd stop."

"I'll have a word with her," Joe said. He took Jane's arm to guide her up the steps.

"I'll put the kettle on," Mary said.

They gathered in the homey kitchen. Like the outside it held the clutter of a life well lived. Over the sink was a window. Filling it was the cow's large head. Once again, she seemed to be staring at Macdara.

"She's a curious one," Siobhán said. She nudged Dara. "I think she's in love with you."

"What are you on about?" Macdara said.

"She can't take her eyes off you."

"That's ridiculous." Macdara looked up to once again find the cow staring at him. The tips of Macdara's ears flamed red. For the first time in her life, Siobhán wanted to bring home a cow.

"Aye," Joe answered. "She likes you alright. She thinks she's a dog."

Mary poured them tea, then opened a tin of biscuits and placed them on the table. "Would you like a biscuit with your tea?" Joe said to Jane. "Or milk?"

"Milk, please," she said. "Just a dash." The cow mooed and everyone jumped, then laughed.

"We'd like to help," Joe said. "Is there anything we can do?"

"We can arrange a mass for your mother," Mary said. "Will you be burying her here?"

"I don't know," Jane said. "I haven't thought that far ahead."

Macdara cleared his throat. "I thought we'd have her

service in Kilbane. Me mam might want her buried there as well."

"Right," Jane said. "I'm sorry they never got the chance to sort things out. I won't argue about where she's to be buried."

The sun hit a bottle of Powers whiskey sitting on the counter and for a second Siobhán was lost in a beam of gold. Macdara and Jane would need to have a sit-down and hash out the burial arrangements. It was messy business, death, and yet mourners were forced to deal with logistics. Siobhán didn't envy them.

"We could still have a small memorial for her here," Joe said.

"Don't be silly," Mary said, placing a hand on her husband's shoulder. "We'll come out to Kilbane."

"Of course," Joe said. "We will, of course."

Siobhán was dying for the pleasantries to end. They'd save so much time if everyone just said what was on their mind. Macdara must have agreed for he spoke first.

"We'd like to know the last time you saw Ellen, plus an account of everything you did over the weekend."

"You're not guards," Joe said. He was smiling, but there was an edge to his voice. After he spoke his gaze shifted to Jane as if waiting to see whose side she was on.

"They are guards," Mary said. "They said they were guards."

Joe treated his wife to a searing look. She bowed her head. "They have no jurisdiction here. Why don't you let our guards do the questioning?"

"Please," Jane said. "I asked them to help."

"I don't see how we can help," Joe said.

Siobhán cut in. "Just tell us about the last time you saw Ellen."

Joe and Mary exchanged looks. "They mean for sure," Joe said. "When are we sure we saw her?"

Mary tilted her head up. "Was it Wednesday we were at the shops? Or Thursday?"

"You didn't see her on Friday?" Jane said. "Not coming or going?"

Siobhán was wondering the same thing. The front of the cottage was in clear view from their front porch. Especially when Joe was "bird-watching." Siobhán turned to Joe. "What did you mean a minute ago? Was there a time you might have seen her but you weren't sure?"

He folded his arms across his chest. "I'd rather get into this with our guards if you don't mind."

Siobhán sighed. It would be easier to get answers from the cow.

"I mind," Jane said. "I want to know. No. I *need* to know."

"We know something strange went on Friday night over the hill," Siobhán said. "Some people in town said they saw a figure running across the field. Did you see it too?"

"The witch," a voice said from the foot of the table. The little girl was standing there, holding a doll in each hand by the neck. "She was screaming."

"Hush," Mary said.

Siobhán was dying to ask the child more, but she wasn't going to step on a mother's toes.

"Talk to my mam," Joe said. "She was the one who saw her."

"Joe wasn't home Friday night," Mary said. "I was with their nana with the children. But it was Geraldine who saw the figure in the field."

"I was out of town," Joe confirmed. Siobhán opened her mouth to ask where when he cut in. "Farming business."

Had to see a man about a horse? She kept that to herself. "Oh?"

"We need new equipment. I tested some tractors."

"Did you buy any?"

"Couldn't come to an agreement."

She was dying to dig into his alibi, as she felt he was spinning a lie, but she could see from the set of his mouth that he wouldn't reveal anything more. Sometimes questioning suspects was like a game of poker. You had to know when to fold them. This little family had already concocted their responses and they were sticking to the script. With the exception of Lilly, who had plenty to say, but she wasn't going to be allowed to say it. Siobhán would pass Joe's alibi along to Danny to scrub. "Where does your mother live?"

"Just beyond the cottage," Jane said. "In the other direction. Walking distance in fact."

"How did she see anything?" Macdara asked.

"She stayed here Friday night," Joe said.

Mary nodded. "I don't like to be alone when he's away."

"Did you see Ellen before you left?" Siobhán addressed the question to Joe, but Mary responded by brushing a strand of hair out of her face with a shaking hand. Siobhán wondered if her limbs always vibrated, or if the questions were making her nervous.

"Just tell them," she said, chewing on her lip.

"We saw the big black car," Lilly said. She thumped the dolls' heads on the edge of the table. Siobhán was starting to pray that this one never had children of her own. On the other hand, Lilly and the cow seemed the only two willing to be open.

"A big black car?" Siobhán asked. She glanced at Jane. "Was it Ellen's?"

"We only have the old truck," Jane said. "We barely used it."

Siobhán had almost forgotten about the truck. No-where to be seen. Had the killer taken it? Why on earth would they do that? For a quick escape? It seemed if they were going to drive away in the truck, they would have taken her body with them. The investigation would be for a missing person instead of a murder, which could have bought them time. She turned to Jane. "Was there any-where else your mam would park the truck? Or anyone she could have lent it to?"

"The truck is missing?" Joe Madigan sounded sur-prised.

"Have you seen it?" Macdara asked.

"No, no," Joe said quickly. He stood. "Sorry we couldn't help." He threw his wife a look, and she stood.

"Joe thinks someone spent the night in our barn Friday night."

"Mary!"

"It could be important. What if it was the killer?"

Macdara was on high alert. "What's the story?"

Joe stared at the floor for a minute, then looked up and crossed his arms. "The hay in the loft of the barn was dis-turbed. It appeared as if someone had slept there."

"Have you told the guards?"

"Not yet, was waiting for them to come to me."

Macdara pulled out his mobile. "I'll give them a heads-up. Was there anything else? Anything at all?"

Lilly tugged on her father's shirt. "Tell them about all the dead micey."

"What?" Siobhán wasn't sure which one of them spoke first, for the question came from her and Macdara.

Joe shook his head. "We had a problem with field mice."

"Yikes," Siobhán said. Mice could be cute, from a distance, say out in a field. Her affection shifted the moment the wee things wanted to share walls and a roof.

"We'll say prayers for Ellen. And you," Mary said, reaching out and grabbing Jane's hand. Jane snatched hers away.

Macdara rose, but Jane remained sitting. Macdara leaned down and whispered into her ear, then helped her up.

"I don't know of any fairy stories that involve big black cars," Siobhán said when they reached the doorway. "Do you know what your daughter was referring to?"

"She's highly imaginative," Joe said. He opened the door and they all filed out onto the porch. "It's no secret we wanted the cottage bulldozed. Now I wish we'd gotten our way. I'm very sorry, Jane. I'm sorry we couldn't help."

"I understand," Jane said. "Thank you anyway."

"I'll walk you out," Joe said, shooing them down the steps of the porch, and herding them down the driveway like they were stray sheep in need of a good shepherd.

"You've lived here for how long?" Siobhán asked.

"I was born here," Joe said. "Like my father and grandfather before me."

As they walked, the cow followed behind Macdara, nudging her nose into his ear. He was trying to be a good sport about it, but the tips of his ears were still bright red. Siobhán knew she shouldn't tease him about it later, and also knew that would be impossible. The cow was in love. She was going to tease him the rest of his life. "Play hard to get," she said to the cow. "Don't be giving that milk away for free."

Macdara would have glowed in the dark. "Hilarious."

She laughed and turned her attention back to Joe Madigan, who was leading them off his property at a fast clip. What had spooked him? Mentioning the truck? "Since you've lived here all your life, I assume you know the history of the cottage?" Siobhán hoped if she kept poking, he'd say something he'd regret.

"Aye."

"Can you tell us about it?"

"Lived here all me life. If that cottage isn't cursed, I'd hate to see a structure that is."

"It must be tough to live so close to it."

He sighed. "If it's ghost stories you want it's my mam you should speak with." They'd reached the end of the lane. "Let us know when the funeral is planned, and we'll pay our respects. Give us a bell if you need anything. Anything at all."

Yeah right, anything. Anything, as long as it amounted to nothing. Only the cow seemed sorry to see them go.

Chapter 11

Siobhán had three items on her agenda: pay a visit to Geraldine Madigan, hear her ghost stories, then check out Mary Madigan and Joe's alibi. Time was of the essence. The less time suspects had to confer with each other the better.

Macdara had grudgingly agreed that he should take Jane into town to get any necessities she required before making the trip back to Kilbane. "And where are you off to?"

She told him her plan to visit Geraldine Madigan. "I think it will be easier to have a chat with our suspects without the victim's daughter in tow."

He nodded. "I wouldn't mind having a crack at them myself."

"They may react the same to you," Siobhán said. "You're the victim's nephew."

"I'm not saying you're wrong, but I don't like it." He sighed. "Jane is going to head back with me to my car. We'll find a better place to park it."

"Good idea."

"I have to admit, I'm feeling a bit left out here."

She kissed him on the cheek and set off in the direction of Geraldine's house. She stopped when she was in the clear and texted Danny.

Free to show me the sink?
Too many about. Will text soon.

On the way to Geraldine's house, Siobhán neared the fairy tree, the one they'd first spotted from the road. Beyond it, a patch of woods framed the scene, like the popular children were keeping their distance from an outcast. She stood by the tree for a moment and sent out positive thoughts, just in case anyone was listening. It was so peaceful underneath, looking out at the rolling hills, breathing the summer air. It was nearly impossible to believe anything sinister or supernatural had occurred here the other day. And no one should ever cut such a gorgeous tree down, no matter what the reasons. If stories had been used throughout time to protect the things that grew on this land, then hats off to the stories. She wished she could sit under the fairy tree all day and daydream, but she had a killer to catch. Now that she was on the hill, she could make out a small house on the other side of the woods. *To grandmother's house we go*, she thought, and continued along her way.

It was a small house painted yellow with a bright blue door. Geraldine, it seemed, was just as colorful as her walking sticks. Her garden burst with flowers, sporting every color in the rainbow. Siobhán vowed then and there to become a better gardener. This was a granny you wanted to visit, unless of course she was the type to not only make walking sticks but beat you with them as well. Siobhán laughed at the thought, and then chided herself for it, as she was pretty sure those children were well looked after, and no stick had been used to harm them. The minute Siobhán stepped up to the door, the smells of cooking wafted out.

She knocked, then waited. Moments later the door was thrown open, and in front of her stood Geraldine clad in an apron, bits of flour clinging to her cheeks. The delicious aroma spilled into the summer air.

"Hello," Siobhán said. "I hope I'm not bothering you."

"I'm preparing a feed for Jane," Geraldine said. "But it's nowhere near ready."

"That's so thoughtful," Siobhán said. "But we're heading to Kilbane later today."

"I see." Geraldine wiped her apron. "Come in then. I'll see what I can have ready for you, and I'll bring the rest to church."

"It smells delicious." Siobhán followed her into an expansive kitchen. The house was larger than it appeared on the outside, and no expense had been spared in the kitchen. Granite counters, a kitchen island with stool, and a giant cooker took center stage. Fresh flowers, Siobhán assumed from the garden, spilled out of a vase on the island. Above the farmhouse sink, a large window looked out onto the fairy tree. Geraldine moved amongst bowls and chopping boards as Siobhán hung back like a specter watching her work.

"Kettle is on," Geraldine said. She nodded to a plate of cookies on the island. "Just baked."

Siobhán's stomach growled. She'd had nothing but tea and biscuits all day. She snuck a cookie, secretly wishing for a sandwich and a cappuccino. The delicious morsel melted in her mouth and she couldn't help but hum a little. "Do you need any help?" she asked, eyeing the plate piled high with the scrumptious treats.

"Heavens, no, too many cooks and all that."

"What are you making?"

"I've got bacon and cabbage, and shepherd's pie, and oxtail stew, and potato and leek soup, and a sherry trifle and cookies."

"That is . . . a ton of food."

"Everyone is going to need comfort after these past few days. No one will have the energy to cook."

"You obviously enjoy it, and it smells divine."

"I hear you run a bistro back in Kilbane."

Gossip, faster than the Internet. "Naomi's Bistro," Siobhán confirmed. "My parents ran it and we took it over after they passed. My brothers mostly run it. I'm in charge of the brown bread, but I don't get much time anymore to do any proper cooking." *Or gardening. Or whittling. Or cleaning. Or child minding.*

"That's a shame," Geraldine said, clicking her tongue. "I find it soothing, especially at times like these."

She certainly was prepared. The countertops were filled with crates of fruit and veg; she must have cleaned up at the farmers' market. After a few moments of enjoying the smells and exchanging pleasantries, Siobhán dived in. "Can you walk me through everything that happened this past weekend beginning with Friday morning?"

"I suppose, although I don't know how it will help." Geraldine continued to chop and stir, moving seamlessly between tasks.

"You never know," Siobhán said. *The Devil was in the details.*

"The long and the short of it is I spent the weekend being a grandmother."

"I've met them," Siobhán said. "They're adorable."

"They're my life."

"Did they stay here?"

"Heavens, no. They wouldn't last very long away from their things. And their animals needed tending too."

Mary Madigan had made it sound like she was also present, but Geraldine was behaving as if she alone was taking care of the farm. Which one of them was lying? "I'm sure Mary appreciated you being there," Siobhán said. She kept her voice pleasant and casual.

"She deserves a break now and then; they both do."

If Geraldine was telling the truth, and Siobhán had the feeling she was, then Mary Madigan had lied. She'd left the children with Geraldine. Hadn't she pretended she'd spent the weekend with them? Where did she go? "What did she do with her break?"

Geraldine stopped and frowned for the first time. "That sounds like a personal question. For Mary."

"I was just making conversation. One day I'd like to take the day off and go to a spa. Feet up, nails polished, face shined."

"She did not go to a spa."

"Shopping?"

"As I said, it's none of my business, and it's certainly none of yours."

"The guards will ask." Siobhán kept her voice upbeat,

but it hardly mattered now; Geraldine was on guard. The shriek of the tea kettle made her jump.

"Let them ask then." Geraldine flicked off the burner, then poured two cups of tea. "My daughter-in-law is quite the artist if Annabel is to be believed." Her hand was shaking. Interesting, like mother-in-law, like daughter-in-law. Siobhán decided to push it.

"This is delicate to say, but we were just at Joe and Mary's house, and your son seems to be under the impression that Mary spent the weekend with you."

Geraldine slammed the kettle down. "She deserves her time off. I insisted. Blame me. Don't tell me you're going to tattle, upset a marriage over nothing?"

For a moment, Siobhán felt sorry for Joe Madigan. Both his wife and his mother had no problem keeping secrets from him. There must be a reason for it. Was he too strict otherwise? Geraldine either really liked her daughter-in-law, or perhaps she wanted to be alone with the children for the weekend. "The guards won't find out from me," Siobhán said, "but they will find out."

"Why do you say that?"

"It's a murder inquiry. Alibis will be collected. I wouldn't advise anyone to lie."

"Of course not," Geraldine said, quite unconvincingly. "If I were to guess, she was off somewhere, painting. Annabel has been putting silly notions in her head."

"What kind of silly notions?"

Geraldine waved it off. "'Tis only supposed to be a hobby."

"Do you know for a fact that's what Mary was doing? She was with Annabel?"

Geraldine smiled. "I have no clue and I didn't care. I just wanted time alone with my babies. I will tell you where she *wasn't*. She wasn't anywhere near that dreadful cottage."

"Mary said she was with the painting class on Friday evening."

"There you go."

"That is near the cottage."

Geraldine turned to the cooker to stir a pot. "My daughter-in-law doesn't have a violent bone in her body. If you want her alibi you'll have to ask her."

"Lilly had a lot to say."

Geraldine's head snapped around. "What are you on about?"

"I think she saw something that evening."

"You're dead wrong."

"You haven't even heard what she said."

"My granddaughter was asleep at half seven."

"Does her window face the cottage?" Geraldine slammed pots into the sink and began muttering to herself. "Do you believe in the supernatural?"

"Piseog," Geraldine said with a nod. "'Course I do."

"I don't think that's what killed poor Ellen."

"We can sit here and argue about fairies and ghosts all day long, but that doesn't change the fact that the inhabitants of that cottage have met with mysterious deaths one after the other. It needs to come down!"

"It won't be coming down anytime soon. It's a crime scene."

"Some things just weren't meant to be, and that cottage is one of them."

"I've noticed that you own the land on one side of the cottage, and your son on the other."

"Your point?"

"Did your family own the cottage at one point?"

Geraldine pursed her lips. "My grandfather owned it back in the day. He sold it when he was a young man starting out. Partly because of the cottage, I suppose. If you're suggesting he should have taken it down, I won't argue with that. Now the land is worthless. Once the cottage comes down, what can one really do with it?"

"You've lived here through all the mysterious deaths."

"I have indeed. 'Tis terrible." She wiped her hands on the apron. "You should see the way my divining sticks react when they're anywhere near the cottage." She shuddered.

"I didn't know you had divining sticks."

Geraldine nodded. "They reacted immediately. A very strong warning."

"What do you use them for?" Siobhán knew they were used to locate water, and for some . . . divining purposes, but she had never met anyone who used them.

"When you're trained, you can use them to feel out troubled spots and try to perform a healing."

"I see."

"One day I may become a member of the Irish Society of Diviners. I've taken a course."

"Well done."

Geraldine raised an eyebrow, as if trying to ascertain whether or not Siobhán was being sarcastic, then let it go. "I showed Ellen. She saw the sticks quiver with her own eyes near dat cottage, and she still scoffed." Geraldine wiped her hands on her apron, twisting it violently.

"When was this?"

"Just after they moved in."

"She saw the sticks react?"

"With her own eyes. It quivered like I've never seen

before in me life. Bent over so much I thought it was going to snap in two."

"Can you give me a demonstration?" Siobhán asked.

"I won't be able to show you the dowsing stick today," Geraldine said. "As you've stated—the area around the cottage is a crime scene."

"Can't you demonstrate it elsewhere?"

"I could, of course, but it only reacts if I'm near the cottage."

How convenient. "I'd like to see your walking sticks," Siobhán said. "I didn't get to buy one at the market."

"Let me get this in the cooker," she said, maneuvering another pan into its depths. "You can have your pick."

Geraldine wasn't joking. Her back room was chock full of decorative walking sticks. Many were woven with colorful string like the one Geraldine carried, others were painted, and one with a round base was covered in thick rope. Geraldine noticed Siobhán staring at the circular bottom. "It's a walker," she said, lifting it out of the corner. She clunked it down. "It's good in the spring when the mud runs thick, or walking near the bog."

"You're very talented."

Geraldine waved her hand as if to dismiss the compliment, but her cheeks took on a rosy hue. Siobhán eventually chose a masculine staff with a darker hue and a green crystal set on top.

"Beautiful," Geraldine said, as if complimenting Siobhán for having such good taste. "That will be forty euro."

Siobhán dug the cash out of her handbag, relieved that she had it. Macdara was going to have to pay for lunch. It spurred another thought, the perfect use for the walking stick—she couldn't wait to present it to Macdara as an engagement gift. His engagement stick. If he wanted to walk around spreading the news of their betrothal, off to it then.

"Can you please take me through the weekend?" Siobhán said. They were now standing outside so that Siobhán could try out her purchase. It was fun to navigate the terrain with it at her side.

"As I stated, I was with my grandchildren at the farm."

"Just take me through it, please." They came to a rest on the other side of Geraldine's flower garden, bursting with color. "Was there anything? Anything out of the ordinary at all?"

"I don't know if this bit of news will be of any interest to you," Geraldine said. She glanced around as if the fairies might be listening.

"Go on."

"Ellen had a visitor Friday morning. A very curious visitor indeed."

Chapter 12

"It is of great interest," Siobhán said, dying to hear about Ellen's mysterious visitor, but trying not to sound too eager.

"I have to tend to the garden. We can chat while I work." Geraldine switched her kitchen apron for a gardening smock, and even had matching gloves, and an adorable basket. "It must have been someone important," Geraldine said as she moved seamlessly amongst the flowers pulling up weeds.

"Why do you say that?"

"A limousine in this village stands out."

Siobhán remembered what Mary's young daughter had said. *"We saw the big black car!"* It seemed the little girl didn't have an overactive imagination after all. "A limousine?"

"It pulled up to the gate, then shut off while the driver got out and made his way up to the cottage."

"Describe him."

"He was a short man, alright."

Siobhán waited but that seemed to be all she remembered about his appearance. "You saw him get out of the limo?"

"I said so, did I not?"

Siobhán clenched her fist and took a deep breath. She needed to start carrying a few whittling tools in her handbag. She'd like to take a knife to wood right about now. "Repetition is helpful to guards, Mrs. Madigan. I'm sure it's frustrating for you, but I do wish you'd adjust your tone."

Instead, Geraldine took the opportunity to adjust her floppy hat, then nodded. "He barged up to Ellen's door and banged on it. Ellen let him in. A few minutes later he hurried out, practically running to his car." She stopped yanking weeds and stood straight. "Do you think that was him? The murderer?" Siobhán's reprimand had done the trick; Geraldine was no longer barking at her.

"What time was this?"

"I believe it was around half ten in the morning."

"A limousine. On Friday morning?"

"Odd, isn't it?"

Yes, it was. Siobhán thought everything she'd seen and heard in this village so far had been odd. She'd keep that opinion to herself as well. "Are you sure of the time?"

"Ah, sure. I was with the young ones in the front yard. I was still trying to get them to eat their breakfast." Siobhán could imagine them out in the yard, watching the limo pull up. "She was going somewhere fancy, we know that."

The image of Ellen in her red dress rose in her mind. "You saw her?"

Geraldine scanned the environment as if the flowers had just sprouted eyes and ears and were intent on eavesdropping. "Aye. I stopped in for a cuppa to see if she would mention the fancy limousine."

"How soon after you first spotted the limo was this?"

"I'd say about an hour. The children had been fed, and were in their beds for a lie-down, and the limo was gone. I decided to find out what that was all about."

"Did Ellen answer?"

"She did. And she lied straight to my face."

"How so?"

"I asked her where she planned on going in that fancy limousine and she had the nerve to say—'what limousine?'"

"Is it possible she hadn't seen it?"

"Not a chance. The driver walked right up to her door and I saw her answer it. Were you not listening?" So much for the truce. Geraldine was prickly once more.

"I give you she saw the driver, but perhaps she didn't see the limousine."

"Well, then I hope she asked the man dressed in black with a driver's cap what he was doing at her door, like."

"Please continue."

"I asked her if it had pulled up for directions—maybe it was someone who heard stories about fairies, a looky-loo. That's all we need is tourists coming to gawk."

"What did she say?"

"She told me she knew nothing about it." Geraldine

stopped pulling weeds and blew on a strand of her hair that had fallen in the way. "But I saw her answer the door, like."

"I see."

"And then there's this." Geraldine took off her gloves and reached under the apron into the pocket of her dress. She pulled out a calling card and held it up for Siobhán to see: PRIMO LIMO. "This was on Ellen's counter."

"On the counter? Are you sure?" Didn't Jane say that Ellen loathed anything cluttering the counter? First the stack of papers, now this. Maybe Ellen only kept things neat when Jane was around. Perhaps she was a more relaxed housekeeper when she was alone? Or someone else was cluttering up the cottage. The killer?

"Yes," Geraldine said, watching Siobhán intently. "Is that important?"

"I don't know," Siobhán answered honestly. "Did you see anything else on the counter?"

Geraldine pondered the question. "No. Just the card."

"Which you plucked?"

Geraldine stared at her shoes. "I don't know why I took it. I really don't."

She not only took it, she was keeping it close. "You know why."

Geraldine's face twisted into a sour expression. "I don't like liars. Ellen Delaney lied straight to my face."

Perhaps she thought it was none of your business. "What was she wearing?"

"Heavens, I wouldn't be able to tell you dat."

"Was she dressed up?"

"No. A housecoat of some sort. That's all I know."

"Then why did you say she must have been going somewhere fancy?"

If Geraldine were a portrait she would be titled: *Woman Who Swallowed a Live Fish*. It took her a moment to recover. "Why, because of the limo, of course."

"Maybe the driver was lost. Asking for directions." Siobhán didn't believe this for a second, but Geraldine was hiding something, she was sure of it.

"She was so upset when I brought up the limo she didn't even let me finish me tea and biscuit. Rushed me out of the house saying she had to take care of something right away." She handed Siobhán the calling card. "Maybe yer man can shed some light on the situation."

Siobhán tucked the card away. "Thank you. Before I leave—can you please tell me your version of the strange events of Friday night?"

"I was standing out on the porch catching the evening breeze when strange lights appeared in the distance, followed by lilting music. Flutes. I saw a figure trudging across the field. At the time I had no idea who it was, although I realize now it must have been Ellen."

"Where do you think she was going?"

"To spend the night near the fairy tree."

This story had just taken a strange turn. "Why do you think that?"

Geraldine tapped her lip with her finger. "I heard a rumor."

Or you're about to start one. . . . "Go on."

"Someone bet Ellen that she couldn't spend the entire night near the fairy tree."

"Who was this someone?"

Geraldine shook her head. "I can't say for sure."

Siobhán doubted that. "Where did you hear this rumor?"

"My daughter-in-law. She heard someone in her painting class mention it."

Yet another reason Siobhán needed to meet this Annabel. "Why do you think Ellen would make a bet like that?"

"Ellen Delaney was on a mission to prove the town wrong about the fairies and therefore save the cottage. If she had managed to spend an entire night near the fairy tree and fairy ring, she could have presented that as proof that either the fairies don't exist, or they had no quarrel with her." She sighed. "I take no pleasure in saying I told her so."

There was a lot of detail in Geraldine's *guess*. "Is this pure conjecture on your part or did Ellen tell you she planned on spending the night near the fairy ring?" It was a very specific theory. Too specific.

Geraldine began to blink rapidly. "I'm just connecting the dots."

"I see." Siobhán didn't know anyone who would come up with those dots let alone connect them. She had a feeling Geraldine was indeed the one who had goaded Ellen into the bet. Was there more to her plan? "Then what?"

"I was awoken in the middle of the night by the music. Flutes. I put on my robe and slippers and stepped outside. You should have seen the lights. The skies were glowing, as if responding to the music. It was the most beautiful thing I'd ever seen. And then came the scream." She shuddered. "The wail of a banshee. That's when I saw Ellen flying through the meadow on her way back to the cottage."

"If it was evening how could you see her so clearly?"

"It was the summer solstice. The longest day of the year. Not to mention the light of the full moon."

"Did you see anyone following her?"

"No. But the scream woke the children up, so I was tending to them."

"Maybe that's when Lilly saw the pretty lights and people dancing?" Geraldine yanked weeds out with a vengeance, sending dirt flying in Siobhán's direction. Mention of her granddaughter only made her clam up. Siobhán edged closer. "Why didn't you go over to the cottage to see if Ellen was okay?" Wasn't that the point of living in a small village? Neighbor looking out for neighbor?

Geraldine stared and blinked some more. "I should have. But I was terrified. I wasn't going to leave the children."

"But that morning you left them having a lie-in and walked over to Ellen's cottage."

"That's different. In the light of day it's alright. Different story in the dark of night. You know yourself."

Ireland did fall to black at night, but earlier Geraldine had argued that there was plenty of light on this eve. "Why didn't you call her? Or the guards?"

Beads of sweat broke out on Geraldine's cheeks. "I don't know. Do you think it would have helped? That she wouldn't have been killed?"

Siobhán had no intention of consoling her. She should have called the guards. "Did you see anyone snooping around the cottage? Did you hear glass breaking?"

"Is it the window you're on about?"

"'Tis."

"I didn't hear it break. I noticed it the next morning when I passed the cottage."

"You didn't knock then, see if she was home? See if she was alright?"

Geraldine dropped her basket and shears and took off her gloves. She wiped her brow. "I thought she was playing a trick on me." Her lip quivered. "That's why I didn't check on her. And I'll regret it the rest of me life." Tears spilled down her cheeks.

"A trick?"

"Yes. First she insists she's going to spend the night by the fairy tree—"

"Insists?"

"I'm not saying any more."

"It could help catch a killer."

"I've told you all I know. You didn't know Ellen. But she wasn't the type who wanted neighborly help. I knew whatever went on that night was either a trick that she orchestrated herself, or it was the work of the fairies. When I found out she was dead, I had my answer."

"I see. I hope you'll tell the guards the unvarnished truth."

"You want the truth? That cottage is coming down now even if I have to set it on fire myself."

"I wouldn't advise that."

"If you want to catch Ellen Delaney's killer, you should start with her stalker."

Despite the sun beating down on them, the words sent a chill through Siobhán. "Stalker?"

"Yes, didn't Jane mention it?" Geraldine frowned. "Or did Ellen tell me not to mention it to Jane? Was she keeping her out of it? I forget."

"What do you remember?"

"Ellen said something about a man in Waterford who wouldn't leave her alone. She said he showed up everywhere—the post office, the market, even followed her to her doctor's appointment one day. She was so afraid of him that she left town." Geraldine sighed. "And yet, she died anyway. Maybe when it's your time, it doesn't matter how you go, just that you go."

If everyone had that attitude, justice would never be done. "Did she say anything else about this stalker?"

Geraldine cocked her head. "Like what?"

"Like who he was? Like if she ever saw him here in Ballysiogdun. Like—did she call the guards?"

"I can see you're disappointed in me for not asking. You see, I didn't even know whether or not I believed her. I mean . . . she's not your typical stalking victim, is she?"

"I'm not sure what you mean by that."

"She wasn't some pretty young thing. If you told me you had a stalker, or several, I'd believe you. But her? Why on earth would anyone be following her around, like?"

Chapter 13

"Engagement stick?" Macdara arched his eyebrow as he stared at her gift.

"Brilliant, isn't it?" They stood on the footpath in front of the chemist. Jane was inside, getting any essentials she would need. Siobhán had almost volunteered that they had a chemist in Kilbane as well, when she realized that Jane probably felt more comfortable in her home stores, where she had an understanding of the layout and where everything was located. There were so many little things that sighted people took for granted.

Macdara twirled his engagement stick, then pounded the ground several times. "You shouldn't have." From the tone of his voice, he really meant it.

"Don't mention it." She took the stick back.

"What are you doing?"

"I'm just going to use it while we're here." She grinned; he shook his head.

"You two are adorable," a voice said. Siobhán turned to find Jane standing in front of her, holding her bags from the chemist.

Macdara took the bags. "Right then. Are we off?"

Siobhán was anxious to get back to Kilbane and away from all this talk of fairies. But her stomach growled. "I'm so hungry I could eat a small horse."

Macdara nodded to the public house across the street. "Why don't we have lunch before we head off." Siobhán planned on contacting Primo Limo as soon as possible, but she would have to do it in private. She'd quickly learned that even when you thought Jane wasn't paying attention, she was actually absorbing every word. Because of that, Siobhán was not yet ready to ask Jane about Geraldine's account of the calling card on the counter, the bet to spend the night near the fairy tree, or the mention of a stalker in Waterford. Siobhán was going to have to speak to Macdara first, or more likely—Danny. He never did get a chance to show her whatever was in the sink, and if Siobhán tried to make up an excuse to delay their return to Kilbane, Macdara would see right through it. Should she just tell him?

Jane was usually by his side. Macdara would not like it if Siobhán went around him for information—who was she kidding, he would loathe it—but she could not give Jane any more ammunition than necessary. Not until she was cleared as a suspect. And as horrible as it was to imagine a daughter killing her own mother, statistics proved that murders were often committed by those closest to the victim. No one could push buttons like your family could. And from the sounds of it, Ellen Delaney had treated her grown daughter like a child. Siobhán could see how that might drive a person to her breaking point. Jane was a suspect, there was no getting around it.

The seanchaí from the farmers' market was guarding the entrance to the pub, using his theatrical voice to entice people inside. "Listen to the tales of yore."

"Eddie Doolan," Jane said with a slight snarl. "Don't encourage him, he's a bit soft in the head."

Storytellers. The bearers of old lore. In ancient times, Celtic lore was never written down. Neither was history for that matter. Or laws until the monks started to keep records. Before that, stories were kept by colorful characters memorizing long lyric poems, which were to be recited by bards. The seanchaíthe would rise to carry on that tradition. Storytelling became an art form, passed from one generation to the next, enthralling crowds with legends, myths, and history. In modern day the few who practiced the craft did so mostly at festivals.

"Hurry, hurry," he said, dancing after them as they tried to pass. "There's no time to waste now—the fairies are out for revenge. The cottage, she must come down." He thrust a tin cup at them. Siobhán dug in her handbag for some change, then tossed it in. He flashed a grin, two-stepped, and bowed.

Jane whirled on him. "You should be ashamed of yourself."

He jumped as if he hadn't realized who she was until she was standing right in front of him. Siobhán glanced at Macdara to see if he would try and temper his cousin, but he was staring off into the distance, clearly wishing he was anywhere but here. It wasn't his place to teach his cousin manners, but head-in-the-sand was not his best look.

"Please," Eddie Doolan said, leaning in. His breath reeked of onions. "The winds have been stirred, death is still near. Do you dare and defy the fairies now?"

"Where are you from?" Siobhán asked.

He frowned as if you weren't supposed to talk to him like he was a person. "I go where I'm needed," he said at last. "I'm only doing me job."

"You're not needed here," Jane said.

"How long have you been here?" Siobhán continued.

His eyes darted left and right as if he couldn't bear to look her in the eye. "I travel often for work," he said. "Originally I'm a Mayo man."

"Lovely." He was talking and she wanted to keep that going. "Do you have family or friends here?"

"Can we go inside?" Jane said. "I'm famished."

"Find us a good spot, I'll be right in," Siobhán said.

"Does she ever take a break?" Jane asked, turning to Macdara.

Dara lifted his head. "Believe me, you should be happy she doesn't." He locked eyes with Siobhán and gave her a nod. Thank goodness. The Dara she knew and loved was still in there.

Jane wagged her finger at Siobhán. "Remember he's a storyteller. He'll spin whatever tale he thinks you want to hear."

"I love hearing tales," Siobhán said. Were there any stories in particular that Jane didn't want the seanchaí to spill?

"You and I need to catch up on everything soon," Macdara said to Siobhán as he opened the door for Jane. "Don't be long."

Eddie relaxed the moment Jane was out of sight. "She's blind," he said, leaning in as if it were breaking news.

"She is," Siobhán agreed. "She's also a very capable woman."

He frowned as if that didn't compute. "She can't see."

"That is the definition of blind."

He shook his head and leaned in. Siobhán was forced to take a step back. "She can't see the truth."

"What is the truth?"

"She's in danger here. She must not stay."

"Danger?" Siobhán looked him in the eye. "From you?"

He leaned back theatrically, whipping his cape around as he poked his own chest. "Me? From me?"

"Are you threatening her?"

He took the side of his cloak and bowed low. "I am but the messenger."

Siobhán did not know what to make of him. Bumbling, and sweet, and theatrical, and as much as she hated the way Jane put it—maybe he had some cognitive delays. At the least, he seemed confident in his storytelling, but cripplingly shy when it came to real conversation. So much drama for such a little village. "Did you see the mysterious events of Friday evening?"

He straightened up, his hair now standing straight from static. "Your hair is gorgeous," he said. As he reached out to touch it, she brought her arm up and blocked him. "I want to touch it."

"No, thank you." He withdrew his hand as if he'd been

scalded. "It's not just you. I don't allow any strangers to touch my hair."

"I'm a stranger," he admitted. Then nodded as if he'd just figured it out.

"My name is Siobhán. Or, if you prefer, Garda O'Sullivan." He took a step back. "Your name is Eddie?"

He blinked. "I don't remember names. I never remember names."

"It's okay."

"I remember songs. I sing."

"You are very talented."

He gave a bow, then stood and flamboyantly gestured to the door. "They're waiting." His demeanor had changed instantly the minute she said she was a guard.

"I'd like to hear more of your stories."

He turned and bolted, his coins rattling in his cup as he ran.

Dark wood paneling and sconce lighting gave the pub a homey feel. A small group of trad players were set up in the corner, their instruments ringing out with jaunty tunes. Siobhán ordered a ham-and-cheese toastie, curried chips, and a mineral. She really wanted two ham-and-cheese toasties, but resisted. This way she could have a slice of pie for dessert. There was something about this village that just made her want to sit down and eat comfort food. Macdara ordered fish and chips and a Guinness, and Jane sat in front of her potato-and-leek soup barely touching it. Siobhán's heart squeezed for her. "You know," she said. "Why not get something indulgent? A slice of pie?"

"Pie," Jane said as if she'd never heard the word. She waved the publican over. Siobhán felt a silly flush of pride. "I'll have a pint of Guinness."

Macdara and Jane exchanged a look. "I'll have a slice of lemon meringue pie, as well, like," Macdara said as he slid his Guinness over to Jane. "And she's sorted with this pint."

"We're engaged," Siobhán said.

"Congrats," said the publican. "One slice of pie and one Guinness coming up."

"Two slices of pie, please," Siobhán said. "And a Guinness for me too."

"If you're having Guinness and pie, then I'm having Guinness and pie," Macdara said, clearly outraged.

Jane slid the pint back to Macdara. "Three slices of pie, and two pints of Guinness."

He nodded and hurried away before they could change the order again.

"How did it go with Geraldine?" Jane was eager for details.

"I'm going to speak with Danny," Siobhán said. "If there are any inconsistencies between her account and that of Joe and Mary Madigan, I'll make sure he knows about it."

Jane slapped the table and laughed. "Are you listening to this, Dara? She's a sly one."

"Honestly, that's not my intent," Siobhán said. "But it's best not to engage in rumors while in the middle of an investigation."

"I'm not asking you to engage in rumors, I'm asking you what Geraldine said. Word for word." Siobhán shot Macdara a look, hoping for a little emotional backup, but he was suddenly examining the walking stick as if it was speaking to him. "You can't keep it from me. She's my mam."

"I'm sorry. My goal is the same as yours. To find your mother's killer. I can't bring you into the investigation."

She shook her head. "Cousin Dara will tell me. Unless you're going to keep it from him as well, like?" Siobhán didn't answer; she was too busy mentally whittling the words "MEAN GIRL." Jane reached out for Macdara's hand. "Are you okay with your fiancée keeping secrets from you?"

"We're just here to enjoy our lunch," Macdara said, setting the walking stick down. The tip of his boot nudged Siobhán's toe under the table. He was *not* okay with her keeping secrets from him. What did he want her to do?

"Maybe you can help me," Siobhán said. "What can you tell me about Eddie the seanchaí?"

"Why? Did he say something?" Jane leaned forward eagerly.

"It's what he didn't say. I tried to talk to him and when I wouldn't let him touch my hair, he bolted."

"Touch your hair?" Macdara said.

She shrugged. "It's a thing."

"You let me touch your hair," Jane said with a smirk.

"Different situation entirely."

Jane laughed, but quickly sobered up. "As far as I know, his name is Eddie Doolan and he's homeless."

"As far as you know?"

"Don't tell me you didn't smell him."

"I did."

"And?"

"It's quite possible he's homeless." Siobhán hoped she didn't sound as judgmental as Jane. She was not the type of person who looked down on others' hardships. She was grateful for the roof over her head and the food that was always on her plate, and despite sharing it with five siblings—which meant the water was often cold by the time it was her turn—she was grateful for their shower and bathtub. It didn't make her a better person that she had these things, it made her a luckier person. And although it could be argued that one made their own luck, it was equally true that fate could be a cruel mistress. As her mam used to say, "*There but for the Grace of God, go I.*" She teared up just thinking about it.

"He sleeps outside," Jane continued. "I've heard people throw coins into his cup, but it's either not enough to get a place to sleep or he doesn't want to."

"Is he a local?"

"No. He arrived just after we did."

Another new resident in this tiny village? What were the odds of that? "Strange," Siobhán said. "Do you know why?"

"All I know is that he's the only person in this village that is hated more than Mam and I."

"Is there a chance you know Eddie from Waterford?" *Could he be Ellen's stalker?*

Jane's head jerked up. "No. Why on earth would I know him from Waterford?"

"Have you learned something?" Macdara asked.

"It seems they all arrived in the village around the same time," Siobhán said. "That seems curious." If Jane was aware that her mother had a stalker, now would be the perfect opportunity to bring it up.

"I'll leave that to you," Jane replied. She wrung her hands. "I guess now it's just me and Eddie left for this village to hate. I keep forgetting Mam's gone."

Siobhán reached over and patted her hand. "That's normal, pet. It takes a while."

Their pie and pints arrived and for a moment everyone buried themselves in them, each preferring it to the discussion at hand. Siobhán was wondering what brought Eddie the wandering storyteller into town at the same time as Ellen and Jane. She was going to have to dig into Eddie Doolan a bit more.

"Get out!" The reprimand came from the publican. Their heads swiveled to the bar.

"Speak of the Devil," Macdara said, filling Jane in on what was happening.

Eddie was back, pleading a case to the publican. "Picture this, story night!"

"I said no." The publican stood with his arms folded across his chest. "Off with ya."

"A nice turf fire, pints all around, some music, and a story that will enthrall ye." He raised his voice to a theatrical level, gesturing around.

"My mother was murdered and all you can talk about is story time?" Jane rose from her chair, matching Eddie's theatrical tone.

Eddie lumbered toward them, his eyes wide, his hands reaching. "Murdered?" Although he was a performer by trade, his shock seemed genuine to Siobhán. He leaned in. "Was it the fairies?"

"No," Siobhán said. "It was a person. A human being."

"They can look like humans," Eddie said, clasping his hands to his chest, his eyes darting around as sweat dripped down his broad face.

"It happened last night," Siobhán said. "You hadn't heard?" That seemed nearly impossible. She had to remind herself he was a performer, an actor. Was he acting now?

He looked to the ground. "I heard she died. I thought . . . well, she was an older woman, a bit on the heavy side—"

"She was only in her sixties!" Jane said.

"A bit on the heavy side," he repeated.

Jane turned her head toward Macdara and Siobhán. "Eddie feels big to me. Is he big?"

"He's . . ." Macdara said, looking up at the gentle giant.

"Big," Eddie said. "I'm big too."

He reminded Siobhán of a child. A giant child in desperate need of a wash.

"And wide," Jane said. She waited. "There you have it, no denials."

Eddie smiled as if he hadn't copped on that Jane wasn't being nice. "Who murdered Mrs. Delaney?"

"The guards are looking into it," Macdara said. "Where were you Friday night and Saturday day?"

"Me?" Eddie repeatedly poked at his chest with his finger. He stammered the words, revealing a slight stutter that seemed to disappear when he was in storytelling mode. "M-m-m-m me?"

"Yes, y-y-y-y-you!" Jane said.

Siobhán gasped. Macdara shook his head at his cousin, although Siobhán had no idea whether Jane could see it. The verdict was in. Jane Delaney was not a nice person and, cousin or not, she was no longer invited to the wedding. Making fun of a man's impediment was just downright cruel. As a blind woman, didn't she realize how the worst part of a disability was dealing with the ignorance of well-meaning people? Even well-meaning stupid people would be hard to take. "It's okay, pet," Siobhán said to Eddie. She reached into her handbag and handed him twenty euro. "You can tell the official guards where you were, luv, and in the meantime, the pie here is delicious."

He clasped the money in his hands and bowed. "My d-d-d-d-d-eepest sympathies," he said.

"You should try singing," Jane said. "It will help with the stutter."

"I kn-kn-kn-know." He bobbed his head. "I can s-s-s-sing."

"Save it for the shower," Jane said, turning her back to him.

"Your mother," Eddie said, slightly singing it. "Your mother was murdered." It sounded so eerie in his singsong voice.

"You catch on quick," Jane said.

Eddie nodded, his lips moving silently as if he was singing to himself, before he turned and fled yet again.

Chapter 14

There was a moment of silence as if Eddie Doolan had suctioned all the thoughts out of their poor heads when he departed.

"Is it me or is there something a little off about that man?" Macdara said at last.

"Mental illness is common among the homeless," Jane said.

Siobhán squirmed in her seat. Was there any heart underneath that cold exterior? She wished she had her scooter so she wouldn't have to be trapped in a car with her. "He seemed genuinely frightened."

Jane pushed back from the table. "You're falling for his stories then."

"Shall we get our legs under us?" Siobhán was tired of Jane, tired of this village, and couldn't wait to get home. "I'm going to hit the jax before we leave."

On her way to the restroom, Siobhán stopped at the corner of the bar where calling cards were piled up. She scanned to see if there were any from Primo Limo. She did not see any for them but there were several others: a jeweler, a furniture maker, a charity shop, and Annabel's art classes.

"Can I help you, luv?" the publican said. "Is everything alright?"

"Just having a nose around," she said. "Where is the jax?"

"That-a-way." He pointed to the restrooms, situated at the back of the bar.

She pocketed several of the calling cards and gave him a nod. "Cheers."

Before they could leave for Kilbane, Danny and Sergeant Eegan summoned Macdara and Siobhán to Molly's Café. To Siobhán's relief, Jane seemed happy to have more time to shop, and didn't put up a fuss about not being invited. They had just reached the café when Macdara gently pulled Siobhán aside. "Now?" Siobhán said, with a glance in the window. Danny and Sergeant were standing, looking at the paintings, waiting for them.

"It's hard to get you alone," Macdara said. "You seem angry with me." Siobhán had trouble meeting his gaze. "Did you learn something from Geraldine?"

"Has your cousin always been so . . . harsh?"

Macdara shoved his hands in his pockets. "I don't know her that well. My guess is that she's always been this way."

"Doesn't it bother you?"

"Of course. Why do you think we were estranged? My

mam barely talked to her own sister. They weren't easy to get along with."

"I think Jane is lying about her alibi."

"Do you?"

"Have you seen proof that she was in Dublin?"

"No. But she hasn't been able to get her luggage bag. I assume there's something in there."

"She had ages to open it before the guards arrived. Or she could tell us the name of the conference, the hotel where she stayed. Anything."

"I hear you. But her mother was just murdered. I understand if it's not the first thing on her mind."

Siobhán chose her words carefully. Her quarrel was not with Dara. "I have cousins I haven't seen in ages. I'm trying to understand."

"Trying?"

"She's a manipulator and you're different around her."

His jaw tightened. "I see."

"Dara." She'd hurt him. Before they could resolve it, a tap sounded on the window next to them. They both jumped and turned to see Danny motioning them inside.

"Ironic," Macdara said, pointing a finger-gun at Danny and heading for the door. "Because you're different around him." Danny, not to be outdone, produced two finger-guns, and he twirled, then blew on them before sticking them into imaginary holsters.

Sergeant Eegan waved them over to the counter the minute they entered. He was jotting things down in a notebook. Siobhán filled them in on everything she'd learned from Geraldine—how Mary Madigan had lied about being with her mother-in-law for the weekend, and the story about Primo Limo, and the odd mention of Ellen staying the night near the fairy tree as if that would somehow settle the dispute. Lastly, she filled them in on the rumor that in Waterford Ellen had a stalker.

"Stalker?" Macdara said. "Is that the exact word she used?"

"'Tis."

"It's true," Garda Eegan said. "At least I heard it from a few other heads, who supposedly heard it from her."

"Heard what exactly?" Macdara was on high alert. Relations must have been strained if Ellen hadn't even reached out to him when she was in danger.

Garda Eegan shook his head. "I'm short on the details. Heard she had a stalker, some kind of nuisance on her doorstep in Waterford. Here for a fresh start."

Macdara turned to Siobhán. "Is that why you were asking Jane about Eddie Doolan?"

"Eddie?" Garda Eegan said. "The storyteller? The beggar?"

Siobhán nodded. "He came to town the same time as Ellen and Jane."

Garda Eegan rubbed his beard. "Ellen and Jane were here a good year before Eddie showed up."

Danny leaned forward. "Are you suggesting Eddie Doolan is her stalker?"

"Do you know where he's from?" Siobhán asked.

"He said he's a Mayo man," Danny answered.

If that was a lie, at least he was telling consistent stories. "Did you ever look into him?"

Garda Eegan waved his hand. "I've moved him along when I've found him sleeping on the footpath. But mostly he isn't a bother. Some folks like his storytelling."

"Maybe you'll have a look at him now?" Macdara said. His hands were clenched; he was dying to get involved.

"We will," Danny said. Instead of comforting Macdara, the utterance from Danny seemed to perturb him more.

"What about Primo Limo?" Siobhán said, wanting to ease the tension.

"They're not part of Ballysiogdun," Sergeant Eegan said, examining the calling card she'd handed him. "They're out of Cork City. We'll give them a bell." He practically crumpled the card as he shoved it in his shirt pocket, and Siobhán was relieved she'd taken the number down for herself.

"Jane mentioned that Aiden Cunningham holds a lot of power here. Especially when it comes to the cottage."

"What about our councilman?" Eegan asked. "You're not accusing him of being a killer, are you?" He leaned back with a hearty laugh.

Danny gave Siobhán a reassuring look. "We'll question everyone and we won't close our options until alibis are checked and rechecked."

"Thank you," Siobhán said. Sergeant Eegan could learn from Danny if he wasn't so threatened by the younger guard. From an investigative perspective, everyone should be considered equally guilty until proven innocent. Otherwise, you could be misled by your own bias. Everyone was capable of killing.

"When can we hold the service?" Macdara asked.

The sergeant nodded his understanding of the question. "The pathologist is expected tomorrow."

"That's good," Siobhán said. The sooner the better.

Macdara stood. "We're heading back to Kilbane now. We'll start on the preliminary arrangements."

"We'd like to be there," Sergeant Eegan said. "Keep us informed."

"Good," Macdara said. "I was hoping you'd say that."

"In case our killer will be there too," Danny said. He caught the stares-all-around. "I'm stating the obvious again, aren't I?"

Macdara patted him on the back. A smidge too hard from Siobhán's observation. "And, unfortunately for our killer," Macdara said, "we'll be watching him."

"Or her," Siobhán said.

Macdara nodded. "Or her," he agreed.

Chapter 15

It was late Saturday afternoon when the sight of Saint Mary's steeple rising above the stone walls of Kilbane welcomed them back. The minute they drove through the Ballygate entrance, the knot in Siobhán's stomach loosened. *Home.* "Mam should be checked into the Kilbane Inn by now," Macdara said.

"Bring her to the bistro."

"That's the plan."

"Do I sense tension?" Jane asked. Everyone had been quiet on the drive home, like boxers retreating to their corners before the next round.

"Not at all," Siobhán said. *Except I don't think she likes me and that was before she knew I was going to marry the golden boy.*

"I'm sure Mam is looking forward to seeing you as well," Macdara said to Jane.

It would be a few days before Ellen's body was released, but in the meantime they could comfort one another, dedicate a mass to Ellen Delaney, and even hold a wake. Macdara dropped Jane and Siobhán off at the bistro, then headed for the inn. The bell dinged as they stepped into Naomi's, giving Siobhán a mini shot of joy. She could hear chattering as she walked in, and was overjoyed when they stepped into the dining room to find that all her siblings were home, even James. Jane's demeanor immediately brightened as she was introduced to the rest of the O'Sullivan Six, as they were affectionately nicknamed by the town. She squeezed Ciarán and Ann, and allowed Gráinne to make style suggestions as they guided her by the fire that James was tending.

Eoin and Bridie were in the kitchen as the bistro was filled, which was slightly unusual for after lunch, but not surprising given the news of Macdara's aunt being murdered in Ballysiogdun had already spread through Kilbane. Siobhán entered the kitchen to see how the pair was holding up. Pans of food lined the counters.

"What's this?" Siobhán asked, nosing around.

"What do you think?" Eoin said. "The neighbors. We look busy, but mostly we're selling tea and brown bread because everyone is bringing their own food."

"Good," Siobhán said. "Why don't you two take a break? We'll officially close and just let everyone help themselves." Eoin and Bridie were happy with that, and Siobhán took over cleaning up the kitchen—it was the least she could do. In fact, she soon found that scrubbing pots and pans and washing down the cooker and the counters was calming. Before she knew it at least an hour had passed, and she returned to the dining room to join the others and fix herself a much-needed cappuccino. It seemed as if twice as many folks were now in the bistro, and discussing not only the murders—fairies were on the lips of her neighbors here as well. The bell dinged, and moments later Macdara entered with his mam. Nancy Flannery, a petite woman with the same brown curls as Macdara, was wearing a linen rose-colored skirt and suit jacket and a white blouse. Suddenly feeling under-dressed in her denims and a T-shirt, Siobhán went to hug her, but Nancy stepped to the side as if she feared being run over.

"Sorry," Siobhán said, going in for the hug again. Nancy barely hugged her back, just a quick pat to the back. There was definitely work to do on this relationship.

"Jane, my love," Nancy said the moment she spotted her niece.

"Aunt Nancy," Jane said. Her tone was polite but guarded, reminding Siobhán that they had been estranged. "How are you?"

Nancy strode to her niece and wrapped Jane in the hug that Siobhán had longed for. "I'm so sorry, petal. My sister." Siobhán's future mother-in-law inhaled and dabbed at her eyes with a handkerchief. "If I had known. We were fools, the pair of us. I should have stepped up and mended fences."

"She could have done the same," Jane said. "There's no use torturing yourself now." Siobhán was relieved to see Jane behaving like a decent human being. Maybe it was the village that had turned her sour. People were like plants, seeking their best environments to thrive. When this nightmare was behind them, if she was found inno-cent, Jane would be free to move on to a place where she fared better.

"What happened? Who did this to my sister?" Nancy Flannery turned to Macdara, her hands clasping the handkerchief. "Tell me you've caught him, luv."

Or her. Siobhán wasn't about to correct her future mother-in-law. Nancy hadn't congratulated either of them on the engagement yet. Maybe Macdara had yet to break the news.

"I'm sorry," Macdara said. "It's not our case."

"But we're going to help them," Siobhán said. "We'll do everything we can."

Nancy cried out, squeezing the handkerchief even harder.

Siobhán felt eyes on them and turned to find her brood hovering nearby, unsure of how to deal with their sobbing guest.

"Tea?" Siobhán said. "And brown bread?"

"On it," Gráinne said, pushing her way into the kitchen.

"Everyone sit," Siobhán said. "A cup of tea will do everyone good." On her way to the kitchen she ambushed Ciarán with a squeeze, then turned and did the same to Ann, Eoin, and then James. She pulled back from her older brother and searched his face.

"Are you alright?" They both knew what she meant: Had he started drinking again?

He ruffled her hair. "I'm fine, Garda," he said affectionately. "Just nursing my wounds."

"It's good to see you. We've missed you around here."

"Sounds like you've been keeping busy," James said. "Will you give us the details later?"

"I'll try," she whispered. Her brood had inquisitive minds and more than once they had helped her work through a case. At the least, they were spending time together, and in the end that was the most important bit of all.

Gráinne waited until after they'd all had a family supper, a hearty plate of lamb chops, potato, and veg, to announce her news. "I have a job."

Siobhán's heart leapt into her throat as she imagined the possibilities and how to talk her out of them. "Where?"

Gráinne pointed out the window. "Sheila's Hair Salon. I'm the new nail girl." She flashed them all a look at her own nails, hot pink to match Sheila's sign. "She said it won't be long before I move up to personal stylist."

James was the first to break the awkward silence. "Congrats," he said, lifting his mineral. "You won't have a far commute either." They all glanced across the street. The salon was closed, the neon pink sign muted for the night. Sheila was a large woman whose bite could be as bad as her bark. Siobhán worried that the two combative personalities would be a bad mix. But there were worse jobs for Gráinne, and she did love style. She had even talked Jane into letting her paint her nails bright red, and Siobhán had already noticed her bringing them up to her eyes. She had mentioned she had some sight. Siobhán wondered what life for her was like. Although it couldn't be easy, she seemed to have accepted it, and had no problem getting around. But if she could make out the red in her nails, wouldn't she have noticed that her mother had been wearing a red dress?

She had acted surprised, even asked Siobhán if the killer had dressed her. Had it all been an act? Macdara wouldn't like it if Siobhán pressed Jane for details about her sight, and he certainly wouldn't like the fact that Siobhán was considering her a suspect, but she had no choice. Jane had been stonewalling when it came to proving her alibi. Siobhán had Googled herbal conferences in Dublin, apothecary conferences in Dublin, and even "plant conference" in Dublin and she hadn't found anything for the days Jane purported to be there.

As the plates were cleared and dessert served—they had an array of options brought by their generous neighbors, including a toffee pudding that Siobhán found delightful—thunder rumbled and the rain started to come down in buckets. It was late in the evening, later than they usually ate, but the murder had them all wide awake. Everyone yearned for some levity, so despite the weather, conversation turned to summer and their plans. Siobhán was pleased to hear Eoin tell Nancy that he would be applying to colleges and he wanted to study art. It conjured up Geraldine's comment about her daughter-in-law. *"Annabel has been putting silly notions in her head."* It was unfair, how people went out of their way to squash other people's dreams. Did Mary Madigan think her pursuit was a silly notion?

"I'm bored," Ciarán said. "May I be excused?"

"Off with ya," Siobhán said.

He swiped his plate to take to the kitchen and let out a "Yes!"

"Me too," Ann said, grabbing her plate and following.

She would need to figure out ways to keep Ann and Ciarán occupied for the summer. Her time off work was going to fly by, and she'd be a terrible sister if she spent it all on the case. Why not take her brood with her when she returned to Ballysiogdun?

For she would return, she knew it in her bones. The

case had a grip on her, and she had no intention of letting go. They could stroll the farmers' market and take hikes, and visit the fairy tree. And yes, she'd be working too, but at least they'd be together. A little family time, a holiday of sorts. Even if it was in a village where they believed in fairies and a woman was recently murdered. Imagine that on the postcard.

Not a bother—her brood was sadly used to it. And they would never be alone. When was the last time they'd taken a holiday as a family? She'd talk to Bridie about hiring extra help in the bistro for the summer, and then see if she could talk her siblings into it.

Macdara announced he was taking personal leave for the funeral, and conversation soon turned to the memorial. Everyone agreed that they should have a public memorial service as soon as possible, and then a private funeral and burial once the pathologist released the body, so the date for the public service was set a few days from now. That would give everyone in Ballysiogdun time to travel to Kilbane. In the meantime, Siobhán had learned that Dylan Kelly would be giving a lecture at Lough Gur. The historical park was practically in their backyard, and it was the perfect way for all of them to get their minds off the murder—everyone but Siobhán, who was hoping after the lecture she could steal a little of the professor's time. On the ride home, she had Googled him, and none of her searches turned up any mention of a book on fairies slated for publication. Or any book for that matter. Had it all been a ruse? If he wasn't in Ballysiogdun to research a book, what exactly was he doing there?

Chapter 16

The words carved into the wooden oval sign read:
BEWARE OF FAIRIES AND 100 STEPS! Siobhán wasn't
sure about the fairies, but there were indeed one hundred
stone steps that led to the fairy village on top of the hill at
Lough Gur. It was lovely to hear Ann and Ciarán giggle
as they read the sign, then sprinted for the top as only
children would do. Lough Gur not only boasted the proximity of Grange Stone Circle (Ireland's largest stone circle, three hundred meters west of the park), it was also
considered one of the most magical places in Ireland. At
least according to their website. And although it was in
County Limerick, Siobhán counted herself as a local sup-
porter of the nearby historical park. How could she not?
Framed by a horseshoe-shaped lake with Knockadoon
Hill on one side and Knockfennel Lake on the other, it

packed a six-thousand-year-history into its rugged and magical land.

The Iron Age, the Bronze Age, Stone-Aged houses, ringforts, hillforts, megalithic remains, and if those archaeological treasures weren't enough, legend had it the park was home to Fer Fí, the King of the Fairies. The Red Cellar Cave high up on the steep side of Knockfennel Hill was where he dwelled. Not to be outdone, where there is a king, there is a queen, and her name was Áine. She lived in the hill of Knockainey, the Goddess of Summer, Wealth, and Sovereignty, aka Queen of the Fairies. She spent most of her time in the lake, fed from underground springs, beneath which dwelled a realm to the other world. She was not a queen to be messed with. As one of the myths went, the King of Munster forced himself on her, resulting in her biting off his ear, therefore rendering him "blemished" and unfit to be king. That was Siobhán's definition of a queen, leading her own #MeToo movement way ahead of her time.

Every civilization was represented here. There was no shortage of stories, and variations of the stories. Regardless, one could not argue that it was a mystical place, and Siobhán was not surprised that Dylan Kelly chose this location for a tour and a talk. Siobhán loved killing two proverbial birds with one magical stone.

They had already strolled around the horseshoe-shaped lake, joined hands inside the stone circle, then slipped into the Heritage Center for Dylan's tour. Now they were out in the fresh air finishing up the Fairy and Tricky Tree Trail where stone fairy houses were built into the path, delighting children as they stumbled upon each one. Ireland was home to twenty-two native species of trees and every single one of them was planted within these special grounds.

When the official tour ended, Ciarán and Ann were filled with questions, and Siobhán was happy to let them kick off the interrogation of Dylan Kelly.

"What exactly is a fairy?" Ciarán asked, his voice laced with doubt.

"'Fairy' is a broad term for an array of creatures," Dylan said. "It started with the Tuatha Dé Danann. When mankind arrived, the fairies agreed to go underground and let the mortals live above-ground among them. When the sun is up they stick to their hiding places. But when darkness falls and the moon rises, that's when they come out to play."

"Play?" Ciarán said. "So they're playful?"

"Of course, lad. They're tricksters."

"That's good. I'd probably like them then. Don't you think?"

Dylan Kelly leaned in. "If you're picturing the Disney fairies with glitter and wings, you'd be best heading off to America, for the Irish fairies are no such thing. Fairies are independent of religion and you'll find them in all cultures. We've got two types here in Ireland. The trooping fairies and the solitary fairies. The trooping fairies are social. You'll find them dancing around the hawthorn trees. The solitary fairies are like they sound. They just want to be left well enough alone." Ciarán had begun to zone out, and Siobhán could tell he was done with the lecture. "Sounds a bit like human beings, does it not? That's the thing about fairies, they can change shapes."

"Change shapes?" And just like that, his interest was back. Ciarán's voice seemed to be going through the change, hitting a high octave and cracking low in the same breath.

"Ah, sure. A fire-breathing horse with a dragon tail and eagle wings, if you like."

"I would not like," Ann said. "Not at all."

"Why do they change shapes?" Ciarán asked.

"So that one could be sitting next to you and you'd never know it."

Ciarán turned and stared at Siobhán intently.

"I'm not a fairy, luv. Neither are you."

"The fairy world and the human world overlap, you see. The fairies are going about their life doing as they please, and all they ask of us is a bit of respect."

"He believes it," Ciarán said as he openly pointed at Dylan Kelly. "And he's wearing a *suit*."

A wolf in sheep's clothing? "He's part entertainer, luv," Siobhán whispered into Ciarán's ear. "And the suit doesn't look very dear." She probably shouldn't have added that bit, but she didn't like how the professor seemed to enjoy getting children riled up. As if to prove her point, Dylan Kelly continued.

"The problem is us human beings have a habit of walking into their realm and disturbing them. That's when you'd best watch your back, or your head before it gets lopped off."

Ciarán did a double-take. "They chop off heads?" He patted his own head, as if trying to assure himself it was still firmly attached.

"They'd rip your throat out if you crossed them."

"Professor, please. These are children."

"I'm not a child." Ciarán reached up and rubbed his throat. "Where can I see a fairy?"

"Look for the hawthorn tree. The sacred tree of the sidhe."

"She?" Ciarán scrunched up his nose. "All fairies are girls? Is that why they're so browned off?"

Siobhán inwardly groaned. She was going to have to spend more time at home.

"Not 'she.' The Irish word s-i-d-h-e. Its meaning is a hillside. It's come to mean the fairies."

"Why would a hillside mean the fairies?" Ciarán rolled his eyes.

"Where there is nature, there are fairies. Look for hill mounds, hillocks, or raths surrounded by a ring of stones, or wild mushrooms." Dylan leaned down and peered into Ciarán's face. "Do you like to read, lad?" Ciarán simply blinked, no doubt wondering if the fairies would punish him for lying.

"I like to read," Ann said.

Dylan straightened as he lifted his finger in the air. "Carolyn White in *A History of Irish Fairies* says that there are three types of humans most likely to interact with the fairies. The poor. The simple. And the sincere."

"You'd better watch out," Gráinne said, leaning into Siobhán. "You're three for three."

"Not believing in them is the worst offense of all," Professor Kelly continued.

"Well done, Professor," Siobhán said, clapping. She gently shoved Ciarán and Ann out of his path. "Have a look around; we're leaving in ten minutes." They raced off, presumably in search of fairies. Siobhán turned to the professor. "I'd love to hear more about this book you're writing."

He straightened up, like a peacock offering his feathers. "I'm researching remote villages, getting to know the people, visiting the fairy rings, and fairy forts, documenting the stories."

"Then Ballysiogdun must be a dream come true. For your book that is."

He pushed his glasses up his nose and grinned. "I never expected such an explosive turn."

"The murder?"

"Yes. I intend to follow it closely. As it seems will you."

"I'm trying to catch a killer."

"Don't be surprised if you never do."

"Pardon?"

"Strange things tend to happen when it involves the Good People."

"Drop the act. It's just us. You can't really believe in them. Can you?"

"I've heard stories. Most I don't believe. But there have been a handful that I couldn't disprove. I went to the places, you know? I talked to the people. I've stood by fairy forts, and fairy rings, and fairy trees. But never has it felt so powerful as the energy in Ballysiogdun. And that cottage! Tell me, how do you explain all those mysterious deaths? Sent shivers up me spine. I may not entirely believe, but I certainly wouldn't chance it. Tell me. Would you ever disturb a fairy ring?"

Siobhán felt like a butterfly that had just been pinned to a board. She wanted to lie—after all she was needling him about his beliefs—but the truth was of course she wouldn't disturb a fairy ring. And if it had been her, she would have moved out of the cottage. Better safe than sorry. "Normally? No."

"What do you mean—*normally?*"

"To catch a killer, I might disturb a lot of things. If it was necessary." She probably wouldn't. She would try really hard not to.

"You'd best think on it carefully. Or you, or the ones you love, may never have a bit of peace again."

"Are you threatening me, Professor?"

"Threatening you?" He stepped back as if to distance himself from her. "Why on earth would I do that?"

"You tell me."

"My dear. I'm trying to *save* you."

"I wish you luck there. I hear I'm a handful."

He blinked rather than laugh, as if her humor was beneath him. "I too bore witness that night. I wrote about it. I'll show you me pages." He leaned in even though no one was listening. "You cannot tell anyone else. I have a photo."

Now he had her attention. "A photo?"

"Quite possibly the only photo that exists of that night."

He was going to tease her to death. She wanted to frisk him immediately, see if the photo was hidden in one of his suit pockets, turn him upside down and shake him like a rug. "What is it of?"

"The hawthorn tree under the full moon. And there, right next to it, I swear on me father's grave, you can see an ethereal figure."

"An ethereal figure."

"I believe I captured a fairy. It's remarkable."

"May I see it?" She held out her hand. He stared at it as if he was expecting *her* to produce something.

"I'm afraid it's not quite ready to show to the public."

That was an abrupt turnaround. "You just said I could see it."

"Patience, my dear."

"It's Garda O'Sullivan."

His blink was back. "I'll put you down for an advanced reading copy, Garda."

"How advanced?"

"Closer to the publication date, I'm afraid." He didn't seem afraid. He seemed quite proud of himself.

"And when is that?"

"Eager for it, are you?" He grinned.

"I'd like to see that photo now."

"I'm going to have it authenticated first."

"You should at least show it to the guards." If he was telling the truth. If Dylan Kelly was the killer, his motive was practically written in swooping letters over his big head: "best seller." He was hyping his book, using the tragedy to wind people up. *Shameful.* "Who is your publisher?"

"Why?"

"I looked you up. I didn't see any mention of the book."

He stood straighter. "They're a small press."

"They still have a name, don't they?"

"You seem unaware of the dangers of sharing too much information," he lectured. "It puts my idea at risk."

"I think a murder investigation trumps protecting your ideas, don't you?"

He shook his head. "Believe me, there's no clue to a murder in the photo."

"You don't know that. If the photo shows a figure— hours before a murder occurred—it could either be our victim, or her killer."

"No, no, it's not human, it's ethereal."

"So, you say. Why don't you hold it up for me to have

a little peek? I won't even touch it." She eyed his pockets again.

"I'm sure skeptics will try and rip it apart, but this is the proof that's going to rocket the book to fame."

"That's a high bar."

"I was called here. Destiny, Garda, it's destiny that I happened to be there researching fairies when the terrible event occurred."

"A human being killed Ellen Delaney, Professor, and you're one of the few people in the village who can help spread that truth instead of riling them up with these stories."

"I believe now."

"You only believe in selling your book."

"You must watch your step."

She could not believe a professor was speaking like this, but he had best-selling book on the brain and he was sticking to his part like glue. "Has *anyone* had an early read?"

"Of course not." He tilted his head away from her and looked at her sideways as if he was a parrot instead of a man.

"Are you sure?" With his ego, he'd definitely shown someone or several someones early drafts of his book.

"I'm quite sure."

She wasn't. He was lying about it, that's what she was sure of. The question was . . . why?

The professor pushed his glasses up yet again, making Siobhán want to tape them to his head. "I see that you're determined," he said. "So if I mention something to you, something that is most likely quite innocent, I trust you'd treat it with the discretion it requires?"

"You have my word."

He sighed. "The last time I remember seeing Ellen Delaney was after a council meeting." He paused. "She was in a heated argument. I couldn't make out the words, but she was quite irate, reading someone the riot act as it were."

Siobhán stepped closer. "Reading who the riot act?"

The professor lifted his head. "The councilman. The subject of Ellen Delaney's rage was Aiden Cunningham."

Chapter 17

The bells of Saint Mary's cathedral rang into the air and the large crowd gathered on the steps awaiting a special mass dedicated to Ellen Delaney. After, everyone would be welcome to take a walking tour of Kilbane, including a chance to walk around the town square and the abbey, then lunch would be served at Naomi's, and finally they would end the evening at O'Rourke's Pub, where they would hold a wake for the mother, sister, aunt, and neighbor they'd lost.

Siobhán had to give the people of Ballysiogdun credit; they all showed up to pay their respects, and so far everyone was on their best behavior. Siobhán couldn't help but wonder if part of it was fueled by guilt for not treating Ellen well when she was alive, and the other part driven by an insatiable need to stay close to the case. There was safety in numbers, and one amongst them was a killer.

Sergeant Eegan and Garda Danny MacGregor were in attendance as well, and folks knew that suspicion might be drawn to anyone who did not show up. Everyone was watching everyone else, bringing a sharp edge of paranoia into the gathering. It was so palpable, Siobhán could feel it, the way some could feel rain in their bones.

Father Kearney gave a lovely mass, and a few even shed tears as they exited. Siobhán noticed several taking in the cathedral and she felt a swell of pride. Built in 1879, it boasted ten gorgeous stained-glass windows, three of which were modeled on the windows of their abbey, bright colors intersecting into a five-light arch.

Joe and Mary Madigan were accompanied by Geraldine and the children. Annabel the art teacher, as Siobhán had dubbed her, was flitting between groups of people like a social butterfly. Aiden Cunningham (despite proclaiming a busy schedule) was one of the first to arrive. And Professor Kelly, who really had no excuse given his recent talk at nearby Lough Gur, seemed the most uncomfortable with the crowd. Siobhán got the feeling that unless the subject revolved around his book, he was not a people person. The most surprising attendee of all was Eddie Doolan. He had put on a suit, which while slightly too big, looked clean and pressed, and he smelled, thankfully, recently washed. He was even carrying a small bouquet of daisies, which he presented to Jane at his first opportunity. Gone was the theatrical storyteller; Eddie looked like a young lad asking a girl on a date for the first time. He even seemed to be humming a little tune to himself as he thrust the bouquet at her.

Jane brought them up to her nose and grimaced. The minute Eddie shuffled away, a shy grin on his face, she tossed them to the ground. Siobhán picked them up and handed them to Ann, who agreed to put them in water back at the bistro.

The crowd gathered at the underpass to King John's Castle, where, to Siobhán's delight, her brood seemed willing to give the villagers the oral history of the magnificent four-story tower. Over time it had been an arsenal, a hospital, a depot, and even a blacksmith. Now it was a local treasure. Although the interior of the structure was no longer open to the public, folks liked to traverse the underpass, where voices would echo beneath the damp stones.

It was there that Siobhán caught two male voices speaking in hushed tones. Professor Kelly and Aiden Cunningham were in the shadows, heads bowed together. Suddenly, the mumbled conversation came to an end with the last sentence ringing out as clear as a bell.

"You scratch my back and I'll scratch yours!" Aiden Cunningham finished his proclamation and then strode away. Professor Kelly whirled around and took off in the other direction. Siobhán looked around but everyone else was making their way to the abbey. She had no other witnesses to the odd exchange. Scratching each other's back. In what way exactly?

She hurried after Aiden Cunningham, intending to find out.

The councilman was keeping a brisk pace, heading down Sarsfield Street, away from the church and in the opposite direction of the abbey, where the rest were making their way. Siobhán hung back, keeping close to the shops, but if he was aware he was being followed, he gave no signs.

He stopped at the corner where there was a rubbish bin. Siobhán squeezed against Liam's Hardware shop as Aiden removed a piece of paper from the pocket of his suit and dropped it into the rubbish bin. *Great.* Digging through garbage, a delightful part of her job. She prayed the bin wasn't too full.

He hurried along, crossing before the light, causing the car turning to beep and swear at him. He reached the other side, then his hand dove into his suit pocket again, only this time he produced a pack of cigarettes. He began to smoke, staring at the rubbish bin, as if he knew Siobhán was waiting to dive in.

Siobhán moved toward it. Given she was now on the same side of the street as the bin, even if he spotted her, she would reach it first. She didn't have her gloves on her, so she popped into Liam's Hardware to buy a box of disposables. She opened the box, stuffed several in her handbag, and left the rest with a puzzled Liam, telling him she'd be back for them. She then hurried to the rubbish bin. Aiden Cunningham was no longer staking it out; he'd moved on down the street.

Siobhán put on a pair of the gloves, then dove into the bin, which now she wished *was* full because she practically had to bend into it to retrieve the paper. What she brought out seemed to be a boilerplate agreement. It was between Ellen Delaney and Geraldine Madigan. Notarized and witnessed by Aiden Cunningham. She scanned it. Just as she suspected, Geraldine was the woman behind the bet that Friday evening. If Ellen Delaney spent the entire night, Geraldine agreed she would drop all efforts to have the cottage bulldozed. Likewise, Ellen agreed to move out if she was unsuccessful at spending the entire night.

Siobhán shook the letter off, then folded it and placed it in her handbag. Why was he hiding this? She wasn't even sure it would hold up legally, and all terms were moot considering what had happened. . . . Was he protecting himself or Geraldine? This was a step they were taking to solve the problem, which suggested that none of them had reached any murderous crescendo—in a way wouldn't this agreement vindicate both Aiden Cunningham and Geraldine Madigan? After all, if Ellen had lost the bet by scurrying home that evening, then Geraldine could have claimed a victory. And Aiden could claim that no fool would murder a woman on the very eve of the agreement.

It was his behavior now that made him look suspicious. Geraldine had also lied, although it had been quite obvious to Siobhán that she had been involved in the bet. Should Siobhán confront Aiden right away or take it to Danny and Sergeant Eegan?

Or Macdara . . .

If she took it to Danny it would be a good excuse to remind him that she still wanted to get into the cottage and see what was in the sink. If evidence had been removed she hoped he'd show her the crime scene photos. Yes. Like it or not, Danny MacGregor was the man to see. She turned and headed back for the abbey, stopping in for a quick basket of heavenly curried chips from the chipper.

By the time she arrived at the abbey, the guests were spread out, exploring the historical ruins and the grounds. Siobhán found Eddie Doolan standing in the middle of the structure, in the section that used to be the kitchen. The storyteller seemed mesmerized by the remains of the fireplace. Although he was alone, he was telling a story, his arms gesturing, his legs twitching to move. Siobhán felt a stab of pity for him. It was as if this chosen profession was his entire reason for being, and he didn't know how to just be Eddie—he always had to be performing. Or maybe he'd been lonely for too long and was comforted by the sound of his own voice.

"How do you like our abbey?" Siobhán asked, when he finally noticed her. Their twelfth-century Dominican priory, with a fifteenth-century Franciscan bell tower, was always a striking vision, set back in a field, with a river in front where the monks used to brew beer. The sun was starting to set, sending shards of sunlight beaming through the gaps in the ancient stone.

The ground floor held the church, the refectory, the kitchen, and the Tomb of the White Knight. The upper floor made up the monks' dormitories, and a final set of stairs led to the bell tower. Although just the bones of the structure remained, there were still carved stone heads tucked in walls, gorgeous arches, ornate recessed niches, and of course the remains of the five-light window, said to be the most gorgeous in Ireland. Siobhán was always thrilled to show it to visitors.

"Remarkable," Eddie said, throwing up his hands. "So many stories here."

"Indeed." Siobhán wished she knew them all. "I think it's admirable that you became a seanchaí."

"You do?" He seemed leery of her compliment.

"I do. Did you start the practice to help improve your speech?" She wanted to be sensitive about his stutter, but she was curious.

"First singing. Singing helped a lot."

"Wonderful."

"Do you like to sing?"

"Only after a few pints." Siobhán laughed at her own joke. None of the O'Sullivans were very musical, something she lamented. Of all of them, James probably had the best singing voice, but you never heard him using it. Gráinne liked to belt out tunes, but she'd need some training to help with the high notes. "Who taught you to sing?"

"I had a teacher." He was suddenly looking everywhere but directly at her.

"Wonderful." *A teacher.*

His head snapped up, and this time he did make eye contact. His dark eyes swam with pain. "Who mocked me."

"Oh." She'd answered too quickly. "I'm sorry." Was Ellen Delaney his teacher? Was this her stalker? A former tortured student?

"*She's* sorry," he said. His voice took on a threatening tone.

"Your teacher?"

He nodded. Siobhán stepped up. "Eddie? Was Ellen Delaney your teacher?"

"We sang a lot of nursery rhymes to practice," Eddie said. "Do you like nursery rhymes?"

"I don't sing them much. I like Christy Moore."

"He's a storyteller and singer."

"He is indeed." Siobhán tried to find Macdara or the other guards in the crowd. Finally, Danny caught her eye and after a quick nod headed over.

"How ya?" he said as he approached.

Eddie started to leave. Siobhán touched his arm. "Stay." She used a polite but firm voice.

"What's the story?" Danny said.

People were starting to gather around the Tomb of the White Knight. Eddie looked ready to flee. They wouldn't have much more time alone with their storyteller.

"Why did you move to Ballysiogdun?" she asked Eddie, now that Danny was listening.

He put his finger up to his lips, then looked around. "It's a secret."

"Go on. We love secrets."

He glanced at Danny. "I can't tell you."

"I'm very good at keeping secrets," Danny said. He jerked his thumb to Siobhán. "And I went to garda training with this one. She's even better at it than I am."

Eddie was starting to visibly sweat. "You don't talk ill of the dead. You *do not.*"

Siobhán smiled at him, a difficult feat given her heartbeat had picked up, her blood was pumping. Eddie had a very important piece of this puzzle; he was holding that piece in plain view, but dangling it over a cliff. One wrong word, one misstep, and he'd drop it into oblivion. She had to get him to hand her the piece. "In our line of work, we investigate stories." Eddie arched an eyebrow, and his body was still turned away from them, but he was listening. "Ellen Delaney, our victim, has a story that needs to be told. A story about what happened to her. And every little piece of the story helps. You of all people should know that." She gave Danny a look.

"Yes," Danny said. "He's a professional. Of course he knows that."

"Okay, okay," Eddie said, a smile overtaking his wide mouth. He held his hands up as if they were applauding

and he was begging them to stop. "Yes. Yes. Ellen Delaney was my teacher." His face immediately turned red
and he curled his hands into fists. "And she was a bad,
bad teacher. Very, very, bad."

They gathered in the Kilbane Garda Station in Interview Room 1. Next to them in Interview Room 2 was
Eddie Doolan. Siobhán made sure he had a nice cup of
tea and a slice of pie, and she put him in there with a tape
recorder in case he wanted to practice. This seemed to
cheer him up, and every time she glanced through the
window between the rooms, she could see his lips moving. Back in Interview Room 1, they were all fixated on
the speakerphone in the middle of the table. The sergeant
in the Waterford Garda Station was announcing that he
was sending over the report that Ellen Delaney had filed
before they moved. The clerk should have it any minute
now via e-mail. Yes, he confirmed, Ellen Delaney had
claimed she was being stalked. By a strange man, a large
man, possibly a homeless man. The description fit Eddie
Doolan. He'd been questioned by the guards at the time,
but he'd insisted he wasn't stalking her, he was performing for her, waiting for her to recognize him. To recognize that this was the same stuttering boy she used to
mock. That he'd been practicing. That singing and then
storytelling had helped him overcome his stutter. When
Ellen Delaney was informed of the latest development,
that her stalker was a student she used to mock, days
later, a moving truck pulled up outside Ellen's home, and
a day after that she was gone. Eddie Doolan remained in
Waterford for the next year. The sergeant informed them

that they had no reports of violence on Eddie, and that most in town put up with his odd ways, and threw him a few bob for his stories. They had done their due diligence and confirmed that Eddie Doolan had been a student of Mrs. Delaney, back in primary school. They ended the meeting by agreeing that despite Eddie's lack of a criminal record, Ellen's accusation of stalking may have been more serious than they realized, given that Eddie had followed her to Ballysiogdun.

"She never came to us," Sergeant Eegan said. "She had to have recognized him."

"It must have come as quite a shock when Eddie Doolan was suddenly in town."

"Jane has never mentioned anything about her mother having a stalker—has she said anything to you about Eddie Doolan?" The question came from Danny and was directed at Siobhán.

"It's not clear how much she knows," Macdara interjected. "But I don't think my aunt shared it with her."

"Jane mocked Eddie," Siobhán said quietly. *Just like her mother.* "At the pub in Ballysiogdun." Was it because she knew who he was and what he'd done, or was it simply part of her nature? Unfortunately, Siobhán suspected the latter.

"I don't think she knows who he is," Macdara said. "Even though Jane is a grown woman, I think my aunt treated her like a child. I'm only guessing, and I'll dig further into it, but I repeat—I don't think Jane knew anything about this."

"I can see why Ellen wouldn't be proud of it," Siobhán said. "And in Waterford when she tried to report him, they had to let him go. Maybe this time . . ."

"She decided to take matters into her own hands," Danny finished for her.

"How exactly?" Macdara asked.

"That's what we need to find out," Sergeant Eegan said. He glanced through the window over to Eddie, who was full-on into a story, hands moving, pacing the room, voice raised as he performed for the recorder. "I'm not convinced he's dealing with a full deck."

They all turned to Eddie, who seemed to sense it. He stopped, his head whipped around to see them. Then, he dove under the interview table.

"You may have a point there, boss," Macdara said.

Siobhán sighed. He was quirky, and troubled, but Siobhán liked Eddie. But after today, they all agreed, Eddie Doolan had just jumped to the top of their suspect list.

Siobhán caught up to Danny on their way out. They stepped to the side of the garda station, just behind the iron street lamp. "I happened by Aiden Cunningham after mass, and he dropped this." She handed him the notarized agreement. Danny arched an eyebrow, regarding her as if he suspected there was more to the story. He'd always been keen on competition; he had the same look in his eye he would get whenever she bested him at Templemore.

"Dropped it?"

She shrugged. "In the rubbish bin."

He smiled and shook his head, then read it. "The plot thickens."

"Why do you think they're hiding this?"

"They're paranoid it doesn't look good."

"I thought the opposite."

"How so?"

"Why make a bet with the victim, one you go to the trouble to notarize, and then murder that same victim before it's said and done?"

Danny nodded his comprehension as he read over the agreement again. "If Geraldine or Aiden is our killer, maybe they were trying to distract Ellen from their malicious intent?"

"Quite a complicated distraction."

"Maybe they were simply trying to get her out of the cottage that evening."

"To what end?"

"Perhaps that is the question we should be chasing."

Siobhán pointed to the agreement. "At the least this proves that both Geraldine and Aiden knew where Ellen planned on being that evening. And by *not* coming forward with this, aren't they obstructing your investigation?"

Danny nodded. "Believe me, we'll bring them in." Danny started to head off with a salute.

"One more thing." He smiled and gave a soft shake of his head, then waited. "How was Ellen supposed to prove that she'd spent the night outside?"

He tapped his head with his index finger. "Good thinking. We'll make sure to ask them."

"They could have been watching her. Or *sent* someone to watch her." Someone like Eddie Doolan? She kept that suspicion to herself. It was dangerous to throw out rumors, and this was nothing more than wild speculation.

Danny glanced to the other side of the building where

Macdara stood conferring with some of his guards. "Who else have you shown this to?"

Siobhán hated the question, mostly because the answer brought up complex feelings of guilt. "Only you." What choice did she have? Danny was the guard officially involved in this investigation, not Macdara. She would fill him in on everything when she was able.

"Good," Danny said. "Let's keep it that way for now." He patted her shoulder, and glanced once more at Macdara as he passed, leaving Siobhán to wonder if his motives were purely about protecting the case.

Chapter 18

The rest of the day flew by, and finally it was time to gather at O'Rourke's for the wake. Although there were plenty of pubs in Kilbane, Siobhán was partial to her local. Not only because it was close to the bistro, but because of the publican himself. Declan O'Rourke was a powerhouse of spirit. From the windows boasting his collection of Laurel and Hardy memorabilia, to the interior filled with posters of John Wayne doing his thing, this pub was like a second home. Declan was probably pushing eighty now (although she'd never dare to ask) and she loved everything about him from the wrinkles in his broad face, to his gapped-tooth mouth, and most of all how he could fill a room with that boisterous laugh of his where one couldn't help but laugh back. He was a man seasoned in the language of operas, and plays, and movies. It was fitting, his job front and center as a publican, for Declan had been entertaining the folks in Kilbane for the past fifty years. He was a kind soul, the first to offer an ossified lad a ride home, but he was just as quick to cut down any lad who got too big for his britches. Declan, like most institutions, demanded a fair amount of respect. He was equally loved and feared. As the mourners entered, Declan was the first to welcome them.

Siobhán's best friend, Maria, stood behind the counter lining pint glasses up for the onslaught, and they exchanged a quick hug.

"So much for your holiday," Maria said. She had a little body and a big voice. Her dark hair was up in a ponytail.

"Death never takes a holiday."

Maria rolled her eyes and gave Siobhán a little shove. "You're not death, which means you can take a holiday."

"It's Macdara's aunt, luv."

"Right, so. Work away then."

"We will holiday soon. You and me."

"From your mouth to God's ears." Maria gave her another shove before disappearing behind the counter.

Minutes later Jane stood on the little stage where musicians usually reigned, her pint raised. "To my mother, Ellen Delaney."

"Hear, hear." Glasses were raised.

"May she rest in peace."

Joe Madigan stood up, smoothing down his suit. It was jarring to see him without his hat, or in flannel for that matter, especially seeing as how he had a full head of thick, dark hair that most men (and women) would be proud to show off. "Ellen Delaney was a good neighbor. She was a woman who spoke her mind, but she played fair. They kept a wonderful garden out back, and my wife attests that she was quite a good painter as well." Mary Madigan looked startled to be mentioned, but then recovered and began to nod vigorously.

"Lovely," she said. "I was lucky enough to see them up close, and you could tell she was very passionate about her work. Very protective of them too. Like they were her children." She swallowed, then looked around, as if hoping for approval. "May she rest in peace." Mary crossed herself and then kept her head bowed.

"Amen," Joe said. He raised his glass once again. "We may have had our differences about the cottage, but now we must all agree that the cottage can be bulldozed. We must never let anything like this happen again."

"Hear, hear!" Cheers from the residents of Ballysiogdun rang out.

"How dare you," Jane said. "It's the killer we should all be focused on, not the cottage." Siobhán sunk her head into her hands. She couldn't believe this lot. So much for honoring Ellen's memory. Then again, new information often spilled when tempers flared.

"I didn't mean to upset you," Joe said. "Maybe this discussion should wait."

"You think?" Jane said. "It's my mother's wake."

"I apologize. I should have left it at 'good neighbor,' and 'rest in peace.'" He hurried offstage and to his wife's side where he slid down into his chair as if he hoped to disappear. Jane, from the look on her face, was steaming mad.

Nancy Flannery, who was sitting to Siobhán's right, turned to her. "Bulldoze her cottage? What in heaven's name are they on about?"

"I'll explain later, Mam," Macdara said.

"It's in the middle of a fairy path," Siobhán said lightly.

Nancy Flannery's eyes widened and then she shook her head and crossed herself. "What was she thinking?"

"You as well?" Jane said. "It's utter nonsense. Mam knew it and so does everyone else in this room. All this talk of fairies and curses while real evil is walking among us."

"Why didn't she call me? I'm her sister. I would have helped. You could have lived with me."

"It doesn't matter anymore," Jane said. "Even I don't want to live in that cottage now. Let them bulldoze it."

"That settles that," Aiden Cunningham said. "The cottage will come down. We'll do it for Ellen."

Nancy stood. "That's *not* what my sister would want, and it's not your decision to make." Aiden Cunningham looked completely startled; this was a man who was used to wielding power over others, and this woman had just confronted him publicly. Siobhán felt a swell of pride for her future mother-in-law.

"Who are you?" he asked.

"I'm Nancy Flannery, and Ellen was my sister."

Aiden Cunningham gave a stilted bow. "I'm sorry for your loss."

"Then you'll stop all talk of bulldozing her home. This once."

"Yes, ma'am. Quite right, we'll take this up at our next town meeting." He removed a handkerchief from his suit pocket and mopped his brow.

"You'll be hearing from my solicitor before that," Nancy said.

Siobhán only realized her jaw was hanging open when

she glanced over at Macdara and saw that his was too. This fired-up persona was a rare side of Nancy Flannery and it was somewhat remarkable to witness. Siobhán nearly wanted to cheer: "You go girl."

Nancy turned to her son and gripped his arm. "You won't let them do anything to the cottage, will you?"

Macdara looked as confused as Siobhán at his mother's outburst. "We'll have a chat about this later," he said to her. "Do you mind?" His voice was soft and loving.

Nancy patted his hand. "You'll fix this, pet," she said. "I know you will."

Fix what? Macdara seemed to settle back to normal, but Siobhán couldn't help but think there was something about Nancy Flannery's outburst that required more digging. She'd have to see if she could get her alone later to have more of a chat.

"I have more to say," announced Jane, thunking down her pint and popping up again. *Oh no.* The crowd hushed. "My mother was not an easy person to love. But as Joe Madigan stated, my mam was a fair person. And in the end, she did not receive fairness. I would like to talk directly to the killer. If I had been home, would you have killed me too? Or spared me because I could not see you? Was my mother your target, or did she simply get in the way of something else you were doing? I do not think I can keep living without knowing who killed my mother, but what I really need to know is why? Why did you do it?" Jane paused as if she fully expected the killer to stand up and respond. Heads began to swivel, as neighbor regarded neighbor. "Did you think at all about the people who loved her? Her daughter. Her sister. Her nephew?" She paused as if trying to come up with more names.

"What about us? Where is our justice? You will not get away with this. Do you hear me?"

The stunned crowd stared back. Siobhán caught the pained look on both Macdara's and Nancy's faces. If Jane was the killer, this was an award-winning act. She was lying about her alibi too. Siobhán felt it in her bones. Would digging into it infuriate her future husband?

Macdara stood and lifted his pint glass. "I promise you, Aunt Ellen, we will honor your memory. We will seek justice. We will find your killer." He gave a nod to Declan, who signaled to the musicians, congregating at a table, killing time with pints. "Let's remember this is also a celebration of a life. What do you say we freshen our pints and bring the lads up for some tunes?"

Tuesday morning was the first chance Siobhán had to sit down with Macdara's mam. They took their breakfast to the back patio so Nancy could watch the birds. The air was fresh, the sun shining just enough overhead to add warmth, but not drive them mental. They arranged their teacups, passed milk back and forth, spooned, or watched each other spoon sugar into the tea, waiting to see who would speak first. "I'm so sorry about your sister." It was an awkward thing to say, but something needed to be said to break the ice between them, and Siobhán had just realized she'd never come out and said it.

"We were barely speaking," Nancy said, her voice low and mournful.

"That must make it even more painful." Siobhán meant it. Platitudes, such as "never go to bed angry," existed for a reason. She couldn't imagine one of her siblings not speaking to her. She would not be able to function. She'd hardly done things perfectly the past few years, but she hoped her mam and da would be proud that at the least the O'Sullivan Six had each other's backs. They were mostly grown up now, and it was too jarring to imagine a day where she wasn't surrounded by her family. By the time one's journey was over, all that really mattered were the people you loved and the way you treated them. Then again, Ellen Delaney, from all accounts, was not a warm and fuzzy person. Siobhán also had the feeling that the estrangement had more to do with Ellen Delaney's rigid personality than her more demure sister's, but that didn't stop the wound from festering. Siobhán laid her hand on top of Nancy's. "She knows you loved her. Try and let the negative bits go."

"I don't know."

"I heard Ellen could be quite . . ."

"Yes. She could."

"Did you ever visit them in Waterford?"

"Once. And she called me from Ballysiogdun several times. We were slowly making our way back to each other." She patted her face as if she expected tears to be there, and when she found none, she picked up her spoon again and placed it on the other side of the saucer.

"I'm aware it might be painful to remember, but the more I learn about Ellen, the easier it might be to find her killer."

"She brought it on herself—is that what you're saying to me?"

"No, of course not."

"Of course she did," Nancy said.

Siobhán sighed. She had a feeling no matter what came out of her piehole, Macdara's mam was going to find a way to twist it. "The cottage," Siobhán mused. "I keep wondering why she didn't just pick up and move. Could it have been worth all the bother?"

Nancy twirled her teacup. "It was the cottage that seemed to bring her around."

"What do you mean?"

"She called me after they'd moved in. She seemed so happy. A wee cottage in the middle of nowhere, but I'm telling you, my sister was over the moon about it." She smiled at the memory. "If only she had loathed it, we wouldn't be here right now."

"Don't tell me you believe in fairies now too?"

"I said nothing of the sort. But someone killed her over that cottage. You can't deny it was causing a fuss."

"It was indeed." She sighed. "Did you know how bad things were?"

"No. But it wouldn't have mattered if I had. I wouldn't have talked her into going."

"No?"

"Why on earth would she leave her own property?"

"I'd hardly call renting a place the same as owning a place."

"Exactly."

Siobhán frowned. She was missing something yet again. "What are you saying?"

"What are *you* saying?"

"It sounds as if you think that your sister owned the cottage." Why was this conversation going sideways? Arse-backward was more like it.

"She did."

"No, luv. The village owned the cottage and rented it to her."

Nancy Flannery shook her head. "Why do you think my sister called me after all these years? Just to be nice?

You didn't know her, but that wasn't her style. She called me because she wanted help in purchasing it. She said her 'man friend' was offering her a chance to purchase it. And so I lent her the money and that's what she did." Even more jarring than the confirmation that Ellen Delaney had a "man friend" was listening to Nancy Flannery repeatedly say "man friend."

"Man friend?" Siobhán knew that may not have been the most explosive bit about what Nancy had just revealed, but it was a piece of the puzzle that Siobhán was dying to have.

"I suppose the cottage was an even split between the two of us, but I have no claims on it. I suppose it belongs to Jane and Dara now."

Siobhán stared at her, waiting for a punch line to a joke she was having trouble following. "You're saying that Aiden Cunningham sold that cottage to you and your sister, and that he was Ellen's"—Siobhán leaned forward and used air quotes—"'man friend.'"

"She always did like a businessman." Nancy pursed her lips as if that wouldn't quite be her taste. "But to be fair, I never did get his name. She simply said her 'man friend.'"

"You and Ellen are the owners of the cottage?" Siobhán was like a stuck record, unable to move on.

"Why else would she continue to live there with all that bother?"

Why indeed. Siobhán was fuming. This was a vital piece of information. Two vital pieces of information. Every single person she'd spoken with was either lying or under the impression that the cottage belonged to the village, and therefore they had the right to decide its fate. Yet Aiden had used his position in the village to allow

Ellen to buy it. And he was her man friend. Siobhán needed another cappuccino and a slice of pie. She'd resist but she really wanted them. "Do you have any paperwork?"

"Paperwork?" Nancy sounded horrified, as if Siobhán was asking her to do homework.

"Proof of ownership? Deed of sale?"

Nancy Flannery moved her spoon to the other side of the cup. "No."

They would either find proof among Ellen's things or they would have to confront Aiden Cunningham. This was another secret he was keeping from the guards. Unless they already knew about this and they were simply keeping a tight lid on their findings. She chewed on this. Danny MacGregor was a friend and colleague. But that didn't mean he was keeping her fully apprised of their inquiries. She couldn't blame him. She'd have handled it the same way if the murder had occurred in Kilbane. On the other hand, right now she had no other choice but to go to the Ballysiogdun guards, and by association, the Cork City guards, with this new information. Aiden Cunningham was a politician alright, playing every side for whatever leverage he could get. "Does Macdara know?"

Nancy's eyebrow shot up. "Does he know what?"

"That Ellen owned the cottage?"

"I assumed he did. I assumed you did too."

"We were not aware—have you mentioned it to him since you've arrived?"

Nancy shook her head. "There's been no time."

"Who else knows that Ellen owns the cottage?"

"If she wanted it kept secret, I'd say no one but those involved directly in the sale."

What if someone had found out? Was that a motive for

the murder? Was there a poor soul in that village who was so superstitious that they would kill in order to have the cottage torn down? It seemed ludicrous. Yet . . . this new information had to have *some* meaning. A hidden ownership. Hard to pull off in a small village.

As Siobhán pondered these troubling new revelations, Nancy pushed back from the table. "Such messy business. Who would want that old thing now? If the village offers me what we paid for it, and Jane and Dara agree, I'm going to just take it and let them do what they will. There will be no peace in that cottage."

"Listen to me." Siobhán stood and rushed to Nancy's side. "You cannot tell anyone else about this. And you should never be alone. Do you understand?"

"What are you on about?" Panic rose in her voice, and Siobhán wished it didn't have to be that way, but it was better than placing Macdara's mam squarely in danger.

"It's not safe to discuss this with anyone right now. Even Jane." *Especially Jane.*

"What are you on about?"

"The cottage is at the center of the murder. Until we have a killer behind bars, you must not let anyone know that you own it."

"I will certainly tell my son."

Siobhán nodded. "Of course. We will tell Macdara straight away, and the guards. But you cannot let anyone else know." She stopped. "Does Jane *already* know?"

Nancy shook her head. "Not from me. I wouldn't put it past Ellen to keep her in the dark." She paused. "I didn't mean it like that."

"Of course not." What if Jane found out? How betrayed would she have felt? Even now Nancy Flannery was speaking as if the cottage now belonged equally to

Macdara. Had Jane found out her mother owned the cottage, then killed her thinking it would all be hers?

The thought was chilling, but not as chilling as the next thought. Were Macdara and his mam now in the crosshairs of a killer?

Nancy Flannery looked posed to cry. Siobhán reached for her hand again, determined to bring the mood up, at least for a bit. "At least our engagement is something to celebrate," she said. As soon as the words were out of her mouth, she gasped. What an eejit! It was all this stress, making her blurt out secrets. Maybe Nancy Flannery was going deaf and hadn't heard her. Macdara was going to kill her for spilling the beans. To his *mam*. Butterflies swirled in Siobhán's stomach. She could pretend she had said something else. What rhymed with "engagement"?

"Engagement?" Nancy said, raising her voice, sounding the most alarmed she had all weekend.

"Arrangement?" Siobhán said, as if that's what she'd said and now didn't know why.

"You said 'engagement.'"

"Did I?"

"Yes, Siobhán. You did." It was Eoin's voice. Siobhán turned to find her siblings, all five of them, huddled in the back doorway, gawking at her with a strong dose of suspicion and enough hurt to let Siobhán know she hadn't just fumbled the engagement ball, she'd completely obliterated it, and her brood looked as if they wanted to shove her in the penalty box for life.

Chapter 19

It was hardly the time for an emergency family meeting, but there was no other way around it. They were all gathered in the dining room of the bistro, her brood standing in front of her like a firing squad. A phrase from an American show on telly rose to mind: "Whoops. My bad." She was smart enough to keep her piehole shut. Speaking of pie, she could really use a slice right now. She'd already given in on the second cappuccino, and was currently clutching it like a security blanket. She was now wearing her engagement ring, trying to be chipper. Nearly an impossible task given that both Nancy Flannery and Ann were crying. Nancy, definitely not in a good way, and Siobhán wasn't so sure about Ann. When she pressed her, she just said, "I can't believe you didn't tell us." Macdara stood near his mam, his head bowed.

His skin tone had turned green when he'd learned what Siobhán had accidentally revealed.

"I love all of you, we both do," Siobhán said. "It's just that—it's going to be a very long engagement and so there wasn't any need to spill the beans just yet."

"And yet you did," Macdara muttered.

"Just popped out!" she said with a cheer she didn't feel.

Nancy's head swiveled from Macdara to Siobhán like a heat-seeking missile. "How long of an engagement?" She looked eager, as if wanting every extra day to try and figure out how to put a stop to it.

"Months," Macdara said.

"Years," Siobhán said at the same time. They looked at each other.

"Well, which is it?" Nancy looked to her son.

He sighed. "We've both been busy. We haven't had time to sit down and properly plan it out."

"We will," Siobhán said. "But you must all forgive us and let us focus on getting justice, solving this case." *Months? What was he on about—months?*

"When you get married are you going to stop solving cases?" Ciarán asked.

"Of course," Nancy Flannery said.

"Of course not," Siobhán said.

Heads ping-ponged from her to her future mother-in-law. "You're going to remain a guard and try to be a wife and mother?" Nancy sounded like a judge, clearly ready to deliver her verdict.

Siobhán groaned. This was why she hadn't told any-one, this right here. She would be the one expected to do it all. The planning, quit her job, stay home and have babies. That wasn't going to be her exact path. "I'm still going to work. We're not in any hurry."

"Are you both going to live here?" Ann asked.

"Here?" Nancy said. "Surely you'll want to get a bigger place. Or . . . a place of your own."

Siobhán tapped Macdara on the shoulder. "Why don't you show them your engagement stick?" *And if one more person says one more thing, beat them over the head with it.*

"Everyone stop talking," Gráinne said. "It's an engagement. We should have a party."

"We'll celebrate when we catch the killer," Macdara said. "Can we move on to the other topic on the agenda?"

Siobhán glanced at Nancy, who was suddenly looking around the bistro as if inspecting it for flaws.

"Can I wear that ring when you're not?" Gráinne asked.

"Not on your life," Siobhán said. "I mean it."

"Okay, okay." Gráinne was still staring at it.

"You have no idea how serious I am."

Gráinne rolled her eyes, but Siobhán could tell the message had landed.

Nancy stood. "Jane. Are you aware that your mother and Aunt Nancy purchased the cottage?"

Oh no. No, no, no, no. Siobhán wished she was holding that engagement stick now more than ever. She had just begged Nancy not to mention that to anyone. Her future mother-in-law had no respect for her. It was proof whether Siobhán wanted to admit it or not.

Jane's face scrunched. "What cottage?"

"The one in Ballysiogdun."

"You're joking me," Macdara said. His eyes found Siobhán's and she wondered if he saw panic in them.

"There's no way," Jane said. She tapped her cane as if sending out an SOS.

"Your mother called me. I paid for half of it. It wasn't that dear."

The price was hardly the point. Jane began to pace, her cane swinging wildly. "You were fine to leave me out of it?"

"The subject never came up. I assumed if your mother wanted you to know, she would tell you."

"I am so sick of being treated like a child."

Macdara approached his mam. "How much?"

"I understand this is a shock," Siobhán said. "But this information must not leave this room." She tried catching everyone's eyes as if to hammer in the warning, but they were all consumed with the revelation to understand how dangerous it was.

"Mam?" Macdara was determined.

Nancy Flannery brushed her hand in the air as if waving away a bothersome fly. "Fifteen thousand euro, luv."

"Why didn't you come to me first?"

"I don't need your permission to lend my sister money."

"I don't like anyone taking advantage of you, even if that someone is your own sister."

"Now my mother is a shrew, is that it?" Jane barked.

Macdara didn't reply or even look at Jane.

"I'm happy I helped out," Nancy said, lifting her chin into the air. "Otherwise the guilt would be eating me alive right now."

"Someone in that village assumed the cottage would be bulldozed," Siobhán said, hoping Jane and Macdara would calm down and focus. "But what if they discovered the cottage now belonged to Ellen Delaney and—"

"They took matters into their own hands." Macdara was back on the trail.

"It's possible they tried negotiating with her first. And when that didn't work . . ." Siobhán didn't need to repeat the gory details.

"This is outrageous. We never intended to stay that long." Jane was still stuck on the betrayal. Siobhán felt for her, but prayed she'd realize that all hurt feelings had to be put aside until the killer was caught. Being overly emotional could get a person deeper into danger. "Why?" Jane said, pacing across the bistro, her cane tapping furiously. "Why did she keep it from me?"

"We'll be probing into the details with the guards," Siobhán said, raising her voice to be heard. "But I must stress something. There is a chance that this is dangerous information." Did she have to whip out a pail of red paint and splash "DANGER" across the bistro?

"Danger?" Ciarán's interest was piqued.

"See?" Nancy said. "This is how you want to raise your children?"

Siobhán could feel herself vibrating with anger.

"Mother," Macdara said.

"What's wrong with how she's raising us?" Ann piped up. Her tone was feisty and protective.

"Nothing at all," James said, placing an arm around Ann. "We're doing just fine."

"Better than fine." Eoin grinned. "We're deadly."

"She's definitely not the worst," Gráinne said with a wink to her older sister. "Apart from hounding me about uni when I'm meant to be a stylist to the stars." She raked her eyes over Nancy. "There's no discount for family, although I still may be able to help you."

Nancy blinked, then turned to Macdara. "You could

have married that nice Australian girl. She had such a lovely, petite figure."

Siobhán no longer wanted to eat pie; she wanted to plant it in Nancy Flannery's face. There. She said it. Or at least thought it. She had to keep it under control. This was no time for a family blowout. "Until we know who killed Ellen Delaney and why, I am simply asking—no, begging—you not to speak of this again. Not even to each other, not when someone could be listening." She stared at Nancy until they made eye contact. "And you may not approve of my profession, but my siblings, despite everything life has thrown at them, are doing just fine."

The O'Sullivan Six stepped closer to Siobhán.

"We're all fine," Macdara said. "Please, let's all calm down."

"I'm going to have a word with Aiden Cunningham," Jane said. "You bet I am."

Siobhán threw her most desperate look to Macdara. This was what she was afraid of. Mouths racing like a flame along a wick. Attached to a bomb.

"No," Macdara said. "You won't say a word." Jane's chin remained thrust in the air. "Siobhán is right. Leave the investigating to us. Your lives depend on it."

"Does my mother have a will?" Jane asked.

"We'll sort that all out," Macdara said. "I need your word, all of you, that you will not share any of this information."

One by one, everyone gave their word. Jane's lips were terse, her answer gruff. "Fine."

Siobhán hesitated. There was one more possible secret that was being kept from Jane, and now that the dangerous bit was already out, she was curious to see Jane's reaction. "It has also come to my attention that Ellen may have been romantically involved with Aiden Cunningham."

"More secrets." Jane sounded like she wanted to start swinging her cane at their suspects. But this time she didn't sound surprised. Just resigned.

"Is it possible?"

Jane chewed on her lip. "I doubt it was true love. But if Mother wanted something from him, it's not out of the realm of possibility."

How romantic. Siobhán glanced over at Macdara, now sitting near his mammy. All his lecturing about her not telling anyone about the engagement, yet all the while, he hadn't mentioned it to his own mother. If he had, this drama could have, should have been avoided. Then again, Siobhán was the one who had wanted to keep it a secret, and he was just honoring her wishes. This was her fault; she just hated to admit it. But just like she warned Jane against letting her emotions get the best of her, Siobhán needed a clear head for this inquiry. She would have to sort this out with Macdara later.

Macdara's mobile rang and Siobhán was so relieved for the interruption she wanted to marry the caller. "Yes. Yes. Here? She'll be there." He clicked off. "Jeanie Brady is on her way to Butler's with Ellen's body," Macdara said. "She wants you to meet her there."

Not marry the caller. Perhaps buy her some pistachios. Siobhan grabbed her handbag, this time housing her trusty notebook. It was preferable to the mobile where it felt like her notes were buried in the ether. "What about you?"

"I want to look into the purchase of the cottage. Make sure it's legit."

"Be careful." Even looking into the matter could draw the attention of the killer.

"Keep me posted."

"You do the same."

He walked her to the door, and then held her back. "About my mam . . ."

"Not now, Dara."

There was way too much to say, too little time. "Later, boss."

Chapter 20

Jeanie Brady was waiting for Siobhán on the footpath outside Butler's Undertaker, Lounge, and Pub. "Can we take a walk?" Jeanie said the minute Siobhán approached. "I need to stretch me legs."

"Of course." They headed in the direction of the town square, Jeanie taking the lead. She was a brisk walker, and Siobhán had to double-step it to keep up.

"I'm confident she was poisoned and that it caused her to fall ill, foam at the mouth, and possibly be in a state of delirium."

There was hesitation in her voice. "But?"

"There were no traces of poison in the teacup."

"Is it possible that the tea was poisoned but it wouldn't leave a trace in the cup?"

"Not remotely possible." Jeanie Brady's eyes gleamed. "Do you want to know why?"

"I certainly do."

"There wasn't even a trace of *tea* in the cup."

A red herring. Either Ellen Delaney was in the habit of having a clean teacup next to her bed, or the killer thought it was a good distraction. He or she hadn't picked it up off the floor because the killer had *placed* it on the floor.

"Then why are you suspecting poison? The foam?"

"She had a high level of alcohol in her blood. Whiskey."

"You think her whiskey was poisoned?"

"I do."

"Yet we didn't recover a bottle."

"Exactly."

Siobhán stopped walking. "She was rumored to be out in the woods that night. Something about spending the night near the fairy tree to prove no harm would come to her."

Jeanie Brady visibly shuddered. "That didn't work out so well."

"We need to search that area for a bottle of whiskey."

"I would say that's a good use of your time." She jabbed her finger at Siobhán. "Better you than me."

"You don't believe in fairies and curses, do you?"

Jeanie gave a nervous laugh. "Me?"

"You seem a bit . . . on edge."

Jeanie sighed. "It's not fairies or the dead we should fear. It's the living."

As Jeanie continued through town, Siobhán could see where they were headed—Annmarie's gift shop. It was originally called "Courtney's" after her late sister, but even though the sign hadn't changed, people now simply referred to it as Annmarie's. Jeanie was being led to the imported pistachios that Annmarie kept in stock. Siobhán had the feeling she was about to lose Jeanie Brady's attention. She stopped her on the footpath just outside the shop. "What else did you find?"

"Her official cause of death is suffocation."

"The pillow?"

"Yes."

"Could it have been done without the poison?"

"I believe they worked in tandem. The alcohol rendered her helpless, unable to fight back." She gazed longingly into the window of the gift shop. "Grisly business."

"Do you have samples from the plants in her garden?" Siobhán had no idea what kind of investigation the guards were running, and so far she'd resisted hounding Danny for facts.

Jeanie shook her head. "I'll put in a request to do just that. But those tests can take ages. And that's when we know which poison to look for. You know yourself—*anything* can be poisonous. The difference between medication and poison is . . . ?" She left it hanging, waiting for Siobhán to answer.

"The dose," Siobhán said.

"Correct! The difference is in the dose. But with a poisonous herb garden right at the crime scene, it would be helpful if we could narrow our suspect list." Plants. Plants were their suspects. Jeanie gestured to the store. "I'm going to just pop in; are you coming?"

"No, thank you," Siobhán said. "I'll be right out here." Jeanie nodded and hurried into the shop.

Whiskey. Did the killer steal the whiskey bottle? Is that why he or she planted the cup of tea on the floor of her bedroom? So they wouldn't look for a missing whiskey bottle? Moments later, Jeanie returned with several bags of pistachios. They began to walk as Jeanie cracked into them. "Would you like to come to Naomi's for a cup of tea?"

"That would be lovely," Jeanie said. "However . . . I have some paperwork to finish up and I don't know about you, but I could use something a little stronger."

"It's half ten in the morning," Siobhán said.

"Perfect!" Jeanie said. "Shall we?"

Siobhán laughed. "Absolutely." They headed back to Butler's Undertaker, Lounge, and Pub.

"Anything to suggest she fought back?" Siobhán asked. "Anything underneath her fingernails?"

"No. That's why I'm assuming the poison did its job."

"Would she have been able to taste the poison?"

"Not if it was added to the whiskey and was the type hard to detect. Or—by the time she did—it may have been too late."

Maybe that was what sent her racing across the meadow that evening. Had she figured out she'd been poisoned? Was she trying to get help? "Everyone heard an awful scream that night, then saw her tearing across the field toward her cottage."

Jeanie nodded. "The sense of terror boosts my theory of poison. Several of our suspected poisons can cause hallucinations. Especially when mixed with alcohol."

Siobhán struggled to piece it together. Ellen had been outside, presumably to spend the night near the fairy tree. Something spooked her, and she ran back to the cottage. Perhaps it was the poison, making her hallucinate. She would not have dressed up to spend the night in a tent. Was someone else through her cottage that evening, expecting her to be gone? Had she interrupted a robbery? Maybe Ellen didn't have just one gold coin, maybe she had piles of them. The pile of dirt by the side of the cottage flashed in her mind. What if Ellen had found coins buried on her property? Was that why she was so keen on purchasing the cottage?

They entered the pub and mortuary under the large oval sign with a painting of a distinguished gent drinking a pint: BUTLER'S, UNDERTAKER, LOUNGE, AND PUB. The punch line, which was often displayed on a chalkboard on the footpath: IF YOU'RE NOT IN ONE, YOU'RE IN THE OTHER. Today, there was no sign, but the door to the stone building opened with a creak.

It was dim inside, but Jeanie brushed past the opening bar and sitting room filled with flowered sofas, parted the velvet curtain, and stepped into a smaller bar devoid of all props for the mourners. John Butler was the lone soul behind the bar, glued to a horse race on the telly. He turned with a nod as Jeanie and Siobhán propped themselves on stools.

"Greetings." John Butler, a formal man with a shock of slicked-back white hair, and suits that seemed more appropriate for the Elizabethan age than modern day, very much looked the part of an old-fashioned undertaker. In his spare time he was an actor with the Kilbane Players, and Siobhán always got the sense that he operated as if all the world was a stage. Good on him. Undertaking and acting. They may not be bound for the big stage but at least the Kilbane Players were much more lively than the poor souls he usually worked with.

"Two pints of the black stuff," Jeanie said. Siobhán hadn't planned on drinking, but she wanted to keep Jeanie on her good side, especially since it was apparent Jeanie only had eyes for her nuts.

"Let's talk about her clothing," Siobhán said, once they'd settled in.

Jeanie stopped cracking and raised an eyebrow. "How did you know?"

"Pardon?"

"From the way you asked the question, I thought you knew."

Siobhán leaned forward. "Knew what?"

Jeanie Brady glanced to see if John Butler was listening, and he probably was, but his eyes were glued to the telly. "We're just two friends chatting here."

"Yes, we are." Siobhán smiled, suddenly wishing she had purchased the pistachios for Jeanie.

"The guards made it clear that you're not on the case." Jeanie's eyes locked with Siobhán as she sipped her pint.

"I'm sure they did." Siobhán shrugged as if it were a small matter.

Jeanie set down her pint. "She had *two* outfits on."

"Pardon?"

"Underneath the red dress—she was in a sleeping gown."

Someone had dressed her. Over her night dress. Why on earth would they do that? "That doesn't make any sense." She'd spent part of the night in the woods. Ran home. If she was in her sleeping outfit, then where were the clothes she'd worn camping? And why on earth would she put on a fancy red dress over her sleeping gown? "Do you know if the guards found dirty clothes?"

"I asked the same question and was told they did not."

"That's perplexing." The killer leaves a teacup that never held any tea. They also don't bother to remove the feather stuck to her cheek. Yet they take her dirty clothes and her truck?

"What's most unusual is that poisons are chosen because a killer is hoping they will go undetected," Jeanie Brady said. "The body will only be screened for them if there's reason to *suspect* poisoning."

"And poison is usually chosen because of the hope that it will be so subtle, it won't be revealed as the cause of death," Siobhán joined in.

"Correct. In smaller doses, especially over a longer period of time."

Such as a daughter slowly killing her mother. "But this killer is drawing a red arrow to the causes of death," Siobhán mused.

"Exactly. The killer did not attempt to wipe the foam from Ellen's mouth, or remove the feather from her cheek."

But they planted the teacup. Either this was purposeful because the killer wanted to get caught—or they had been interrupted. . . . "If those clues hadn't been present at the scene, would you have suspected poison?"

"No. I more likely would have attributed her death to the suffocation and the alcohol in her system. The foam and the teacup—even though it turns out not to be the source of the poison—and the rumors of a woman screaming, and racing across the meadow were the clues that led me to suspect hallucination and poisoning. Mother-daughter relationships are complex, wouldn't you say?" Jeanie Brady's voice was light. She didn't ever wade too far into theories, but this case seemed to fascinate her.

"Yes, I would. But what are you saying?"

"Either the killer wanted the daughter to be a top suspect in the murder. Or . . . the murderer wants to be caught."

"Meaning that Jane may have killed her mother, and she's also trying to tell us that loud and clear?"

Jeanie seemed to be humming to herself, or perhaps she was serenading the pistachios. "It's a possibility that cannot be ignored."

"She's blind. Legally. But technically she has some vision. Isn't is possible she wasn't able to see the foam or the feather?"

"Yes, that's possible."

"Jane developed the garden using a system to help her know where to find everything. She relies on the placement of her plants and the signs in the garden."

"Yes?" Jeanie could tell Siobhán was going somewhere.

"What if . . . someone switched them?"

"Meaning Jane could have accidentally poisoned her mother?"

"Is it possible?"

Jeanie sighed. "It's all possible. However . . . we're not talking about picking out a few leafs and putting them in tea. Most poisons from plants have to be carefully curated."

Carefully curated. "So accidental poisoning is out."

"Correct."

Premeditated. "There goes my theory."

"It may actually help the daughter."

"How so?"

"A loved one usually poisons a little at a time. Ellen was killed with one dose."

"How can you be sure?"

"The foaming of the mouth was an immediate reaction. Something that took hours, not days, to hit her system."

"The killer is someone who knew she would take a bottle of whiskey on her overnight adventure," Siobhán said out loud.

"What do you make of the daughter's alibi?"

"She's yet to offer proof of it." They could no longer allow Jane to deflect on this very important aspect of the case.

Jeanie drained her pint and stood. Siobhán pushed the remainder of hers away. "I'll get that paperwork sorted and then let's go to Ballysiogdun and see this garden."

"You want to identify the poison?"

"That and I'm dying to have a look at the cottage in the middle of a fairy path." She popped a pistachio and grinned. "How are you at identifying plants?"

"Useless," Siobhán said. "But I've got just the person."

Chapter 21

Two guards stood on the periphery of the garden watching as Jane began to walk through the delineated sections, Bridie following close behind. Since Bridie wasn't a suspect, and she had two green thumbs, they could trust her to correctly identify the herbs. If any of the plants had been moved, or switched, or plucked, they would soon find out. Everyone near the garden wore gloves.

The sections were clearly developed. Each herb had a corresponding sign, painted in vibrant colors. Mint. Basil. Thyme. Cilantro. Parsley. Rosemary. They started with the kitchen herbs, and as Bridie called them out and examined them, she would mark the sheet in front of her. Thirty minutes later, Bridie had them all marked down.

"Everything is clearly marked apart from the wolfsbane," she announced.

"Wolfsbane?" Jane said. "I didn't plant wolfsbane. Where is it?"

Bridie scanned the garden. "They don't quite fit into the grid." She pointed. Siobhán followed Bridie's finger as it outlined the garden.

"It's at the far edge opposite of where you're standing," Siobhán relayed. There at the edge of the garden, clearly outside the delineated portions, grew the hardy perennial. They had dark glossy leaves and purple flowers shaped like a hood. Some called it friar's cap.

"It must be growing wild," Jane said. "I didn't plant them."

"Well, there's wolfsbane here. And plenty of it."

Siobhán joined Bridie and stared down at the plants. They looked innocent, not out to murder anyone. The same could be said for their human suspects. "They're poisonous?"

"Very," Jane said. "With no healing properties. That's why I didn't plant them."

"Every part of the plant is poisonous," Bridie said. "But the roots are the most deadly."

"What did I tell you?" Jeanie Brady coached from the sidelines. "Carefully curated."

"Do any of them seem missing?" Siobhán asked as she edged in to have a look.

"They're thick in here," Bridie said. "Several plants could have been pulled and we wouldn't know it."

"I'll put in a rush on wolfsbane," Jeanie said. "Looks like we have a winner."

Jane sighed. "I didn't plant them and neither did my mother."

Siobhán left them to continue the discussion and motioned for Jeanie Brady to have a walk with her in private.

"Aconite," Jeanie said as soon as they were alone. "The poison is derived from the roots."

Not as simple as plucking off a few leaves and dropping it into liquid. This murder was premeditated. "Supposing someone knew how to extract the poison from the roots. Would that have done the job?"

"Done it? Half a teaspoon of a tincture of aconite root dropped in a bottle of whiskey would have been enough to kill a very large man."

"And given we have a . . . woman on the heavier side—but it didn't kill her?"

"They didn't get the dose strong enough . . . although . . ."

"Yes?"

"Had she fallen asleep out there, the poison may have very well taken her by morning."

"But because she got back to the cottage and hadn't yet succumbed . . ."

"The killer finished the job with a pillow." *Which meant they were either in a hurry, impatient, or not sure if the poison would do the job.*

"The tincture of an aconite root is an alcohol extract," Jeanie said. "In whiskey it wouldn't have been detected. They call it 'the perfect poison to mask a murder.'"

"So," Siobhán said, picking up on her train of thought. "Someone used the perfect poison, then ruined it by planting clues to it at the crime scene."

"Good luck figuring out why!" Jeanie Brady gave a sarcastic laugh. "And people wonder how I do *my* job." She stared at the cottage, then shuddered.

Siobhán sighed—she had no disagreement there. "How long will it take to test for wolfsbane?"

Jeanie shrugged. "The toxicology is sophisticated. It has to be sent to the best forensic lab. Patience is in order."

Siobhán nodded. "The poison may be sophisticated. But I'm starting to wonder whether or not our killer is."

Siobhán was dying to get inside the cottage again, but the village had placed new locks on the doors and boarded the windows. Jane was prepared to throw a fit, as well she should, but they hadn't had time to fight it. The only window that wasn't boarded was the one looking directly into Ellen's bedroom, but the curtains were firmly closed. Siobhán stood in front of it, pondering. The curtains had been open when they found Ellen's body. Standing here, one would have been able to see right into the bedroom. She was dying for another look inside. The sink . . . she'd almost forgotten. She'd waited long enough. Hopefully Danny was at the garda station and would be able to slip away to let Siobhán have a look. Part of her wondered if he had mentioned it to drive her mental, knowing that the anticipation was killing her. With Macdara back in Kilbane, and Bridie driving Jeanie back to Kilbane any minute now, this was the perfect chance to get back inside the cottage. She headed for the Ballysiogdun Garda Station, located just past the meadow where they held the Saturday farmers' market. She loved that the village was walkable, but had to admit she missed zipping around on her scooter.

The garda station was housed in a small stone building, roughly half the size of the Kilbane Garda Station. Two guards stood outside, smoking and chatting. On her way in, she caught part of their conversation. "Oddest

case I've ever worked. Still can't believe what they found."
They clammed up when they saw her, and she could tell
by the look on their faces that they hadn't meant for her
to hear that last bit. She simply nodded and headed inside.

Danny had let the clerk know that Siobhán was coming, so it wasn't long before she was waiting in an interview room for him.

"How ya," he said when he swept in with a stack of
folders.

"Wolfsbane," she said. "We believe it's the poison that
killed Ellen."

"I thought you were here for me to brief you," he said
with a grin. "Let me write that down."

"It's not official, but we found it planted in the backyard of the cottage. Jane says that neither she nor her
mother planted it. Half a teaspoon of the tincture dropped
in a bottle of whiskey would have been enough to kill."

Danny frowned. "Then why the pillow?"

"Either the killer didn't use enough of the poison, or it
wasn't working fast enough."

Danny nodded, and opened the folder on the top of his
pile. "I can't tell you much."

"Give me a touch then."

Danny shifted in his seat. "Why don't you make some
guesses, and I'll see if I can confirm any of them."

Siobhán understood where he was coming from. He
wasn't supposed to share this investigation with her. But
he also knew she was a good guard, and this case needed
as many cooks in the kitchen as possible. Her mind conjured up the cottage from the moment they entered. "If I
were conducting this case, I'd definitely be interested in
the stack of papers that was on Ellen's counter."

Danny nodded. "And why is that?"

He was encouraging the line of questioning. She was onto something. "Because. Given her tidiness, they didn't seem the sort of thing that she would have out on her counter?" He nodded again. "And they didn't belong to her."

"Quite right."

"But you do know who they belong to. . . ."

He grinned. "How could we not?"

"Because the party's name was on it."

"Indeed."

"Do you have any idea why this person left his or her papers on Ellen's counter?"

"Somebody must have wanted her to have an early read."

He was choosing his words carefully. *An early read.* She gasped. "Professor Kelly's manuscript."

"Quite interesting," he said. "Along with the letter."

"Yes, the letter." Shoot. "Why is the letter interesting?"

Danny shrugged. "I'm not a writer. But if I was a writer, I'd find that part of the process stressful."

That part of the process. "Getting published you mean."

"Indeed."

"Yes, indeed." There was a partial of his manuscript and a letter from a publishing company? "How do you think Professor Kelly felt after reading the letter?"

"I can imagine he was devastated."

Devastated. "Rejection isn't easy."

"Exactly."

Part of Dylan Kelly's manuscript along with his rejection letter had been left on Ellen's countertop. She wanted a time machine so she could go back and slap herself for not looking. Then again if she could go back she might as well just look and save herself the pain. Still. She really wanted to slap the version of herself who didn't look at the papers. Or, presumably, the sink.

Focus. Hadn't Dylan Kelly been crowing about a book deal? *He lied.* But why would he leave his rejection letter and manuscript with Ellen? Or had she stolen it? If she had suspected Professor Kelly was behind wanting the cottage bulldozed, maybe she was using it as leverage. And if she alone knew that his publishing deal had been rejected . . .

Had she threatened him? *Back off the rumors of the cottage or I'll tell everyone you don't have a book deal?*

"You'll be bringing the good professor in for questioning?"

"Of course."

"Have you identified the gold object under the bed?" He nodded. "And?" She was growing tired of the guessing games. Cases were so much easier when she had jurisdiction.

"It does appear to be from a hoard."

"A hoard."

"There have been a number of them found over the years in Ireland, England, Scotland, and Wales. You should look them up."

"I will, of course. You're sure the gold coin is from ancient times?"

"Just like the ones found in Tipperary," he said. "Seventeenth century."

"Those were found in what year?"

"Found in the floorboards of a pub in Carrick-on-Suir in 2013."

"I'll have to look that one up."

"You should."

"Did you find any more in the cottage?"

"We did not."

"And you checked out the side of the cottage where the dirt was piled higher than the rest?"

"It does appear someone had been digging in that spot."

"But there's no longer anything buried there."

"As you say."

One gold coin. "Unusual, is it? To find just one?"

Danny nodded. "If it came from a hoard, then it would be unusual."

"Did the owner of the pub in Carrick-on-Suir get to keep the gold coins he found?"

"No. They all went to the National Museum."

As she thought. The Irish government claimed buried treasures as their own. "That means that anyone who found such treasures wouldn't be able to cash in on them."

"Not if they did their duty and reported them."

"And if they didn't?"

"Definitely wouldn't be easy to find buyers."

"And the coin you found is the exact coin found in Tipperary?"

"'Tis." He closed his folder. Siobhán finished telling him everything she'd learned from their suspects so far. He leaned in. "Jane Delaney hasn't submitted any proof that she was in Dublin this past week."

Siobhán swallowed hard. Then nodded. "I will speak to Macdara."

Danny stood. "You might want to check out the Bally-siogdun Charity Shop."

Charity shop. Why did that sound familiar? She'd plucked the calling card from the local pub, then forgotten all about it. "I will do so." She wasn't sure why he was suggesting it, but there had to be a good reason. Maybe the owner could offer information about the gold coin. Luckily she had a photo of it on her mobile. Siobhán stood as Danny opened the door. Was he messing with her, dragging out the revelation as long as possible, or had he forgotten? "What did they find in her sink?"

His eyes danced. The game was afoot. "I have time for a break. You?"

Siobhán and Danny stood in Ellen's kitchen staring into the sink. Written on the side of the sink in blood were two words: Jane. Tree.

Siobhán was at a loss. "What in the world?"

"Oh, there's more." Danny had dragged along his folder. He opened it and removed a printout of a crime scene photograph, and held it out for her to see. There was something gray and furry in the sink. She leaned in. "Is that a mouse?"

"Yep. A very dead mouse."

If someone had offered her a million guesses she would have never thought for a second there would have been a dead mouse in the sink.

"My God." Siobhán had no other words.

"Notice anything about the poor critter?"

She moved in on the photo. She didn't mean to be cruel, but poor critter was hardly a fitting description. Deformed creature was more like it. Its enlarged face was hard to look away from, but when she did she spotted its stump of a tail with drops of red surrounding it. "Is that blood?" Danny shrugged. She wasn't normally a fan of rodents but she couldn't help but feel sorry for the poor wee thing. "I can't make sense of it."

"Can't make heads or tails?" Danny laughed at his own joke. She didn't blame him. Humor was a much-needed stress reliever when dealing with the macabre.

"Would Ellen kill a mouse and just leave it in her sink?"

"No clue."

"I am at a complete loss." Wasn't she supposed to be a neat and orderly woman? Did she let loose when her daughter was away? Dead rodents in the sink weren't just letting loose, it was darn right mental.

"The detective sergeant is thinking it was some kind of sacrifice."

"You have to be joking me."

"Did Jane ever mention that her mother believes in witches?"

"Witches?" Siobhán glanced around the simple cottage. "Do witches sacrifice mice?"

Danny shrugged and leaned in. "My first murder probe and it's stranger than fiction." He tapped on the specks of blood in the photograph. "Are there certain poisons that cause bleeding?"

Siobhán glanced away, she was already going to see that mouse in her dreams. "Did you find a bloody knife here?"

"No."

"Then maybe poison does cause bleeding, or someone poked at this poor mouse somewhere else."

"Possible."

"Which means it was someone other than Ellen."

"Jane?"

"Because her name is in the sink?"

"Yes. And. You know. She lives here."

"What if someone was trying to send her a message?" *Jane. Tree.* Dead mouse. What kind of deranged message was that? Siobhán tried to work it out. *If Jane messes with the tree she's a dead mouse?* Or was this more of a mobster warning? *You dirty rat.*

Danny folded his arms, looked away from her as he spoke. "Do you want to guess what killed the mouse?"

"Poison," Siobhán said. "Wolfsbane."

His eyebrows shot up. "Why do you think that?"

"If we confirm that Ellen was poisoned with wolfsbane. My guess? The killer was practicing."

"But there's blood evidence." He pointed to the drops in the sink. "Do you think she cut into it?"

Siobhán's stomach turned. "Why on earth would she cut into a dead mouse?"

"I'm still trying to account for the blood. Why is it there?"

Reluctantly, she glanced at the photo again and shrugged. "I would ask him but I don't tink he's going to answer." Siobhán was convinced that Ellen did not leave this poor bloody mouse in her sink. Only one person would want to practice poisoning poor critters. *The killer.*

Was Ellen awake when her killer entered? She might have fought back. Thrown something through the window even. Siobhán headed for the window. It had been patched with boards. "Have you determined that the window was broken from *inside* the cottage?"

"What makes you think that?" There was a twinge of jealousy in his tone, and something else. Admiration. She was right. Ellen threw an object from inside the cottage, maybe aiming at her killer. But the poison was starting to take effect, or maybe the killer ducked.

"The witch," the little Madigan girl had said. *"Dancing."* Had she seen Ellen struggle with her attacker?

If someone poked at the mouse with a knife, and that caused the blood . . . wasn't that overkill? Poison should have been enough. Had he or she *planned* on killing Ellen Delaney with a knife? But Ellen Delaney *wasn't* killed with a knife.

Had the killer *intended* a stabbing versus a smothering? Did she pass out once the poison hit her system and the killer changed the weapon to suit the circumstances? Much neater to kill with a pillow than a knife . . .

Danny was watching Siobhán. "You get this look on your face when you're concentrating," he said. "Just like in college."

"Joe Madigan mentioned something about dead mice at his farm."

Danny perked up. "Were any of them deformed?"

Siobhán shook her head. "I didn't think to ask, but he certainly didn't mention it."

Danny backed away from the sink. "I'll check it out."

"I'll ask Macdara to press Jane on her alibi."

"It won't be good for her if she doesn't offer proof soon," Danny said. "Tickets, photos, witnesses. If she was in Dublin, it should be easy and quick to prove it. So why hasn't she?"

Why indeed. "Tree," Siobhán said. "Fairy tree?" Maybe someone was trying to frame Jane for her mother's murder. "Do you mind if I have a quick look for Ellen's camping outfit?"

"The scene has been processed. Feel free."

Siobhán headed for Ellen's bedroom, but a quick search did not find any dirty clothes. "What about her laptop. Anything come of it?"

"I really can't say." Danny meandered over to the boarded-up window.

"I understand."

"But sometimes I talk out loud."

"Do you?"

"Makes it easier to process."

"I'll just mosey over here." Siobhán wandered to the far wall. Nothing hung on the simple wall, so Siobhán lost herself in the cracks, and lines, and dust. Was Ellen such a sparse decorator because she felt guilty that Jane couldn't see? Or maybe decorating just wasn't her thing. Siobhán loved the little touches that made a house a home. This cottage did not have that welcoming touch. She wondered what the fairies would think about that.

"Let's see," Danny said. "We need to bring Jane in for questioning, because her alibi hasn't been verified, and as the closest kin to the deceased, she'd be very much on our radar as a suspect. We need to know why Dylan Kelly left his manuscript in the cottage. Or, if it wasn't him, we need to know how and why the manuscript was on the counter. We're waiting for the results of the footwear impression we found near the front door. We still don't know how the window was broken, even though we know it was from the inside. Looking like wolfsbane in whiskey is the poison, but there's no whiskey bottle. We've yet to locate Ellen's truck, handbag, or mobile phone. Or the clothes she wore if indeed she was outside to spend the night near the fairy tree. We've requested her phone records—it's unfortunate that everything takes so long. We ran with the recent tip that Ellen had secretly purchased the cottage, but we've verified with the village that she did not. It was never even up for sale."

"She lied to her sister." Siobhán was most definitely not going to be the eejit who delivered that bombshell.

"That makes me wonder why she needed to borrow fifteen thousand euro from her sister," Danny added.

Siobhán began to follow a trail of dust on the wall, one that suddenly took shape as she stepped back. The dust marked a rectangle, as if a large frame had recently been hanging there.

"Danny, look."

He ambled over as she pointed to the wall. "What am I looking at?"

"Doesn't it look as if a painting once hung here?"

"Possibly," Danny said. "Where are you going with this? Are you suggesting it was stolen?"

"No. Jane said she donated a painting—or tried to— for a showing Annabel was hosting at Molly's Café. She said when Ellen found out she was livid."

"Okay . . ."

"Ellen presumably got the painting back. So what did she do with it?"

Danny quickly took in the room. "The guards have been over the place several times. We didn't find a large painting."

"Interesting."

Danny laughed. "I'll let you follow that trail."

"Thank you." She smiled. It was great to work with her old friend. "For everything."

"Don't mention it," he said with a grin. When she didn't reply, his smile faded. "Seriously," he said, as they exited the cottage. "Please don't mention it."

Chapter 22

Siobhán was headed back to the Ballysiogdun Inn when her phone pinged with a text from James.

We're here

Who is we?

Her mobile dinged and a photo came back. Her entire brood was in front of the inn, large grins plastered on their faces.

It takes a village to survive this village

Tears welled in her eyes as she texted back:

Let's go shopping then

Three moving dots appeared on her text and she grinned as she waited for his reply:

Typical

She laughed out loud, her steps lighter as she headed to meet up with them. Her joy was soon muted by the image of a dead, tailless mouse in Ellen's sink. *Sacrifice.*

Witch. How browned off was her fiancé going to be that she was keeping such bizarre discoveries from him? It would be hard to claim that it slipped her mind. She sighed, pondering her options, wishing she had a little person to blame it on.

The Ballysiogdun Charity Shop sold antiques and curiosity items, and after asking around Siobhán learned that the owner was touted as the man to ask about coins, or any Irish treasures, for that matter. It was also a destination if not wildly, at least mildly approved by her brood. The short man tinkering with a clock grinned when they walked in. Ciarán, Ann, Gráinne, Eoin, and James all spread out, going for toys, books, clothes, graphic novels, and Siobhán wasn't sure what James was going to find to occupy himself, but he seemed content to be in their company. She vowed they would go on a proper holiday soon, where murder would be the last thing on their minds.

Siobhán was hoping that a photo of the coin found underneath Ellen's bed would be enough to garner some information. She approached the owner, who was polishing a crystal owl, smiling as if calculating how much they might spend.

"How ye," he said. "If you're looking for jewelry, I've got a nice assortment here." He pointed to a large glass case next to him. She thought of her engagement ring, once again safely tucked away. She wouldn't care if she never owned another piece of jewelry in her life.

"I need a consultation," she said. "I have a photo of a coin. A guinea."

"A guinea?" He plunked the owl down on the counter,

rubbed his hands together, then looked around. "You heard the chatter then?"

"Chatter?"

"If it's a big payout you're looking for, you'll be disappointed. If you found it buried in Ireland, it belongs to the government." His smile was still visible but carried half the power.

"Nothing like that." She pulled out her mobile phone and enlarged the picture of the gold coin. "It's not a perfect picture, but I was wondering if there is any way you could identify it."

He reluctantly took her mobile and brought it up to his eyes. "Hold on." He dug around in a drawer, pulled out a monocle, and looked again. She saw him light up. "A 1773 George the Third. If it's in fine condition, could be around eight hundred euro, or more. They'd have to measure the gold content."

"Eight hundred euro?" Ciarán's voice ricocheted through the shop as he careened over. "Let me see." Siobhán showed him the picture. "Eight hundred euro?" Ciarán repeated. "For that?"

"Imagine if you found a whole pile of them," Siobhán said.

"You'd be handing them over to the government," the clerk repeated.

Chatter. "Has anyone else come into your shop inquiring about this coin?"

"Is this yours?" he asked. She noted that he didn't answer the question.

"It belongs to a friend."

"Did she find a hoard?" Siobhán took note that he said "she."

"I know all about the book that's being written," Siobhán said. "I'm assuming Dylan Kelly has been in to see you."

The clerk nodded. "He showed me an article mentioning rumors of a hoard in Ballysiogdun. Something about 'where the fairies dwell.' But he sure as I'm standing here didn't have anything like that coin to show me. He promised he'd come back in and tell me if he found a hoard."

He'd certainly told someone something about it. Or did he keep it all to himself?

"Hoard?" Ciarán said, scrunching his nose. "What's that?"

"Buried treasures," he said with a wink. "Do you want to hear the stories?"

"Of course." The answer came not from Siobhán, who was about to say the same thing, but from Ann, who was now standing behind her. Soon, all of her brood was gathered, eager to hear the stories.

"Barry Shannon, 2014," he said. "Found himself a fishie buried in his aunt's field."

"A fishie?" Ciarán said. "In a field?"

"Not just any fishie. Not the swimming kind, lad. This was a gold fish from the seventh century."

"A gold fish?"

"Aye. About this long." He held his fingers out three inches. "Might have been part of a belt buckle. You see yer man had been searching as a hobby, like, using one of those metal detectors. 'Twas only a foot beneath the soil—can you imagine? The lad was only twenty-two years of age." He laughed to himself. "Lad was a fisherman, thought it was a spinner, you know, the yoke you have on the end of the line. Even offered it to his cousin. Cousin told the lad to keep it for himself, for his trouble.

He'd been out there all day searching, so he had. Then he takes it to his auntie, who thought nothing of it at first. After a while curiosity starts tickling at her. Who left it? How old was it? Was it worth anything? She decided it would be good to know, if even for a laugh. She gets the name of a fella who might know a ting or two. Lucky she did. Turns out it was a medieval adornment to a belt buckle, determined to be not Irish but Anglo-Saxon. How it ended up in that field we'll never know. Perhaps due to trade back and forth across the Irish Sea."

"How much was it worth?" James asked.

"I don't recall. It was sent for valuation, but similar Anglo-Saxon finds have gone for just under two hundred thousand pounds."

"Does he mean euros?" Ciarán said, crinkling his face.

"You're right, lad," the man said. "The pound is still stuck in me head. And sometimes the quid." He threw his head back and laughed, then laughed even more at the perplexed look on her brother's young face. "There's buried treasure out there, chalices, jewelry, earthenware, even little gold fishies." He leaned in. "But the Irish government is going to take it from ye and stick it in a museum. Yer man there in England, back in 2009, was digging and struck an entire pot of gold coins. Seems they were buried in the third century as an offering to the gods, hoping they'd bless them with good farming conditions. In 2013 there was another fella in Wales, found fourteen coins. Worth about seven hundred fifty euros each. Nice little haul." He was excited now, practically drooling.

"Did he have a metal detector too?" Ciarán asked.

The man scrunched his brow. "I don't rightly know, lad. I suppose he might have."

"I want a metal detector." Ciarán turned to Siobhán. "What's a metal detector?"

"It's an electronic device used to find metal," James said, patting him on the head.

"I'll take one," Ciarán said.

"Won't do you any good now," the man said. "Ireland ruled them against the law."

"Why?" Siobhán asked.

"Probably so your average Joe won't go taking archaeological objects they deem belong to them. If you want to use one you'll need written consent from the minister for Culture, Heritage, and Gaeltracht. Otherwise you'll be prosecuted." He made a horrified face, then winked at Ciarán.

"Do you have his address?" Ciarán asked.

"No metal detectors for us, luv," Siobhán said.

"How many of these does your friend have?" the man asked, rubbing his hands together. "Depending on the worth of the hoard, a farmer might get a few thousand from the government for their trouble."

"I don't know," Siobhán said. Were there any more gold coins? *That was an excellent question.*

"It's possibly an exciting find, but I'd advise them to obey the law."

"I'll pass that along. Thank you very much."

"I'm sure you're going to buy something, now, aren't you, luv?"

"Of course," Siobhán said, then tasked Ciarán and Ann with the troublesome chore of picking out an item. "Under ten euro," she said as they hurried off. "I'm not sitting on a hoard."

* * *

Lunchtime found them back at the local pub, but Siobhán's thoughts were more on the gold coin than her fish and chips. Even though the clerk from the shop made it clear it was against the law to keep buried treasures, the treasure hunter may not have been aware of the law. And even if they were aware of the law, mankind did not always follow the law. She imagined if she owned a piece of property and found buried treasure, she'd be a little incensed with the Irish government claiming it as their own. Then again, didn't archaeological treasures belong in a museum for everyone to appreciate? Ownership was a man-made concept, and at the end of the day, none of it came with you. That didn't stop people from trying, even killing over it. Once again, she was reminded that you never knew what could crack an investigation open. Sometimes it was as simple as the flip of a coin. And who better to know what was buried on that property than someone who had lived there all her life? It was time Siobhán paid another visit to Geraldine Madigan. The cottage was clear. She was owed a divining-stick demonstration.

Geraldine's sticks were crossed, and seemed to be pulling down, toward the ground. The shaking increased. "That's pure energy, that is," Geraldine said, as sweat rolled down the side of her face. They were standing in the exact spot where the dirt rose into a little hill as if something had been buried there. *Or dug up . . .*

"Energy can be good," Siobhán said. If her current theory was correct, it wasn't an accident that Geraldine gravitated to this exact spot with her divining sticks. The question that remained was—had Ellen discovered the hoard first, or Geraldine? Siobhán was starting to think it was the former. And finding that treasure had marked her with an X.

"This cottage kills," Geraldine was saying. "Is that your definition of good?"

"May I hold them?" Siobhán wanted to see if the sticks would react the same way.

Geraldine shook her head. "I don't let others handle me sticks."

"Speaking of sticks . . . I'd like to buy another one. I like the one you have with the round base?"

"That one's not for sale."

"Why is that?"

Geraldine squinted as if trying to read Siobhán's mind. "It took me ages to make."

"I see. I'd still like to have another look at it."

Geraldine looked at her watch. "It won't be today. That is if you're planning on going to the council meeting."

"Another day then," Siobhán said. Not that she needed to have a look now; her theory had just been confirmed. And the meeting wasn't one she was willing to miss. Not when Aiden Cunningham had proved to be so slippery.

"I'll see you there then," Geraldine said, as she hurried away. It was plain as day that the woman was relieved to have an excuse to leave. Siobhán stared after her. She didn't need to see Geraldine's walking stick, the one with a round base, to know what it was. Siobhán had picked it up and recalled it being heavier than the other sticks. That's because it wasn't a stick. Not your typical one anyway. It was a metal detector. And the only reason a person would dress a metal detector in colorful yarn was if they knew that it was illegal to use them. Which meant she didn't care. There were still a million unanswered questions about this case. But Siobhán knew she had a very important piece of it. Geraldine Madigan wanted Ellen and Jane away from the property, not because she thought the cottage was cursed, but because she had been after a buried hoard.

Had Ellen found Geraldine digging on her property when she returned that evening? Had they struggled? Had Ellen yanked the detector away from Geraldine and busted the window with it? Wait. Didn't Danny confirm the window was broken from the inside? Maybe the metal detector ended up there. Siobhán was mostly curious to see if the yoke lit up. If Geraldine and Ellen were struggling and the metal detector was blinking through the colored yarn, that would explain "the pretty lights" and "dancing" witnessed by Lilly from the window. Poor thing thought she was watching fairies dance instead of a prelude to a murder.

Had they wrestled for the coins? Who dropped one under the bed? Would Ellen have had time to take a shower and put on a sleeping dress? Where were her dirty clothes? Why take her truck and not anything else? Siobhán loathed the part of an investigation where a single answered question unleashed nothing but an avalanche of more.

The town meeting was held on the first floor of a storefront building on the main street. Aiden Cunningham started off by welcoming them all and assuring them the murder inquiry into the death of Ellen Delaney was well under way. "What about the cottage?" Geraldine Madigan called out. "When will it be bulldozed?" She was still harping on that. Did that mean she'd yet to strike gold?

"No decisions will be made until the investigation is closed."

"My divining sticks indicated great evil all around the cottage. She saw it for herself, an outsider!"

All eyes turned to Siobhán, which was when she realized that Geraldine Madigan was pointing at her.

"I'm not sure what I saw."

"You saw my stick quiver!"

"There was a bit of a quiver, alright."

"Could have been her hand that was doing the quivering!" someone called out.

"I'm a teetotaler, so just why would me hand be quivering?"

"Old age." Geraldine frowned as several in the crowd laughed.

"The lease on the cottage expires in two months," Aiden Cunningham said. He cleared his throat. "We won't be renewing it."

"Will you be bulldozing it or not?" an older man called out.

Dylan Kelly stepped up to the podium. "Perhaps *preserving* the cottage is a better idea, finding a way to keep the fairies appeased, as well as honoring our beloved folklore. We can come up with a compromise."

"You want the people of the hills to stay enraged, do ye?" Geraldine, face red with fury, scanned the room. "I heard all of you say it. One more death and we'll have to bulldoze it. Are ye going back on your word now? All of ye?"

Sergeant Eegan stood from a chair in the very back. "There's nothing to be decided right now. If I see anyone but Jane Delaney and her family stepping beyond the gate, on the bramble path, or anywhere near the cottage, they'll be arrested straightaway."

"That goes for my property too," Joseph Madigan said. He was sitting up front with Mary, his children, and his mother.

Aiden Cunningham was up for reelection, and trying to appeal to both sides of the argument. Had Ellen given Aiden Cunningham that money for his political campaign, hoping for assurance in return? Did he promise them they could continue to live in the cottage?

Why on earth would they want to?

There was only one possible answer. *Buried treasure.*

Siobhán had been studying Aiden Cunningham, wondering about his relationship with Ellen. If they were lovers, he was foolish not to come out and volunteer the information. Had he given it to the Ballysiogdun guards? No one was required to tell Siobhán anything, and it was a loathsome, powerless feeling. When the meeting was over, she meant to have a word with the councilman, and she was beginning to wonder if he was half man, half eel, for once again he slipped out. He was a curious fella indeed. Not interested in talking, Councilman? That was okay. Siobhán could think of one other place that just might shed some light on the mysterious man.

Chapter 23

Primo Limo was operated out of Cork City. But the man on the phone informed Siobhán that Ballysiogdun had one driver, and he worked out of his home. He gave her the address and Siobhán booked a taxi. When they reached the limestone house thirty minutes away, a black limousine loomed in the circular drive. She asked the taxi to wait. The driver reclined his seat and lit a cigarette. "Not a bother."

Siobhán approached the limo, cupped her hand, and tried to peer into the back, wondering if she'd spot bottles of champagne waiting for the next spoiled rider. The front door of the house flew open, and minutes later a short man dressed all in black strode down the walkway. He waved as he drew closer. "Are you the client who called about a visit?"

"I am indeed," Siobhán said. No harm in a little white

lie. She held out her hand and introduced her civilian-self.

"Would you like to book a ride?" There was an eager-ness to his tone that made her suspect business was slow.

"I'm thinking about it." She'd never been in a limo. None of her close girlfriends had married, so no hen par-ties as of yet. It wasn't long ago they all would have been doomed as spinsters by this point. She was grateful for being born in a time where women were in no rush to have babies. *Tell that to your future mother-in-law.*

"Suit yourself," the driver said. "So why are you here?"

Pleasantries were finished. She introduced her garda-self. "You stopped by Ellen Delaney's cottage on Friday morning?" She glanced at the date in her notebook and recited it just so there was no misunderstanding.

He took a rag out of his pocket and began to polish the side mirrors on his limo. "Who told you dat?"

"Are you saying you didn't?" Quite adept at it herself, Siobhán had very little patience for deflection.

"I'm not saying a thing. I run a discreet business." He moved to the other window and continued his polishing.

"It's the only limousine in town. You were seen."

"I'm saying nothing."

"I'm trying to catch a killer."

"You don't belong here. If the local guards want to question me, so be it."

Siobhán glanced at his windshield. Hanging from the rearview mirror was a medal. She had to lean in to see it. Saint Francis of Assisi. The patron of animals, merchants, and ecology, but also the saint of families. "What if her daughter gives you permission to talk about her mother?"

"The blind daughter?" His interest was piqued.

"Yes. She's hired us to bring justice to her mother." This was a man who respected work and family.

He stopped polishing. "I suppose that would be alright then. Will she be able to hear me?"

"She's blind. Not deaf."

"I see. Will we go to her then?" He glanced back at his house. "I don't have any ramps."

"Why would she need a ramp?"

The driver shrugged. "You're asking the wrong man."

She so was. "Perhaps you can come to Kilbane."

He scrunched his face like it was a dirty word. "Why would I do that?"

"The funeral will take place this weekend. I'm sure your services will be needed." Siobhán felt guilty for fobbing this limo on the residents of Kilbane, but she needed to find out what he knew.

"I could use a change of scenery. These are me rates." He opened the passenger door, rummaged around in the glove compartment, then handed her a sheet.

"I see." He should have been hanging a medal for the Patron Saint of Price Gouging. There had better be champagne. This was going to cost somebody. She tucked the price sheet in her handbag so she would remember to give it to Macdara.

The weekend arrived in no time, so when the limo pulled its long, sleek body up to Naomi's and purred at the curb, mourners spilled out of the bistro and gathered around it like curious moths. Ciarán began bouncing around. "Is it ours?" he asked. "Can we keep it?"

"No," Siobhán said.

The driver got out and hurried over to Jane, who was

standing next to Siobhán. He took off his hat and placed it over his chest. "Hello," he said.

Jane tilted her chin. "Hello."

"How ya?" His tone was as nervous as a lad on a first date. "I'm sorry about your mam."

"Thank you."

Siobhán had filled Jane in on their meeting with the driver, and she knew he was here to hopefully give information, so why was Jane suddenly clamming up? "This is the driver who saw your mother over the weekend," Siobhán said, hoping to move things along. Jane did not respond.

"She hired me for the weekend," the driver said, with a worried glance to Siobhán.

"The entire weekend?" Finally, Jane spoke up.

"It was to be an enjoyable weekend. I'm sorry they didn't get to go."

They. Jane caught it too; it was quick, but Siobhán caught it. She'd flinched.

"It's okay," Siobhán said, leaning in and lowering her voice. "We've spoken to the councilman." This was a pure shot in the dark, not to mention a power move. Jane could immediately dispute it if she wished. Siobhán waited, her heart in her throat. To her relief, Jane did not interrupt the play.

"He was very kind to pay my cancellation fee. Had I known, I would have gone to him instead of Mrs. Delaney. My cancellation policy is very clear. It's written down like." He stared at Jane. "Would you like a copy in braille?"

She snorted. "Do you have a copy in braille?"

"No."

"That's sorted then."

"Why did you go to the cottage Friday morning if the gig had been canceled?" Siobhán asked.

"She owed me for the entire weekend. I came to collect."

"And she sent you to the councilman?"

"Yes. He wasn't in. Which surprised me. I don't know where he went or with who, but I was the one he hired for the weekend."

"Hired to go where?"

"He wouldn't say. I was told there would be multiple destinations, nothing farther than an hour up the road."

"When was this shift to begin?"

"The first pickup was scheduled for Saturday evening, half five."

Sounded like the first stop was out to dinner.

"Are you saying they canceled but you didn't get paid?"

"When I refused to leave the councilman's office, his assistant paid me."

"Did you ever find out why they were canceling?" He shifted his gaze away from them, as if not wanting to answer. Siobhán nudged Jane.

"Please," Jane said. "I need to know."

His gaze was back on Jane. He nodded. "She was rattled by something, I tell you that."

"Rattled how?" Siobhán asked.

"She was shoving things into a bag, an odd assortment of things—she said . . ." He swallowed. "'I'll show them.'"

"What does that mean?" Jane mused. "Who is them? The village?"

"I think she had something to prove and she was going to prove it," the driver said.

Spending the night near the fairy tree.

"If she was going somewhere, and paying you—why didn't she just change the route?" Jane asked.

"I have a feeling she was . . . taking off on foot."

"Why do you say that?"

"The bag she was packing. It was a hiking pack. And she had her Wellies and walking stick out. That's all I can say."

Butler's Undertaker, Lounge, and Pub welcomed the villagers of Ballysiogdun, and Ellen Delaney's funeral was conducted professionally and warmly. It was a short service, as requested by Jane, and no one was allowed to mention the cottage, or fairies, or murder.

The crowd stood back as Jane Delaney approached her mother's coffin. Her hands traveled over her mother's face, causing multiple hands to reach into their handbags for tissues. Jane was touching Ellen's hair. She snatched her handbag as if she'd been scalded. When she turned around, as if searching the shadows in the crowd, she looked panicked. Siobhán hurried up to her.

"What's wrong?"

"We need to speak with the person who arranged her."

"Okay." She waited, thinking that if she was about to complain about the job they'd done arranging her, it wasn't going to be pleasant. "Why?"

"Can anyone hear us?" Jane tilted her head down.

"No, luv."

"Her hair. It's curly."

Siobhán glanced in the coffin. Ellen's hair was curly, but Siobhán did not see why this mattered. "And?"

"I know they probably washed it here, but when you found my mother on the bed, was her hair just like this?"

Siobhán thought back. It was the only time she'd ever laid eyes on Ellen and a lot was going on in the scene. She closed her eyes. The white feather on the cheek, the slack mouth with foam, the gray curls—"Yes. It was curly."

"She was interrupted then. Just after."

"What do you mean?"

"Mam's hair was only curly after she showered. She would then put fat rollers in it to loosen the curls. If her hair was in tight curls like this when you found her, it means she showered but never put in her rollers."

"Is it possible she just didn't feel like it?"

"No," Jane said. "Mam never wavered on this. If she didn't put her curlers in, something interrupted her. Or someone."

One more piece of the puzzle confirmed. Ellen had showered that evening and changed into her sleeping dress. Next step would have been curlers.

This pointed to the killer dressing Ellen, not Ellen dressing herself. Why? Had the outfit been sitting out? After all, she had originally planned on going out that evening with Aiden Cunningham. It had been confirmed that had been canceled, but with Jane away for the weekend, perhaps Ellen wasn't bothered about being tidy. Where were the clothes she wore camping? Siobhán needed time to think this through. "Let's keep this between us for now."

"Why, Siobhán O'Sullivan," Jane said, raising her voice. "Are you still keeping secrets from Cousin Dara?" Jane walked away with a smirk, but the comment was like a gut punch. She'd meant to have a heart-to-heart with Macdara and tell him absolutely everything, especially about the sink, but the right moment had never presented itself. Who was she fooling? The longer she waited, the harder it was going to be. But everyone in their right mind would agree: his aunt's funeral was *not* the time and the place for creepy-dead-mouse confessions.

They gathered in Saint Mary's churchyard for the burial. Nancy Flannery's parents were buried there, and her older sister went into the plot next to them. It was a relief when everyone was back at Naomi's, gathered with mugs of tea, and sandwiches, and pie. The weather was pleasant, and after the feed many decided to have a walkabout. Dylan Kelly was among them. Siobhán wanted to hurry after him, eager to talk to him about the pages they'd found in Ellen's cottage, along with his rejection letter. Hawthorne Publishing, she'd discovered after some digging, had been the name of the publisher. Did he, or did he not have a publishing deal? Macdara was on the phone with them now, pretending to be Dylan Kelly. She waited for him by the fireplace, nearly jumping out of her skin. Would he learn anything?

She was relieved when he bounded into the room, a slight smile on his face. "Come on," she said, grabbing his hand and pulling him to the exit. "He just left."

"How did you know," Macdara asked her when they were out on the footpath, "that I learned something?"

"Your smirk," she said.

He laughed. "You haven't even asked me what it is."

"I'll hear when you confront the good professor."

"You always did like a good cliffhanger," Macdara said, as they ran to catch up with him.

They found the professor on the footpath in front of Gordon's Comics, looking somewhat bewildered by the images of vampires and superheroes in the window.

"Are you a fan of the graphic novel?" Siobhán said pleasantly as they approached from behind, causing him to jump.

He recovered with a laugh, and a cough, then shook his head. "I was hoping to find more of a traditional bookstore."

Siobhán nodded. Secretly, she did too, although now that Eoin was into graphic novels, she had a new appreciation for them. "That makes sense. When is yours due to be published?"

"Very soon, I hope. Very soon." He began to rock on his heels as if consoling himself.

"I'm sure you have a deadline and a publishing date?" She should let Macdara take the lead—he was the one with some news—but she was making the professor nervous, and a nervous suspect was more likely to tip over and spill something out, even unwillingly.

"There's a bit more work to do." He stopped rocking and threw a desperate look down the street as if he'd summoned the cavalry and was searching for any sign of them. "But I'm very, very close." He flashed a disturbing grin.

"Are any of your pages missing?" Macdara asked.

His grin vanished and was just as quickly replaced by

a frown. "How did you know?" He stepped closer to Macdara. "Those pages are mine. They belong to me." If Siobhán wasn't watching it with her own eyes she wouldn't have believed the transformation from nerdy professor to menacing thug. His fists clenched and his dark eyes flashed with anger. Macdara didn't flinch.

"When did you notice they were missing?"

"I'll tell the guards. The *other* guards."

"They're the ones who have them," Macdara said. "And I just had an interesting talk with your publisher." He stopped. "Or should I say—your prospective publisher?"

"They rejected you," Siobhán said. "And yet you're telling everyone you have a book deal. Why?"

"This is outrageous," Dylan Kelly said. "It's an ongoing negotiation."

"Because your story wasn't . . . What was it?" Macdara looked up as if he was struggling to remember. "Relevant enough."

"My, my," Siobhán said. "They wanted something more contemporary?"

"And dramatic," Macdara said. "I've seen some of the titles they publish. I must say—they do like stories that are a little more . . . what's the word?" He turned to Siobhán.

"Sensational?" she said.

Macdara snapped his fingers. "Sensational!" he said. "That's it."

Siobhán shook her head. "I bet Ellen Delaney's murder fits into the sensational category."

"Makes it relevant too," Macdara said. He crossed his arms. "They're very eager for your new pages."

Dylan Kelly's face turned red. "As a writer, a historian, I have a duty to write about the cottage, and it's not like I murdered her just to write a book!"

"Really?" Siobhán said. "Because some might consider yours a very strong motive indeed."

"Not to mention where they found your pages," Macdara said.

Dylan's head snapped toward them. "Where?" He sounded like he was genuinely asking.

"We can't say," Siobhán said. "But Garda Flannery is correct. It looks very bad for you." She glanced across the street where Sergeant Eegan and Danny were taking a stroll. "They must think our killer has shown up for the funeral."

"They're going to stay very close until they solve this case," Macdara agreed. "Breathe down the killer's neck."

"Breathe down everyone's neck," Siobhan said.

Dylan Kelly started to blink rapidly. "Those pages were stolen from me. Including that publishing letter."

"When were they stolen?" Macdara added. Since Dylan was responding better to another male, Siobhán stepped back to let Dara continue the questioning.

"At the town hall. During one of the council meetings."

"Before the murder?"

"Yes. Days before."

"Take us through it."

Dylan Kelly sighed. "Aiden Cunningham introduced me at the meeting, told me to come and say a few quick words. I took the podium for maybe ten minutes . . . it could have been more."

As she listened to him nervously drone on, Siobhán knew it was more. "Go on," Macdara urged.

"I didn't notice that any pages were missing. Not right

away. It wasn't until that evening that I noticed them. My opening chapters and the letter from the publisher gone." Siobhán noted he couldn't bring himself to utter the word "rejection." "I thought maybe . . . I thought someone was playing a trick on me."

He thought it was a fairy. He wouldn't say it, but Siobhán could see that was what he was thinking.

"If someone stole your rejection letter, it's reasonable to assume they did so to blackmail you," Siobhán said.

"Anyone been blackmailing you?" Macdara added.

Dylan Kelly swallowed. "Everyone is jealous when you have a book coming out."

"Unless it turns out you don't really have a book coming out."

"They won't reject this draft," he said passionately.

"Because of the murder," Siobhán said.

He swallowed again. "If you're not the killer," Macdara said, moving in closer, "do you think the killer might be threatened by the thought of a book being written about the murder?"

"How could the killer not be threatened?" Siobhán said. "He or she definitely wanted to get his or her hands on the manuscript."

"Why would they want to do that?" Dylan stammered.

"To make sure there wasn't anything in the book that reveals the killer's identity."

"There's not! I'm certain there's not."

"You don't mention any names in the book?" Macdara challenged.

"You're trying to scare me," Dylan Kelly said. That was true. It was also working. His upper lip was covered in little beads of sweat. "Aiden Cunningham," he croaked out. "The councilman stole my pages."

Chapter 24

"You know," Macdara said, as he stood in the doorway to her bedroom and watched Siobhán pack her bag. "You don't have to stay involved in this case."

Siobhán stopped packing and turned around. "Do you have a fever?"

He smiled. Shook his head. "It's summer. It's your summer holiday." He approached her and took her hands in his. "You said yourself, Garda MacGregor is a good guard. They have help from Cork City and Dublin. Maybe it's not up to us to solve every murder."

"This is personal."

"To me. Not to you."

"We're engaged. Your family is my family."

He sat on the edge of her bed. "Your family holiday consists of funerals and witness interrogations."

Was this toxic residue left over from his mother's tirade? *Do not say it.* "They were all charmed by Ballysiogdun."

"For a few days. Are you actually dragging everyone back now?"

She clenched and unclenched her fists while counting. Never insult a man's mother; there's no coming back from that. "Eoin is staying to run the bistro with Bridie. James is staying—whether it's to work or go back to mooning after Elise, I don't know. Gráinne starts her job with Sheila. I have to take Ciarán and Ann with me."

"You can stay here with Ciarán and Ann."

"I can't. I have to see this through."

"You'll never get this time back."

"I'm doing the best I can." *Was she?* Was lying to the man she was going to marry, a man who happened to be an excellent guard, really the best she could do? She stopped throwing clothes into her suitcase and turned to him. "Remember when you were in Kilbane with your mam and I accompanied Jeanie Brady and Jane back to the cottage?"

"Yes." Macdara lowered himself to a chair and crossed his arms, as if knowing whatever she was about to say was best heard sitting down.

"Danny had something else to show me." Macdara did not respond, he simply waited. "Something we missed. In the sink." Had he blinked? It didn't look as if he was blinking.

"Go on."

She took a breath and filled him in on the macabre scene in the sink, the crime scene photo of the mauled mouse, the words "Jane" and "Tree" in the sink written in mouse blood, the shoe print Danny said they'd lifted from near the cottage, and the dust on the wall where Siobhán believed a painting had hung.

He stood. "Are you joking me?"

"I know. It's bizarre."

"You know what else is bizarre?" His voice was raised. "The amount of times we've seen each other since then, and you didn't think to mention a dead mouse in me aunt's sink!"

She went to him and took his hands. He pulled away. "I'm sorry, but I've been conflicted. You're too close to the victim."

"That didn't stop you when your brother was accused of murder."

He was going back over three years now. "I wasn't a guard then. I didn't know any better."

"Convenient."

"I'm sorry. It's been eating me up. And you can be as browned off as you wish. Later. Because right now I need you."

He rubbed his face, looked to the ceiling. "Joe Madigan mentioned dead mice on his farm."

"Exactly. I think the killer was practicing. With wolfsbane."

"Jane. Tree," Macdara said.

"Tree. Jane," Siobhán corrected.

"Does it matter?"

"I haven't a clue. There's more."

"Your capacity to keep secrets is impressive."

She placed her hand on his chest and backed him back into his chair. In a rare display of affection she plopped herself on his lap, threw her arms around his neck. "I'm sorry. I won't ever do it again. I promise."

"Well played," he said, his voice low.

"You're the best detective I know."

"Don't overplay your hand."

"Honestly. Keeping secrets from you was giving me a constant pain in the head."

"Good."

"I think we need to find a missing painting." She filled him in on her conversation with Jane, and how she'd given Annabel a painting of Ellen's to hang in Molly's Café. "Apparently your aunt went absolutely mental, stormed over to Annabel's, and took back the painting. So where is it now?"

"I have a feeling you know where to look."

"I need to visit Annabel." She jumped up. "Oh!"

"What?"

"I think one of Geraldine's walking sticks is a metal detector and the gold coin is probably from a hoard and alone it's worth around eight hundred euro, but technically would belong to the government, and it's my theory that Ellen found the hoard and that's what got her killed. I think Geraldine didn't realize that Ellen discovered it, and she was in a race to find it. That's why she made a bet with Ellen that she couldn't spend the night by the fairy tree. What she didn't count on was Ellen returning to the cottage in the middle of the night. I think the two of them wrestled while Geraldine was holding the metal detector and that's why Lilly, who was watching from her window, thought she saw dancing and pretty lights."

Macdara's jaw dropped. "I've changed me mind. You should stay out of this."

"We both know I can't."

"We both know you *won't*." He sighed. "Just don't fly too close to the sun." He pulled her to him and kissed her.

"It's Ireland, you eejit," she said softly when they pulled away. "There's hardly ever any sun."

Siobhán entered Molly's Café. Ann and Ciarán loved the small bistro and its friendly owner. They had a pile of books, and notebooks, and games. Despite Macdara's lightly delivered lecture, Siobhán was enjoying her time with her youngest siblings. Yes, she had to be careful what she said and did with them in tow, but they were making the best of it. The lunch hour was over, and with the exception of an older couple reading the newspaper and drinking tea, they were the only other customers.

When Ann and Ciarán were happily eating and reading, Siobhán approached Molly. She ordered pie and tea, finding herself in grave need of creature comforts. "Would you be able to join me for a minute?"

Molly didn't ask why. She knew who she was. She gave a nod and a smile. "I'll be there in a moment with your pie and tea."

Siobhán took the seat furthest from the window. She didn't want folks knowing who she was talking to, and wondering why. Molly removed her apron, set Siobhán's tea and pie in front of her. "Will you be wanting milk and sugar, luv?"

"Yes, please." She probably didn't need the sugar, not with the pie, but maybe just a pinch.

When Molly didn't sit right away, Siobhán gave her a puzzling look.

"There's something here for you."

"For me?" That was odd.

Molly held up her finger. "There's a note here for

you." She returned to the counter and when she appeared again she set down milk, sugar, and a plain envelope. "SIOBHÁN O'SULLIVAN" was typed across it.

When Siobhán didn't make a move to pick it up, Molly pointed at it. "It's you, isn't it?"

"'Tis. I just . . . It's a surprise."

Molly shrugged. "Not in a small village." She sat across from Siobhán and eyed the envelope.

"Fair play." Siobhán wasn't going to open it in front of her. "I heard that Ellen used to come here with her laptop."

"She did, yeah."

"When was the last time you saw her?"

She smoothed her hands across the table and looked up. "Just before the murder. It was Thursday day."

"What can you tell me about that visit?"

She was already shaking her head. "The same as it always was, so. She'd order a cup of tea and sit by the window." She gestured to the window. "Hardly a word exchanged."

"Did anyone else come in and speak with her?"

"I wasn't keeping a close eye. We were busy. If I'd known she was going to be murdered I'd have paid more attention, like."

"She was on her laptop that Thursday?"

"She was." She squinted. "There is one thing. I don't know if it's important."

"Go on."

"She left something behind. I've been waiting to give it to the guards."

"Have you called them?"

She shook her head. "I thought they'd come to see me."

"What did she leave?"

Molly chewed on her bottom lip. "I'd better call the guards."

"Yet you haven't so far."

She blinked. "It was for me. A tip."

"Okay . . ."

"I don't have to turn it over to the guards, do I?"

A flash of gold underneath Ellen's bed rose in Siobhán's mind. "A gold coin."

Molly gasped. "How did you know?"

"Where is it now?"

"In a safe place." She leaned in. "What is it worth?"

"Did she hand it to you?"

Again with the lip biting. "It was left by the table."

"*By* the table?" She was choosing her words carefully.

"It was under the table."

"She dropped it."

"She never came back for it." For a moment she looked stricken. "I just mean . . ."

"It's okay. Either she didn't realize she dropped it, or she meant it as a tip."

Molly exhaled. "Thank you."

"However . . . you must call the guards."

"I will, of course."

"I'm sorry. You have to do it now, or I will."

"Did I do anything wrong?"

"You won't be in trouble for waiting this long, if that's what you mean. But I can't promise you'll get it back."

"Is it a clue? I've never seen anything like it. I've been meaning to take it to the charity shop, see if yer man can appraise it."

"I understand. But it is part of an ongoing investigation."

The petite owner sighed, then rose and headed back to the counter. Siobhán watched her place the call. She tore open the envelope. The letter was typed, most likely on a computer:

When a guard is dating a suspect, how can they promise a fair inquiry?

Siobhán stared at the strange message. Were they talking about her and Macdara? No one here knew them and they weren't officially on the case. Then again, someone had left this note for her, so she'd better rethink it. Besides, neither she nor Macdara was a suspect—unless someone thought otherwise. It could be a crank. Sadly, the garda tip line was often flooded with nefarious calls during murder probes. Liars, gossips, and begrudgers.

Molly returned to Siobhán's table, wringing her hands on her apron. "The guards are sending someone now."

"You've done the right thing." From the look on her face, Molly did not agree. Siobhán held up the envelope. "Who left this for me?"

"I couldn't tell you that. The envelope was slid under me door during the night."

"Do you have a camera inside or outside the shop?"

"No, sorry, luv, we've never had the need for anything like that."

"Has anyone ever slipped a note underneath your door before?"

"This would be the very first."

"Have any of the locals been chatting to you about me, or this case?"

A faint trace of pink flared at her cheeks. "You know how it goes, so."

"Right." They were *all* talking about the outsiders, and the case. "Has anyone behaved out of the ordinary or said anything that struck you as odd?"

"Everything has been odd and out of the ordinary when it comes to that cottage."

"Did you know Ellen Delaney well?"

"We all knew them, but I don't think anyone knew them well. They'd slip in early to mass, and be the first to leave. At the farmers' market, they were all business, didn't seem to like the chin-wagging. They'd barely say hello to you in the shops, or the pub, and although Ellen joined the painting class, she kept to herself."

"Why don't you have Ellen's paintings hanging here?"

"You'll have to ask Annabel; she chose the paintings." She leaned in and lowered her voice. "From what I hear, Ellen Delaney refused for *any* of her work to be shown." She shook her head as if that in itself was a crime. "She must have been jealous."

Siobhán's ears perked up. "Jealous?"

"Of Annabel's star pupil."

"Star pupil?"

Molly nodded. "Annabel sent her over to Geraldine's, to butter her up, can you imagine? Gush about how much she loved Ellen's work so that I could get one of her paintings."

"Why was it that important?"

"Annabel liked showing off her students. It irked her that someone would refuse to participate."

"When was this?"

Molly scrunched her face and stared off into space. Then her mouth widened. "A few days before the murder." Her hands flew up to her mouth. "It's still so shocking. She could have had her work admired while she was still alive. More's the pity."

"And who is this star pupil?"

Molly pointed to the wall, at the center painting. The rotation had changed since Siobhán had been in here previously. This one depicted a little girl kneeling by her bedside, her hands clasped in prayer. Above the bed was a window, through which a full, honey-colored moon was visible. It lit up the child's blond hair. The painting captured innocence and magic. Siobhán knew who painted it even before she looked at the signature: Mary Madigan.

"It's stunning," Siobhán said. She meant it. The work didn't look like someone with a hobby, it looked like someone with a job.

"Annabel said she's been trying to encourage Mary to apply to Glasgow School of Art."

Siobhán nodded. The Scottish institution was renowned. "It's hard to imagine her having the flexibility to attend."

Molly nodded. "That's what Mary told Annabel. Joe Madigan doesn't seem the type to pick up and move so his wife can study art."

Sadly, she concurred. But it wasn't Mary's paintings that Siobhán was focused on. It was Ellen's. The more elusive they were becoming, the more she was dying to see them.

Chapter 25

Siobhán waited until the guards came to take the note and the gold coin before heading back to the inn. Danny or Sergeant Eegan wasn't among them, and since Siobhán had no clue who could have left the note or what it meant, she wasn't required to stay long. Ann and Ciarán, who were bouncing out of their seats an hour ago, seemed to be dragging. They would all have a rest and then Siobhán would schedule an appointment with Annabel. When they entered the lobby, they found Macdara checking in. "Dara."

He turned and grinned. "You're not the only one who can't stay away."

"You don't think I know that?" She tilted her head at the clerk, who was dangling a room key in front of him.

"She booked your room this morning," he announced with a sly grin.

Dara chuckled. "Of course she did." He took the key and saluted her. "Thanks, boss."

Ann and Ciarán headed up to the room for a rest, and Siobhán suspected, to watch telly and eat crisps in bed. Siobhán and Macdara convened by a love seat in the lobby. Sticking to her promise that she wasn't going to leave him out again, she told him about the note someone anonymously slipped under the door of the coffee shop. He frowned. "Relationship with a guard. Were they talking about us?"

"I wondered the same. I don't think so."

"You said your friend Danny had a girlfriend. Who is she?"

"I don't know. The subject hasn't come up." Had they been here under normal circumstances she would have thought to ask. They would have enjoyed a double date, and chatted away about Templemore, and hit the farmers' market and driven home saying what a lovely village it was and how they had to do it again soon. But this visit had been anything but normal.

Macdara stood. "Looks like the subject is up now."

"It might be nothing." They ascended the oak staircase on the way to the room.

Macdara shook his head. "If his lover is one of our suspects, and he hasn't disclosed that, it's definitely not nothing."

"Danny is an honest person."

"The Danny you know."

"Yes, the Danny I know." The stairs were old and steep, and by the time they reached the upper floor she was nearly out of breath. She had missed several mornings of running, and it was starting to show.

"Love makes people do crazy things." Macdara took her hand and squeezed as they headed down the hall.

"I don't even know what this note is accusing him of doing."

"He's one of the lead guards. He could be hiding or changing evidence to protect the woman he's dating. He needs to be taken off the case."

"We don't even know if what's in this letter is true."

"Fine. If it's true—he needs to be taken off the case."

"It's not our decision to make." She let go of his hand, worried that this conversation was about to go off the rails again.

"It wouldn't be easy to hide a love affair in this village," Macdara said as they stopped at their doors. Siobhán was in one room with Ciarán and Ann, and Macdara had the adjoining one.

"Yet multiple people seem to be doing it." *Like your aunt. And maybe your cousin . . .* There were only two good reasons that Jane might be lying about her alibi. She was either the murderer, or she had snuck off with a man.

"If anyone would know how to hide it, it's a guard." He gave her a look.

"Everyone knows we're dating and we tried to hide it."

"Maybe he's better at it."

"What are you getting at? The guards have the note now. I'm sure they'll be questioning everyone, even Danny."

"Wouldn't it be quicker if you just asked him?"

"I will, so." She glanced at the door. They could hear the sound of the telly and bursts of laughter. She took a minute to enjoy it. When she spoke to Macdara again, her voice was a whisper. "There could be another explanation."

"Go on."

"This note is from the killer, and we're getting too close so they're starting a fire somewhere else."

"Let's just make sure we're not the ones who get burned."

While Macdara settled into his room, Siobhán left a message for Danny, asking if they could meet. She got his voice mail and left him a message. Macdara's mission was to speak with Aiden Cunningham. Siobhán, who was determined to investigate *and* entertain her siblings, had another destination in mind. Annabel's. Maybe she'd let Ann and Ciarán do a bit of painting while they chatted. Siobhán could pay for the impromptu lesson. And it just so happened that the art teacher lived in a town house not far from their inn.

Annabel was pretty and petite, much like Siobhán imagined a Disney fairy would look. She grinned when she saw the young ones, then ushered them in and through her living quarters. Landscape and portrait paintings hung on every surface. Hawthorn trees, and fairy rings, and rolling hills. "Are these yours?" Ann and Ciarán examined each one, praising and exclaiming over them, which made Annabel's pixie face light up with joy.

"When I was younger I was embarrassed to hang my own work. Now that I'm older, they've become like old friends."

"I'd hang every one of them in my room," Ciarán said. His voice cracked again, a reminder to Siobhán that the little boy she knew was growing up.

Annabel's laugh was like music. "You're such a love."

"They're gorgeous," Siobhán said, resisting a strong urge to ruffle Ciarán's head. "You're a believer then?"

She laughed. "I love the lore and the legends. I wanted to honor them."

She had artfully dodged the question. "I'll show you the studio." She led them to a back room that seemed to be a recent addition to the older storefront. Easels and canvas and paints were set up, enough stations for ten students. "My partner built this for me when he realized I wasn't going to give up on my little hobby." Siobhán thought of Eoin and wondered how his life as an artist would progress. Annabel set Ann and Ciarán up with paints and canvases, then joined Siobhán at the other end of the studio.

"I'm assuming you want to see Ellen's work."

"Yes," Siobhán said. "And anything you can tell me about your interactions with her."

"I don't normally judge students on their artwork. Expression should be free from labels. However . . ."

"Yes?"

"I'll show you." She headed to the corner of the room where a stack of paintings leaned against the wall. "See for yourself. They're in order with the first painting she ever did on top. You'll find nine of them." She waited, as if expecting Siobhán to react to the number.

"Is that significant?"

Annabel nodded. "In class we've only done four. But Ellen started staying late, painting more. The last few were done feverishly. I thought she was just lonely, or working out her frustrations with the town. But now . . . I'm worried I should have seen the signs of her distress. I should have said something. Maybe . . . she would still be alive." A tear came to Annabel's eyes. "I'm sorry. It's been eating me up."

"I see." Annabel, tears pooling in her eyes, waited expectantly for Siobhán to assure her that she wasn't to blame. And Siobhán wanted to. Non-garda Siobhán would have consoled her. But Garda O'Sullivan had to keep a distance. The more freedom you allowed a suspect, the more they revealed. Anguish was an unfortunate side effect.

Annabel wiped her tears. "When you're finished, I'll be with my two bright, new students." She bounded off to see to Ciarán and Ann. Siobhán turned her attention to the first painting.

As Jane had surmised, the first painting was of the cottage. It was simple but quietly beautiful. The white stone facade, the red door, a glistening meadow. The view was of the cottage from the front at sunrise. Siobhán tried to see if there was anything sinister in the picture, anything that would scream cursed, or fairies, or killer. But no. It was simply a modest painting of a sweet cottage, by a beginner.

The second painting was again of the cottage, this time from a side angle. She seemed to be playing with light and shadows, and once again, nothing stood out as alarming, or unusual, just the side of the cottage. Although, and it was very, very difficult to discern, looking at the cottage from this angle reminded Siobhán of the one patch of dirt she'd observed that seemed to be set up higher. The same patch where Geraldine's dowsing sticks had reacted. Siobhán had yet to tell the Ballysiogdun guards about her suspicion about Geraldine's walking stick. That was going to have to change today.

The third painting was the view from the back of the cottage, and included the lush garden. Siobhán peered closely. She'd included the patches of wolfsbane, the purple hoods appearing innocent of any evildoing. The fourth painting was of the herb garden, and this one put Siobhán on pause. Ellen seemed to be focusing on one particular section: POISON. The sign, skull and crossbones, were rendered in dark shades while the rest was muted by lighter strokes making the sign pop in a sinister way. Ellen was improving as an artist. But was she also painting a message? Could one of the other students have gleaned the idea of using wolfsbane or poison from her paintings?

The fifth and sixth paintings were of fairy trees and fairy rings. They appeared to be the ones on either side of the cottage. The paintings had an ethereal quality about them, as if you could sense the presence of fairies, without actually seeing any in the paintings. Maybe it was the play of light, how parts of the tree and ring seemed to gleam, or maybe it was the brush stokes, playful in some areas, stark in others. But it was the seventh painting that startled Siobhán. Gone were the light colors and idyllic settings. The cottage was dark, and a gnarled and blackened fairy tree hovered directly over it. Hanging from the branches were small but pinched and furious little faces, glaring down at the old stone cottage as if they were intent on causing trouble. In the distance, in the bushes, someone was crouched with binoculars.

Joe Madigan.

Ellen knew all about his "bird-watching".

But that wasn't the most startling bit. Standing in the doorway, in the direct path of the binoculars, her hair shining in the sun, her face turned up and smiling, was

Jane. As if she was enjoying the attention from her not-so-secret admirer. Is that why Ellen didn't want anyone to see her paintings? Was she setting out to reveal everyone's dirty little secrets? Something else struck Siobhán. The look on Jane's face in the painting. She was positively basking in the attention. Ellen must have described Joe's actions to her. Of course she had. She'd confronted him at the farmers' market. At the time, Siobhán hadn't stopped to wonder how Jane knew. Partly because she kept forgetting about her disability. Ellen was clearly conveying that Jane liked the attention. Encouraged it even. Or was it Joe Madigan who Jane Delaney liked? Did this have anything to do with why Jane's name was written in the sink?

Siobhán almost turned to the next painting, when she realized there was one more figure in the current painting. It was easy to miss if you didn't look closely, but a female figure was standing behind Joe, hands on her hips, her face the epitome of the betrayed wife. Ellen was not a master painter, but there was no mistaking the figure was Mary Madigan.

Were Jane and Joe having a secret affair? Joe, Siobhán recalled, was also out of town for the weekend. To look at tractors, he said. Yet he did not buy a tractor. Jane was at a conference for which she'd offered no proof. And Mary Madigan pretended she was with her children and mother-in-law. What if instead she'd been stalking her husband and his lover? Ironically, this would clear all three of them of the murder. What a grave mistake to lie about alibis that could actually clear them.

The eighth painting was of an old hag. The tip of her crooked nose was red. In her hands she was clutching handfuls of gold coins, so many they were spilling out of her palms. Next to her was a colorful walking stick. *Geraldine Madigan.* That solidified it for Siobhán. *Someone* had found a hoard near the cottage. Most likely Ellen. Not only had she found it, she was teasing the Madigans with her discovery. Siobhán eagerly turned to the last painting.

Two men were portrayed in a seedy alley, one standing, one sitting. The first man lurked at the corner, dressed in a tattered cloak. It flew behind him as if lifted by a great wind. His hands were thrown out in a dramatic gesture. Eddie Doolan was well-rendered except for one thing: his face. It had been replaced by a giant gold coin. A guinea. Ellen's skills had improved. Behind him, perched atop a pile of books, writing feverishly, sweat dripping from his large nose, was Dylan Kelly. Mouth open, flat pink tongue lolling out. A gold coin rested on top of his tongue, matching the gleam in the two gold coins he had for eyes.

Chapter 26

Annabel joined Siobhán as they studied the paintings. Siobhán had leaned them against the wall in the order they were painted.

"Her last three paintings," Siobhán said.

"I told you. I should have said something. I've been wringing me hands. I'll never forgive myself."

"Because you didn't ask her about them?"

"I tried."

"And?"

"She told me to keep me nose out of her business."

"That seems harsh."

"I normally pay things like that no mind. Painting should free one from judgment. But they were getting progressively darker."

"Did Mary Madigan see these?"

"Not that I'm aware."

"I heard you sent her over to Geraldine's to convince her to show one of her paintings."

Annabel frowned. "Did I?"

"It doesn't ring a bell?"

She shook her head as if she'd just convinced herself. "I'm sorry, it doesn't. These paintings are the ones Ellen painted after class."

"Jane mentioned an incident where she lent you one of Ellen's paintings to hang?"

"How could I forget."

"But it wasn't Mary Madigan who was sent to fetch it?"

"No, that was me. Jane let me have the painting. Ellen wasn't home."

"I heard Ellen wasn't too happy about that."

"Wasn't happy? She stormed over to Molly's and ripped it from me before I could even hang it."

"Which painting was it?"

Annabel pointed to the one of Eddie with a guinea for a face. Siobhán couldn't puzzle it out. What was she trying to say? Eddie couldn't have the gold coins, could he? Perhaps Ellen had given him one as a tip, but not if she knew he was her stalker.

The paintings were symbolic, not literal. Was she suggesting that Dylan Kelly was using Eddie in some way? Employing him? Was Dylan Kelly paying Eddie Doolan to stir up trouble, whip the village into a frenzy with his stories?

"Was Ellen social in class?"

"Heavens, no. You could tell she used to be a school-teacher. She was constantly criticizing me and the others."

"How so?"

"She was a stickler for time. Always harping about the

fact that my students could walk in late. Her words would pierce you worse than nettles."

Siobhán snapped photos of Ellen's paintings with her mobile, then hurried over to praise Ann and Ciarán's paintings. She was relieved to see their subjects were cheery and innocent. Ann had painted a horse in a meadow. Ciarán was painting a sports car. "Well done," she said to them.

"Can we take them with us?" Ciarán asked.

"Of course you can," Annabel said.

"Can we hang them in the bistro?" Ciarán asked.

"Why not," Siobhán said. "Wherever you'd like." She was anxious to show Macdara the paintings, find out what happened with Aiden Cunningham, and track down Eddie Doolan. Ann slipped her hand into Siobhán's.

"How much more work do you have to do today?"

Siobhán's heart melted. "I'm done for the day." There were a thousand things she needed to do. But family was the most important.

"Really?" Ciarán and Ann exclaimed in stereo.

"Really," Siobhán said. "I'd love to go for a hike. But I left my new walking stick at home."

"Can we get sticks of our own?" Ciarán asked.

That would mean another visit to Geraldine. She meant it when she said she was taking the rest of the day off work. It was hardly her fault if her siblings were dragging her back into it. And since the stick she bought had been designated as Macdara's engagement stick, and they were reasonably priced, she wouldn't mind picking out another one for herself. And, while there, it wouldn't hurt to get a look at the stick she was convinced was a metal detector before going to the guards. Did Geraldine Madigan have any inkling that her son may have been sleeping with Jane Delaney? Had she mentioned it to her daughter-in-law or vice versa? "You know," Siobhán said. "I think that's a fantastic idea."

Siobhán and the young ones were exiting the inn when they ran into a weeping girl trying to barrel past them, cursing and dragging a recalcitrant suitcase. Long black streaks of mascara ran down her face.

"Gráinne!"

Her sister burst into tears. "I was given the boot!"

Oh, no. That made about a day surviving Sheila Mahoney. Longer than Siobhán predicted. "What happened?"

"I was doing me job, that's what. Women shouldn't come in for a makeover if they don't want to hear the truth about what's wrong with them!" Siobhán nodded and murmured. "And there was loads wrong with them!"

"I see."

"Dry hair, blotchy faces, flab everywhere, and don't even get me started on their eyebrows."

"I won't."

"Like furry little caterpillars stuck above sunken eyes!"

"You need not utter another word."

"Is it my fault I go out of my way to serve? From their cankles to their cowlicks?"

"You poor thing. You need a rest." *Please, please, please give it a rest.*

Gráinne stuck her hip out and blew air from her lips, lifting her fringe, which Siobhán just now noticed was streaked neon blue. This was not the time to school Gráinne on tact or style. "We're going for a hike. Dump your bag at the desk, wipe your face, and come with us."

* * *

They were told Geraldine was at her son's farmhouse, but that she had plenty of walking sticks stored at the farmhouse they could look at. Siobhán was disappointed she wouldn't get a look at the metal detector. She texted Danny her suspicions. He'd been kind enough to keep her in the loop, and now that a second gold coin had been found, it was information he needed to know. She held back on mentioning the mysterious note left for her at the café. Surely he'd read it by now and she was hoping he would mention it. Was he the guard mentioned in the note? She was dying to know.

The cow was in the driveway as they trudged up, her big brown eyes scanning their little group like a heat-seeking missile for Macdara. When she didn't find him, she let out a mournful moo. "Sorry," Siobhán said, holding up her hand. "He already put a ring on it."

"Which you never wear," Gráinne chimed in.

"If you touch it, you're dead to me," Siobhán sang back.

Lilly was in the yard smashing her dolls together, wearing a man's shirt, streaked with mud and dirt, hanging off her like a dress. This time wee William was shrieking along with her and running around. Siobhán was relieved to see him successfully detached from his mammy's hip.

Joe's legs stuck out from underneath a tractor near the barn. Mary Madigan stretched to hang clothing on the line, soft fabrics swaying in the warm breeze, and Geraldine had commandeered the front porch, her walking sticks set up behind her like soldiers in formation.

Siobhán and her brood headed for the porch, and once up, began exclaiming over the walking sticks and trying them out. Geraldine's smile was genuine; she was proud of her product.

"Do you believe in fairies?" Ciarán asked her when Siobhán wasn't paying attention.

"I believe there are certain mysteries in life that can't be explained away. Like what happened here the other night."

Gráinne edged closer. "What did you see?" Siobhán was torn. She didn't want Geraldine Madigan riling her siblings up about the supernatural, but then again, it was Ciarán who started it. And it never hurt to have a witness tell a tale a dozen times, see how it changed, if at all, maybe learn something new. And they were as big eyed and attentive as the in-love cow. In the meantime, Siobhán was wondering if there was a subtle way to ask Joe Madigan about those dead mice, specifically if any were missing their tails.

"This is what I saw that night," Geraldine said, as her siblings drew closer. "It was a full moon—we should have known it was coming. I was standing on this porch when I heard a piercing wail. I don't have all my hearing, but it nearly took what's left of it."

She didn't mention the hearing loss the first time she told the tale.

"A wail," Gráinne said. "That's a banshee. Warning of death. Holy Mother of God." Gráinne crossed herself.

Geraldine pointed straight ahead. "If you look you'll see the white bark of the hawthorn tree; the fairy ring is just beyond it. Just there behind the cottage, I saw a woman running, running, running. Right after the wail. 'Twas Ellen Delaney. . . . I know that now."

"She's saying it wasn't a banshee that screamed," Siobhán said. "It was a person."

Geraldine shook her head. "If you think I don't know the wail of banshee when I hear it you have another think coming."

Ciarán turned to Siobhán and gave her a look. "You do. You really do." He wanted the ghost stories. He'd better remember that when he tried crawling into her bed at night poking at her with his ice-cold toes.

"What did you do?" Ann asked.

"I lit a candle and prayed."

That was new too.

"Good woman," Gráinne said. "Safety first."

"When you saw the figure running, did they seem to have a pack on them?" Siobhán asked.

"A pack?"

"Presumably Ellen had gone to the meadow to spend the night. I'm assuming she had a pack with a tent and supplies. Does that fit?"

"From the way she was moving, I'd say she had nothing on her back."

If that was the case, then her things could still be out there. Siobhán knew where she wanted to test out her walking stick.

"Everyone pick out your walking stick," Siobhán said. "Time for a family hike."

"I'm a personal stylist," Gráinne said, zeroing in on Geraldine. "Would you like a makeover?"

Geraldine blushed. "I'm just an old woman."

"Nonsense, you have great bones."

Geraldine's hand fluttered to her cheek. "I do?"

"Underneath all that sagging skin? Absolutely." Geraldine blinked rapidly. "Don't worry. Think of me like a beauty guard here to rescue those cheekbones!" Geraldine patted her cheekbones, still blinking.

Siobhán sighed. "Gráinne O'Sullivan, are you trying to get out of the family hike?"

"I don't want to hike either," Ann said. Now that was a surprise. Of all the girls, Ann was the most athletic. Ann turned to Gráinne. "Can I be your assistant?"

"You can watch and learn," Gráinne said. "Or just watch."

"I want to take a hike," Ciarán said.

"Take a hike!" Ann and Gráinne said in unison.

"Then go jump in a lake," Gráinne added with a snort.

"Is there a lake?" Excitement danced in his eyes.

Siobhán glanced at Geraldine. "Leave them with me," Geraldine said. "We'll get Mary to volunteer too, and she can make over both of us."

Truthfully, Siobhán could cover more ground without her sisters complaining. Ciarán was young and full of energy. He'd keep up no problem. She and Ciarán picked out walking sticks. Siobhán pulled Gráinne aside. "I have a small favor."

"Don't get murdered."

"That too."

"What is it?"

"Keep your ears and eyes open, and . . . if you get a chance please take a photo of the kitchen—the counter near the window. But only if no one is around to see you do it."

"A secret mission. It will cost you." Gráinne cocked a gun-finger at Siobhán and winked. Siobhán was starting to wonder if it was too soon for her to give the boot to Gráinne as well.

"If you get the photos, I'll pay you."

"Why do you want them?"

The last time they were in the kitchen, Siobhán had

seen a bottle of Powers whiskey on the counter. Later, she'd heard Geraldine and others mention they were all teetotalers. The bottle was full, so it hadn't been the one that poisoned Ellen Delaney, but what were teetotalers doing with a full bottle of whiskey on the kitchen counter? She knew if she asked them it would be easy enough to come up with an excuse—a gift from someone who didn't realize they didn't drink—but everyone in this little village would certainly know they didn't. Siobhán wasn't sure what she could prove by a photo—maybe run it by Danny—but she at least wanted to know whether or not it was still there.

"You should come," Ciarán said, popping up. "We're going to see a fairy ring."

"You've seen them at Lough Gur."

"I want to see another one."

"You'll have to stay right with me and if I tell you not to step somewhere you must listen."

Mary Madigan, finished at the clothesline, grappled with Lilly as she struggled to remove the dirty oversized shirt. The child wasn't having it.

"Leave her with it," Geraldine said.

Mary Madigan looked up, her face red. She did not appreciate her mother-in-law reprimanding her. "She cannot snatch clothes off the line."

"I didn't," the girl said. "It's mine."

"That is not yours."

"It's already dirty—what's the harm?" Geraldine said.

"Mine," the girl said. "I find. I keep."

Mary whispered in her daughter's ear, pursed her lips, and joined them at the porch. The little girl stared after them, then went back to smashing her dolls. Mary smiled at Ciarán, enthralled with tapping his new walking stick along the porch. Seconds later he was slicing and jabbing it through the air like a sword. Mary gestured to their yard. "You might want to take a pocket of stones."

Ciarán stopped fencing his invisible enemies and peered at her. "Why?"

Mary smiled. "In case the fairies put a stray on you."

"What's that?"

"Leave him be," Geraldine said.

"'Tis terrible," Mary continued. "You could be standing in your own yard and nothing looks familiar. You'll walk around in a daze not knowing which direction to go."

"What are the stones for?" Siobhán asked. Despite herself she was curious. This was a new side to Mary Madigan, her behavior somewhat snarky, more reminiscent of Ellen or Jane. But Ciarán wasn't easily scared and Siobhán wanted to keep the farmer's wife chatting.

"They're to throw ahead of you so you don't walk into a body of water and drown."

Ciarán started tapping again, although this time he seemed to be scouring the yard for stones. "Why would we walk into a body of water?"

"Because you don't know it's there! That's what a stray is. You lose your sense of things altogether." Mary Madigan sounded surprised that they did not already know this.

Ciarán bounded down the porch steps. "We'd better get stones."

"I'll let you collect them for us," Siobhán said. She turned to her sisters. "I texted Macdara and Garda Mac-Gregor that you're here while we're going on a hike," she said loudly. "We'll be back in two shakes."

"In case you were thinking of murdering us," Gráinne explained to Mary and Geraldine. The two women pursed their lips and blinked but did not respond. Siobhán would have preferred a simple "Of course we won't murder them," but folks in this village had their own way of doing things.

Gráinne raked her eyes over her makeover victims. "This may take a while." She turned back to Siobhán. "Make it three shakes. Or four."

Chapter 27

As they trudged through the field leading away from the Madigan farmhouse, Siobhán was relieved to have Ciarán's company. The sun was muted, but even in the blue-gray light the ragged countryside filled Siobhán with pride, and she hoped Ciarán felt it too. The kind of beauty that could lull you into another world, one where magic danced underneath blooming trees, and hid in full moons.

Ciarán gripped his staff like a young warrior catapulting over dips in the ground. Guilt squeezed her insides that she was the witness to the adventures of his life and not her mam and da. She clung to the belief that somehow they were watching, just as much a part of them as the rocks, and trees, and rolling hills. Maybe that's why they say the hills have eyes. Until one experienced a profound loss of their own it was impossible to explain that sorrow never vanishes. It was a war fought not in long, drawn-out battles, but in the everyday, unexpected moments. She threw a quick hello and kisses to the heavens and forced her mind back to the case.

"I'll show them." That's what the limo driver heard Ellen say. Who was she referring to? Geraldine? Aiden? Joe? It wasn't coincidence that she was killed the same night she undertook this endeavor. If Ellen was going to spend the night outdoors, she would have brought a pack with her. In that pack would have been her bottle of whiskey.

Powers whiskey.

The bottle in the Madigans' house. Was that Ellen's *original* bottle?

Geraldine admitted visiting Ellen after the limo driver left. Did she switch the bottles then?

"I've got twelve stones," Ciarán said, jumping back to her.

"That'll do."

"Are you lost?"

Siobhán laughed. They were barely past the cottage. "Only philosophically."

Ciarán scrunched his face. "You're weird."

"Tank you."

He waggled his finger at her. "In school our teacher says to mind our *h*'s."

"Does she now?"

He nodded. "You don't say 'tank you'; you say 'thank you'." Spit flew from his mouth as he struggled with the pronunciation.

"I tink it's fine," Siobhán said, exaggerating for effect even whilst scolding herself for disagreeing with his teacher. "As long as meaning isn't lost."

"W-h-atever," Ciarán said, isolating the *h*. He raced ahead once more, leaping with the boundless energy of the young.

They stopped at the fairy tree and fairy ring, although Siobhán made them keep a respectful distance.

"It doesn't look scary," Ciarán said.

"It's not," Siobhán agreed. "It's gorgeous, don't you think, petal?"

Ciarán shrugged. "Will they get mad if I don't think it is?"

Siobhán laughed. "I suppose they might be a little offended."

"It's a gorgeous tree, and ring," Ciarán said loudly. "And don't even think of putting a stray on us, because I've got a pocketful of stones."

"Well done, lad," Siobhán said. "Let's keep going."

Just as they passed the fairy tree, Siobhán spotted something on the ground in the distance, in a small valley, nearly hidden by the hill. Ellen's campsite. She could make out a sack lying on the ground and a half-erect tent. Ciarán started for it, but Siobhán was quick to grab ahold of him. "It's a crime scene, luv."

"It is?"

"If it belongs to Ellen Delaney, which I think it does, then yes, it is."

She made Ciarán stay where he was as she removed gloves and booties from her pack.

"Do you always carry those?"

"Rarely leave home without them," she said with a wink.

"Double weird."

Siobhán laughed. "The day is young. I'm going for triple." She donned her booties and gloves and headed slowly toward the campsite. She wouldn't touch anything that she didn't have to, and she'd place a call to the guards as soon as she was sure it was Ellen's site. As she drew closer, a frying pan and the remnants of a fire came into view. An unopened can of beans was propped on a rock with an opener lying next to it. *Abandoned.* Ellen Delaney had arrived at this site. Set up her tent. Built a fire. She was preparing to eat. Or she lost her appetite. And then . . . what? Something frightened her. . . .

Siobhán edged toward the tent. "Hello?" Nothing answered or moved. She reached out with gloved hands and opened the flap. She nearly collapsed with relief to find nothing but a sleeping bag.

Abandoned. And there, in the corner of the tent, was a bottle of Powers whiskey. With only an inch left. An inch of poison. Siobhán was dying to pick up the bottle. Instead, she hurried back to Ciarán as she dialed Danny MacGregor.

"Wait," Ciarán said as she approached. "Stop." Siobhán stopped. "Do you know where you are?" He studied her intently while she tried not to laugh.

"Yes, pet."

"Do you know who you are?"

"Unfortunately."

He crinkled his nose. "Do you need a stone?"

"I do not." He looked disappointed. "Why don't you toss them ahead of us on our walk back, just in case?"

He finally relaxed, nodded, and allowed her to approach. "Why didn't you take the things?" He gestured to the tent.

"I can't touch anything. I called the guards."

"You are a guard."

"This isn't my case, luv."

"Then why are you investigating?"

"Because it's Dara's aunt."

Ciarán nodded. "And because you're like a blood-hound."

"Where did you hear that?"

"Macdara."

Of course.

The guards were sent to process the campsite. Siobhán and Ciarán returned to the Madigan farmhouse to find Geraldine and Mary looking markedly better. She was expecting Gráinne to turn them into trollops or clowns, but her sister's touch was light yet noticeable. Maybe it was because the pair was smiling, the first genuine smiles Siobhán had seen in the village.

Siobhán complimented them and turned to Gráinne. "Well done."

"My biggest victory to date," Gráinne said, snapping their photos. As they headed down the drive, Joe Madigan's voice rang out. "Wash that goop off." Siobhán resisted the urge to return and beat him with her walking stick.

Relief settled into her bones when they were all back at the inn, away from the Madigans' and the fairy cottage. She didn't get a chance to ask Joe about the dead mice or confront Geraldine about the metal detector, or the whiskey bottle on their counter, but she was exhausted. She suspected the only fingerprints they would find at the campsite would be Ellen's, but maybe they'd get lucky.

At the least, they should be able to confirm poison in her whiskey bottle.

Siobhán stretched and reached to the hotel bedside table where she had a little bag of chocolates. She was at the chocolate-eating portion of the inquiry, where every question lead to more questions, and the case was nothing but a tangle of inconsistencies swimming around her poor head. Ciarán was right. She was weird.

The red dress kept circling Siobhán's mind. Even if the killer dressed her for some reason, it was Ellen's dress. One at odds with the rest of the dowdy outfits in her closet. And Jane said she didn't put her rollers in. The killer wanted them to think she was all ready for bed, drinking tea. But she wasn't finished getting ready. The killer wanted the guards to assume her tea was poisoned, hoped they wouldn't dig any further.

Siobhán was convinced Ellen was having a romantic relationship with Aiden Cunningham. The limo was booked for a Saturday night. Which made Siobhán wonder—where was the closest fancy restaurant? Top on the list was the French restaurant in the village run by an Irish woman and her French husband. It looked like a reservation was in order. *Oui.* But first, a nap.

She fell into a deep sleep and dreamed she was caught in a fairy ring guarded by giant mice, wielding their severed tails like whips. She woke up with a scream.

"Easy tiger." Macdara was sitting in a chair by the desk.

Siobhán was relieved to be awake. "How long have I been out?"

"About an hour."

She rubbed her head. "I had a nightmare."

"How about some fresh air?"

What she really wanted was to watch telly in bed with chocolate. "Lovely." She forced herself to her feet. "How did you make out?"

Macdara shook his head. "While you were finding the campsite, I was getting the runaround from Aiden Cunningham and then picking my mam and Jane up at the bus stop."

"They're back?"

"You don't sound thrilled."

"The more the merrier." He couldn't see her fingers crossed at her side.

"Then you'll be happy to hear that I greeted tree folks coming off the bus."

"Don't say that around Ciarán or he'll have you minding your *h*'s."

Macdara frowned. "Long story," she said. "Continue. Who's the turd?"

When he finally got the joke he let out a belly laugh. "Eoin."

"Ah, lovely."

"Nearly your entire brood. Happy?"

"I am." With the exception of Jane and his mam. No need to overshare.

Macdara chuckled. "About time for supper. Everyone is getting hangry."

"I know just the place. Perfect for a date night."

"Date night?"

"Exactly."

"What did you have in mind?" Siobhán filled him in

on the French restaurant. "I'll make a reservation." Macdara took out his mobile phone.

"I already did. Tonight. You and me."

"Romantic." His tone conveyed that he knew there was more to the story.

"And Ciarán, and Ann, and Eoin, and Gráinne, and James, and Jane, and your mam." They would be just the distraction Siobhán needed to slip away and talk to the waiters.

"Be still me heart." Siobhán laughed and took his hand. The sooner this was over, the sooner they could go home and have a real date night.

The French restaurant had a lovely interior with mirrors, and candles, and shelves by the register filled with fresh baked bread. The walls were white and the trim black, giving it a touch of sophistication. They were led to a dining room and sat at the middle table. On the back wall was a mural of the Seine, happy French people strolling alongside it. Siobhán lost herself in it for a moment, as the desire to travel pinged through her. Macdara ordered drinks and starters and soon oysters arrived along with wine and sparkling water.

Macdara's mother stared at the oysters on her plate as if someone had just placed a severed head in front of her. Macdara nodded to the plate. "They aren't going to bite."

"I'll just have soup," Nancy replied. Macdara shrugged and snagged her oysters. Siobhán got the feeling that was his plan all along.

"I want bacon and cabbage," Ciarán said.

"I'm afraid you can't get that here," Siobhán said.

"I'm having the quail," Gráinne announced. Then she threw her head back and laughed.

"Do they have ham-and-cheese toasties?" Ann asked.

"Might as well just close your eyes and point," Gráinne said. "You aren't going to like any of it anyway."

"I'm embarrassed to be with you lot," Eoin said. "I'll have one of everything."

This had been a mistake. Siobhán should have come alone. She stared at the menu trying to pretend she wouldn't rather have a basket of curried chips herself.

"There's a chipper next door," Macdara said. "Why don't you meet us there instead?"

He'd read her mind. Not the first time they'd done it. Or maybe she had a dreamy look on her face from just thinking about curried chips. "Meet you there?"

"Yes," Macdara said. "After you interrogate the staff about me aunt and her love life." His eyes remained steady on hers.

"You're perfect for me." She reached over and gave him a rare public kiss.

"You're going to be disappointed."

"We'll see." To the chagrin of the waiter, all of her crew but Eoin filed out. "I'll eat for the lot of 'em," he said with a grin.

Siobhán squeezed his shoulder. "Good man."

Siobhán hurried to the register. A slim and aloof hostess manned the station, ignoring Siobhán, as if acting like she was above the patrons was a requirement of the job. Siobhán cleared her throat, and finally the woman acknowledged her. "What can I do for you?"

"I'm sorry they had to leave. My fiancé's cousin is grieving. She realized rich food may not be the best for her. I hope it's not too much of a bother."

"You reserved a large table for a Friday night. Why would that be a bother?" Her smile was as plastic as her talon-nails.

"We tried to cheer up a woman who lost her mother. I'm sure you heard of the recent tragedy."

Finally the employee's face relaxed into an expression that bordered on compassion. "The woman who was murdered?"

"Yes." Siobhán hated playing into the human weakness for gossip, but she needed information. "The very same." Siobhán leaned into the counter and lowered her voice, as if sharing a secret just with her. "Did you know her?"

The employee's eyebrows shot up. "The woman who was murdered?"

"Yes."

"Why would you ask me that?" The French wall was back.

Siobhán glanced around. "I have it on good authority she'd been here before."

The woman followed Siobhán's gaze around the restaurant, as if trying to spot a ghost. "I'm new."

"How new?"

"A few months." The woman quickly averted her gaze, staring at a list of reservations as if it would jump off the page and save her. Siobhán's pulse quickened.

"You've seen her then. Haven't you?"

"We get a lot of customers in here." She began fiddling with a bowl of mints.

"She makes an impression then, doesn't she?"

"I'd say you do too."

Siobhán fingered a mint. Next to it sat a stack of business cards. PRIMO LIMO.

"This is her limo service," Siobhán said, plucking up a card as if it was a smoking gun. "Was."

The woman began to blink rapidly. "We only keep those because of the councilman."

"Of course." *Aiden Cunningham.* "He likes to arrive in style."

She nodded. "Is there anything else?"

"Is there anything else you want to tell me?"

She frowned. "No."

"Thank you for a lovely evening."

"You didn't have a lovely evening."

At least the hostess was direct. Siobhán sighed. "My brother is in heaven." She threw a look to Eoin in the dining room.

The hostess gasped. "I'm so sorry."

"What?" Siobhán registered the look of horror on the woman's face.

"No, no, not literally," Siobhán added hastily. *Lost in translation.* "I just mean he's enjoying his feed. Dinner. Proper dinner." *Stop. Just stop chattering.* She pointed to the dining room where Eoin was lording over his banquet for one. He deserved it. Siobhán had a feeling he would be adding new items to the menu at Naomi's Bistro shortly. It may not go over well in Kilbane, but he had a right to be creative. She turned back to the hostess, who looked visibly paler. "The decor is beautiful. And my fiancé and I will be back one day. Just the two of us," she said, tripping over herself to right the ship.

"We look forward to it." *She so didn't.* The phone rang. Siobhán watched her pick it up.

"Yes, yes, of course. How many in your party?" The girl opened a black book near the register and jotted down a name. Siobhán needed to get a look at that book, check the reservations for Saturday night. If the party was a no-show would the entries still be legible? She needed black and white proof that Aiden Cunningham made a reservation for two on Saturday night and then canceled it. He was proving to be the type of man who would lie until you shoved irrefutable proof in his round face.

Siobhán hurried to the jax and wasted a few minutes primping by the mirror. She exited and watched the register. She waited until new customers came in and the hostess moved away to greet them. She slipped the black book off the counter and hurried back into the jax. Taking out her mobile, she flipped to the page for Saturday and took as many photos as she could. She hurried back to find the hostess pawing the counter. Siobhán stuck the book behind her back. When she passed the counter, she dropped it. Siobhán then bent over, retrieved the book, and handed it to her. "You dropped this."

"Merci," the hostess said, with another frown.

"De nada," Siobhán said, forgetting how to say 'You're welcome' in French. She messaged Eoin to meet them at the chipper next door and made a beeline for the door, already regretting she didn't buy a baguette.

Chapter 28

The chipper didn't disappoint. Siobhán found her group at a table piled high with fish and chips, and chicken and chips, and burgers and chips. Ciarán was so thrilled he was humming.

"Where were you?" Gráinne said.

"Just having a chat with one of the employees. She was telling me how much the councilman loves eating there."

Jane laughed. "Typical," she said. "Aiden Cunningham thinks he's a king."

Macdara picked up on the connotation right away, and no longer had the look of a happy man, despite his basket of chips. "I need some air," he said. He turned to Siobhán. "Do you need some air?"

* * *

The back of the chipper had a delightful patio strung with little white lights. "Now it feels like date night," Siobhán said, planting a kiss on Macdara's cheek.

"I love a woman who is easy to please. What did you find?"

Siobhán showed him the photo of the reservation. There it was: 7 P.M., Aiden Cunningham plus guest. A thin line was drawn through the reservation. Underneath someone had scribbled "Must reschedule."

"You're sure his guest was me aunt?"

"It explains the red dress. We should confront Aiden and see if he'll admit it."

Macdara started to pace. "Let's say you're on to something. Aunt Ellen is having an affair with the councilman. They were supposed to go to the French restaurant on Saturday evening but he cancels."

"He made the reservation in advance, along with the limo," Siobhán said. "Remember he didn't cancel that either. That's why the driver came to the cottage." She drummed her fingers on the picnic table. "He was definitely wooing your aunt."

Macdara threw his hands up. "Okay, okay, just stop saying "wooing" and me "aunt" in the same breath."

"Then we have Jane."

"What about Jane?"

"The same weekend your aunt plans this, Jane claims she's going to Dublin."

"Claims?"

"Has she shown you proof?" Macdara crossed his arms and didn't respond. "That's not normal. She's hiding something."

"Let me deal with her. Jane did not kill her mother."

"You know it's possible."

"Continue." He could not refute her statement, but he had no desire to linger on it.

"I believe that Ellen's bottle of whiskey was poisoned with a teaspoon of aconite."

"Aconite?"

"Made from the roots of wolfsbane, which is growing wild behind the cottage."

"You're getting fancy."

"Jeanie Brady agrees with the conclusion."

"Go on."

"Whoever poisoned her knew that she planned on spending the night near the fairy tree, and assumed she'd be taking her bottle of whiskey with her."

"Safe assumption."

"The Madigans are teetotalers. When we first paid them a visit there was an unopened bottle of Powers whiskey on the counter. It's since been removed." Gráinne had managed to get a photo and the bottle was gone. Had one of them noticed Siobhán staring at it?

"If it's a full bottle it's not the one that poisoned Aunt Ellen."

"Correct. But I believe it was her bottle. The original. Then the killer switched it with the poisoned bottle."

"At least they have the bottle to test now, thanks to you."

"You know as well as I do that it may take a while for the results. We can't wait around for them." Siobhán touched Macdara so that he would stop pacing and she could start. This was why she liked to run and think; there was something about keeping the body moving that helped her sort through facts. "Ellen didn't win the bet. The poison—or a person—scared her. Maybe both. She ran back to the cottage."

"Where someone finished the job."

"Correct. I think Ellen found the hoard—gold coins—and was flaunting them."

"How do you figure?"

"She dropped one at Molly's Café, and possibly tipped Eddie with one, and then she paints a gold coin for Eddie's face, and ones for Dylan Kelly's eyes, not to mention his tongue."

"I'm going to need you to repeat that." He held up his hand. "Even though I'd really rather you didn't."

Siobhán filled him in on the visit to Annabel's work-shop and Ellen's increasingly bizarre paintings. He listened intently. "The guards will never consider those paintings evidence."

"I know. We have to use them to find other evidence."

"Who dropped the coin under the bed?"

"I don't know. Either Ellen or her killer."

"How can a simple village be this complicated?" He gazed at the lights on the patio for a moment as if expecting them to answer. For a second Siobhán wished they would too. Instead they just stayed pretty and twinkled.

"Then there's the matter of Dylan Kelly's manuscript left on the counter along with a rejection letter from the publisher. I don't know why Ellen would have those papers. Do you?"

"No."

"Dylan said the only other place he left the manuscript was at the town hall."

Macdara nodded. "Which, if true, brings us back to Aiden Cunningham."

"We definitely need to grill him."

"What else?"

"Eddie Doolan."

Macdara clenched his jaw. "The stalker."

"I got the feeling he just wanted her to know he'd over-come his stutter. 'Stalker' was Ellen's word for it, but what if it was innocent?"

"You like him."

"He's a character. I feel for him."

"We can't dismiss him as a suspect."

"I have one more thing. You're not going to like it."

"Why stop now?"

"I think Jane is having an affair with Joe Madigan."

"Tell me you're joking me."

"And I think the reason Mary Madigan lied about her alibi—to her husband and us—is because she spent the weekend following them."

Macdara sighed. "You have been busy."

"We still have too many suspects."

"But you're getting closer."

"I need you to press Jane—it's not a crime to have an affair. But if she's keeping it quiet to protect her reputation . . ."

Macdara nodded. "She could lose her freedom instead."

Their bellies were full and the mood was jovial as they headed back to the inn. After that feed everyone was ready for a snooze. But as they neared the entrance, somber figures stood blocking it. Danny MacGregor and Sergeant Eegan greeted them without smiles.

"Are they waiting for us?" Ciarán said.

"What's going on?" Jane picked up on the change in the atmosphere right away.

"Garda MacGregor and Sergeant Eegan are here," Macdara said.

"They're here for me." Jane swallowed hard. She grabbed Siobhán's hand and squeezed. "I lied," she said. "But I didn't kill my mother."

Siobhán didn't have time to respond.

"Jane Delaney," Sergeant Eegan said, stepping forward. "You are under arrest for the murder of Ellen Delaney."

"No," Jane said. "I would never."

Danny MacGregor cleared his throat. "You are not obliged to say anything unless you wish to do so, but whatever you say will be taken down in writing and may be given in evidence."

"Can you just give us a minute?" Macdara asked.

Sergeant Eegan gave a quick nod, then stepped aside, allowing Macdara and Siobhán to confer with Jane. She looked more vulnerable than Siobhán had ever seen her, as if the nightmare had finally sunk in. If only she had trusted them from the beginning. Siobhán knew she was lying about her alibi. She should have pressed her more. She would have done so if Jane hadn't been Macdara's cousin.

"Don't say a word," Macdara said. "We'll get you a solicitor."

"Just stay calm, everyone," Nancy Flannery said, her voice an octave higher than normal, her hands clutching her face.

"Why don't you all go into the inn," Siobhán said. Her brood and Nancy backed up but they remained on the footpath.

"I want to see the charging sheet," Macdara said as they detained Jane.

"If you want, you can follow us to the station, Detective Sergeant Flannery."

"I intend to."

Siobhán edged up near Danny. "Is this because of her alibi?"

"Her alibi," Danny confirmed, keeping his voice low. "She wasn't in Dublin at an herbal conference. She was in Ballysiogdun the entire time."

"What do you base this on?"

"We have a witness as well as photographic evidence."

"Who is your witness?" Siobhán asked lightly.

Danny gave her the side eye. "Nice try."

"This village," Jane said from the backseat of the garda car. "Always spying on me."

"Is it true?" Macdara asked. "Did you lie?"

"I did, Dara. I'm sorry."

"Why?" Macdara pleaded. He glanced at Siobhán, then turned back to Jane. "It's not against the law to have an affair."

Jane gasped. "Why do you say that?"

Siobhán stepped up. "There comes a time when you have to stop protecting someone else and start protecting yourself."

"Is there something you'd like to say now?" Sergeant Eegan asked. "Someone else involved?"

"Jane," Macdara said. "Give them the name of your . . . lover."

"I won't."

"Jane."

"I won't."

"How could she have killed anyone?" Gráinne said. "Can you not see that she's *blind*?" Siobhán sighed. Now was not a perfect time to educate Gráinne on stereotypes.

Because arguing that Jane was quite capable of everything sighted people were capable of, including murder,
would not exactly help the current situation.

"I've been speaking with folks here, and there are no
shortage of suspects," Siobhán said. "Including the strange
message I received at Molly's about one of you."

Sergeant Eegan, who was standing outside the guard
car, pounded the hood. "There's no merit to that message.
Are you accusing my guards of not doing their job?"

"I just want to know if you've figured out which guard
the note is referring to. Are one of you dating a suspect?"

"That's none of your business," Sergeant Eegan barked.
"If you keep sticking your nose where it doesn't belong
I'll escort you out of town m'self."

Danny simply stared at her from the passenger seat.
He shook his head slightly, warning her off.

"Have you brought the councilman in for questioning?" This was the hastiest arrest she had ever seen. If all
they had was a false alibi, there should have been multiple suspects arrested. No answer came from the guards.
Sergeant Eegan jumped in the driver's seat and screeched
away, Jane sitting up straight in the back as the rest of
them watched helplessly until the garda car disappeared
from view.

The next morning Siobhán had a lie-in while Macdara
and his mam headed to the garda station to see Jane. To
Siobhán's delight, Eoin and Gráinne were playing big
brother and sister and entertaining Ann and Ciarán. There
was a soft knock on the door, and Siobhán opened it to
see James standing in the hall. "You're here!" She ambushed him with a hug.

"I can't stay away."

"Come in."

She dragged him inside while he plopped down in a lounge chair. "Cup of tea?"

"Sure." She put the kettle on. "I've been speaking with Elise," James said at last.

Siobhán suspected as much, but felt a twinge of worry. James needed stability, not emotional chaos. Then again, he was a recovering alcoholic. Was he latching on to another form of addiction? Chasing after love that wasn't ever going to fulfill him? "Do you think that's wise?"

He folded his arms. "That wasn't why I mentioned it."

Grand. "Why did you mention it then?"

"I asked her to keep her ears open in case anyone was talking about Mrs. Delaney's murder."

Siobhán had nearly forgotten Elise was home in Waterford. Mystery of where James had been disappearing solved. If only every case were that easy. "And?"

"She overheard several heads say 'What a pity. She leaves Waterford to get away from a stalker and she ends up dead.'"

"Yes. I'm aware, and we know who it is."

"You do?"

"Have you seen the seanchaí?"

"No."

"You wouldn't be able to miss him. His name is Eddie Doolan."

"Elise heard something else."

"Go on."

"Ellen Delaney had a reputation as a strict schoolteacher."

"We know that too."

He gave her an admiring look. "You are good at your job."

"Thank you."

"You said he's a storyteller?"

"Yes."

"Elise said he used to drive everyone mental singing children's songs and forcing everyone to solve his riddles."

Siobhán nodded. "He's a character."

"Sounds like more than that to me," James said. "Sounds like a danger."

Chapter 29

Riddles . . . danger . . . children's songs . . . She felt as if someone had whapped her on the side of her head. She sprung from her seat.

"What?" James pointed at her. "What did I say?"

"You've given me a thought. I need to follow up on something." She texted the information to Macdara and then called Danny. She grabbed her handbag and her jacket.

"Can't it wait until you've finished your tea?"

"Not with Jane in jail."

James stood. "I'll come with you."

Siobhán hesitated. She loved the company of her older brother, and everyone needed to feel needed. But she was an official guard now, and didn't like involving any of them when she didn't have to. Besides, her entire brood was here and needed looking after. "I'd feel safer if you stayed here."

James gave her a look. "I don't like you out there by yourself. I get the feeling you're going to confront the seanchaí." That was the problem with family; they knew what you were thinking with just the twitch of an eyebrow.

"I'm still working through it. Please. You just said I'm good at my job. You have to let me do it."

"Don't tell me you're going to confront him alone?"

"No. I promise. I called Danny." James, along with the rest of her siblings, had met Danny MacGregor on several occasions.

"What does Macdara think about Danny?" James called as Siobhán headed for the door.

"I'm sure you can imagine," she called back.

Siobhán was standing by the cottage when a number flashed across her mobile. Danny MacGregor. She'd left him a message, and she was relieved to see how quickly he was calling back. "Where are you?" he asked.

"In a field. Staring at cows." Eddie Doolan hadn't been in any of his usual locations, so she'd come here to ponder it all.

"Are you alone?"

"Yes."

"Give me the location, I'll pick you up."

"I'm at the cottage. What's going on?"

"Someone reported an abandoned truck. I'm on me way to check it out. Thought you might like to join."

"Is it red?"

"It is indeed."

Ellen's truck. "I'll be waiting."

In the far corner of the small parking lot at the bus station, a red pickup was parked diagonally across two spaces. Danny put on gloves and handed a pair to Siobhán. They approached the truck sideways. The back cab was empty and no one was visible in the seats. "Clear," Danny said as he was upon it. He tried the passenger door. Locked. He quickly moved around to the driver's side. It was also locked.

He peered in the window and glanced at Siobhán. "We've got a handbag and a mobile phone on the seat."

"It's Ellen's truck," Siobhán said. "It has to be."

"I'd say it's an emergency then," Danny said, removing a slim file. "Have you learned this trick?"

"No. Did the station teach you?"

"YouTube," Danny said with a grin. "C'm'ere, I'll teach you."

Siobhán joined Danny at the driver's side and watched as he wedged the slim wire down by the window, and after moving it sideways and up and down and sideways again, the lock clicked. "Thankfully it's an old truck. The fancy new ones aren't as easy."

The door opened with a squeak and for a moment they simply stared at the handbag and the phone.

"Why would someone lock the doors but leave the purse and mobile out in the open?" Siobhán mused.

"He or she wanted us to see it, but also wanted us to work for it?" Danny guessed.

"Maybe whoever moved the truck wasn't the killer."

Danny shrugged. "I prefer to deal with facts." He shut

the door to the truck. "As much as I'd love to paw through it, we'll have to call the team out, and place the items in evidence bags first."

Siobhán sighed. He was right. She was dying to have a look, but procedures must be followed. The phone would need to be combed through for recent calls. Did Ellen's purse contain money, or receipts, or notes, or anything that would point to a killer?

"There's something under the passenger seat." He moved around to the other side of the truck. Siobhán followed. He handed her the metal wire. "Your turn."

She slipped it down by the window and calmed her mind, trying to connect to the feel of the wire, and find the latch to trip. Seconds later she heard a pop. Danny whistled. "Besting me. Just like old times."

She opened the door. Danny came around and began his investigation, opening the glove box, checking under the seats. He lifted a newspaper. "Nothing sinister." Siobhán neared the truck again and leaned in. "What are you doing?" There was a distinct odor in the cab.

"What does it smell like to you?"

Danny returned and sniffed. "Cleaner?"

"Leather cleaner," Siobhán said. "Shoe polish."

Danny sniffed again. "You're right." He arched his eyebrow. "And?"

"Jane smelled leather in the cottage when she first found her mam."

"I didn't hear about this."

"Maybe you were too busy booking her for murder."

His face went still. "She lied about her alibi. She was in Ballysiogdun the entire weekend."

"I know. But she certainly didn't drive the truck here."

"We can't be sure of that."

"What?"

"She has some sight, and look how it's parked."

She could hardly argue with him there. And it wasn't going to help to get combative with the one guard here she trusted. "Did the results of the footprint come in?"

"I'll have to check."

"Maybe we can pull CCTV from the bus station?" If any of their suspects were the type to polish their shoes, it was Aiden Cunningham.

Danny looked at his watch. "The guards are going to take their sweet time. I'll drive you back to town."

She hesitated. It was now or never. "Who are you dating, Danny?"

He kicked a stone with the tip of his boot. "Are you accusing me of something?"

"No. But the killer might be."

"Annabel."

"Oh." Her pixie-like face rose before her. "I can see that."

He smiled. "She's . . ." He shook his head. "Couldn't imagine my life without her."

"I get that." She began to pace. "Someone is worried we're getting too close. Creating a diversion."

"And that someone might be sitting in a jail cell right now."

"Or the wrong someone might be sitting in the jail cell."

"We're still following up on Eddie Doolan. But I won't lie. The sergeant likes Jane for this."

"What about Geraldine's metal detector?"

"Did you confirm that or is it still just a theory?"

"All you have to do is go over to her house and find the one with a round base."

He shook his head. "It's going to take hard evidence."

"The councilman and the notarized agreement?"

"He admitted to that. It's not a crime." He stepped closer. "What do you think Jane was up to that weekend? You said something about an affair?"

"I have no proof."

"But you suspect?"

Siobhán hesitated. One of the reasons Jane was sitting in jail was that she had refused to give up the name of her lover. She wouldn't want Siobhán betraying her. But Siobhán's duty was to find a killer. And that meant the truth must come out. "Joe Madigan."

Danny whistled. "You're right. We have a lot of people to keep our eye on."

There was something Siobhán was forgetting. What was it? "Dylan Kelly. Did you follow up on the photograph he told me he had?"

Danny nodded. "It shows a figure near the cottage. We believe it's Eddie Doolan."

Pinpricks of electricity shot up Siobhán's spine. "Where near the cottage?"

Danny frowned. "Near the bedroom window."

He saw the killer. "My God."

"But it's dark. We *think* it's Eddie Doolan because the figure appears to be in a cloak."

"Did you call Eddie in for questioning?"

"Of course."

"And?" She hadn't realized how much they'd been leaving her out of this investigation.

Danny sighed. "His solicitor wanted a mental health evaluation. All he did was speak in story, and riddle. We finally agreed to let the psychologists test him."

That was to the benefit of Eddie Doolan. But the more time they wasted, the easier it was for a killer to get away.

Handbag, mobile phone, gold coins, shoe-polish-smell, abandoned truck. Siobhán often repeated facts in her head, like refrains of favorite songs, especially when something didn't make sense to her. *A riddle.* Mixed messages. Find the truck. But don't make it too easy or obvious. Find the handbag and mobile phone, but lock the doors so they have to work for it. Why?

Poison her, then point to the fact she was poisoned. Inept or cunning?

Someone digs. Someone lies in wait. Someone kills and severs the tail of a mouse and leaves it in the sink with cryptic words. Someone drives the truck to the train station, locks the door, but leaves the handbag and mobile phone out in the open. Someone dresses the victim. Someone leaves Dylan Kelly's manuscript on the counter.

Who would Ellen call as her panic mounts?

Her lover. Who enters and is so startled to find her dead takes off forgetting the manuscript on the counter. Does he also grab her handbag and mobile phone so they wouldn't see he was her last call? Does he drive it to the parking lot, hoping it's enough to throw suspicion off him?

Next, her stalker. When does Eddie appear at the window? Before or after Aiden? Is he the killer? Or did he look through the bedroom window and witness the murder? The villagers were playing a very dangerous game, keeping their secrets. No more.

There was only one way out of this. Everyone who was *not* a killer was going to have to start telling the truth and nothing but. Stop this game of musical suspects until only one of them was left standing. The killer.

Chapter 30

Siobhán waited in the small visiting room at the jail where they were keeping Jane. She had a feeling it would be easier to get her to talk without Macdara in the room. Minutes later, Jane was escorted into the room, using her cane. She took a seat, her eyes focused slightly above Siobhán's head.

"You have to get me out of here," she said. "I didn't kill my mother."

"I want to help you. But first you have to help me."

"I'll do anything."

"Who is your lover?"

Jane chewed on her lip, as if pondering the question. "I won't say."

"He's married then."

"I didn't say that."

"That's the most reasonable explanation." Siobhán

wanted to add that if he was any man at all he would have come forward himself by now. "I think you're having an affair with Joe Madigan."

The lip biting grew worse. "How did you . . . Why do you say that?"

"I think Mary Madigan knows too."

"No!"

"You aren't the only one who lied about your alibi. I think she spent that weekend following Joe."

"Dear God." Jane bowed her head. "I'm not in love. Neither is he. It's just a bit of company."

"You should have come clean from the beginning. Maybe you wouldn't be here."

"I don't want to ruin a marriage."

"Did your mother know?"

"I don't think so. Then again, I didn't think anyone would ever know."

"You weren't the only one keeping a relationship secret."

Jane swallowed. "You mean my mam?"

"Yes."

"You think she was dating Aiden Cunningham."

"I do."

"I was with Joe all weekend. So you can rule him out."

"I need to hear every detail about the weekend. Everything this time. If you lie to me again, I can't help you. Do you understand?"

Jane nodded. "There's not much to tell. I left Thursday after breakfast as I stated. Mam drove me to the bus stop. She insisted on waiting until I got on the bus. I had to take it to the next stop. That's where Joe picked me up."

"In his car?"

"In a taxi."

"And then?"

"Then we went to an inn just outside town."

"That was risky."

Jane sighed. "No one there knew us. Mary Madigan may have tried looking for us, but I don't see how she would know where we were."

"She could have tracked her husband's phone."

Jane shrugged. "I wouldn't know about that."

"Tell your lawyer all of this."

"I can't. I can't do it to Joe."

"It's too late. No more secrets. If you stayed in that inn all weekend as you say, that's your alibi. Everywhere you went, anyone you spoke with, it's all going to come out."

Jane hung her head. "I made a mess of everything. Mam would be so disappointed."

"Everything takes a backseat to finding her killer." Siobhán took a few notes, then looked at Jane. "Now we're going to talk about Joe. If he left you at all during the weekend, you have to tell me." Jane hesitated. "Unless you want to spend the rest of your life behind bars."

"Friday evening he had to call his wife. And his mother. Talk to his children. I fell asleep. I don't know how long he was out."

"When did you see him again?"

Jane swallowed. "Not until morning."

"You slept straight through?"

Jane nodded. "I've always been a heavy sleeper."

"We'll have to talk with the clerk at the inn, to see if they know what time Joe returned." And check the CCTV cameras. "Whose idea was it to stay at the inn?"

"It was Joe's. He wanted to be close in case his children needed him."

"I see." Or was there another reason? Had he wanted

to be close so he could get away with murder? "When are you meeting with your solicitor?"

"Today."

"Good. Tell him everything."

"I promise."

Siobhán stood. "Good. Then I'll do everything I can."

"I remembered something else."

"Go on."

"The leather smell in the cottage. Remember?"

"Yes." Siobhán wanted to tell her they'd just smelled it again in the truck, but she could not. Especially now that Jane was in custody.

"I smelled it again. At the memorial for Mam. When I was standing next to Aiden Cunningham."

Siobhán caught up with Danny outside the station and filled him in on her meeting with Jane, and her affair with Joe Madigan. "I'll get a guard up there to take down her report. It won't look good that she lied to us."

"Maybe so, but if her alibi can be proved, then she'll have to be released."

"I'll get right on it."

Soon everyone would know about the affair. Joe Madigan would be called to the station along with Geraldine and Mary. Secrets always came out. And so did the truth.

"Danny."

"Yes?"

"Annabel was teaching an art class that evening."

"She was."

"Did you see her after?"

He nodded. "We spent the night at her house."

"Where were you before that?"

His eyes hardened. "Are you serious? You're after my alibi now?"

"Someone saw the two of you, or they know something about your romance."

"We're not hiding it."

"Why did they leave me that note?"

"Obviously to turn you against me. I guess the writer of that note thinks you're the better guard."

She ignored the jealous comment. "I was at Annabel's the other day. Ellen had some disturbing paintings. Have you seen them?"

"What were you doing in her studio?"

"Ciarán and Ann were having a lesson."

"Do you expect me to believe that?"

His defenses were up. "I'm not accusing your girl-friend of anything."

He turned away from her. "I was wrong to let you in."

"Don't say that."

"Maybe you should go home."

He started to walk away. "What about Joe's barn?"

He stopped but kept his back to her. "What about it?"

"Did you follow up on his mysterious barn crasher?" She should have paid more attention to this at the time. He'd stated that the night of the murder someone had slept in his barn. Seeking refuge. And there was only one explanation why Siobhán could see the killer, this killer, doing that.

"Go home."

"What about the dead mouse?"

He stopped, turned. "Siobhán. It was good to see you. But you're officially interfering in an active investigation. I'll say it one more time. Go home."

Chapter 31

Siobhán returned to Molly's Café. She scrutinized the paintings along the wall one by one. When she reached the end of the first wall, dust marked the edges of the empty space. A painting had been removed.

Molly was wiping down tables. "Excuse me," Siobhán called to her.

Molly smiled as she recognized Siobhán, drying her hands on her apron as she approached. "How can I help you?"

"I thought none of these paintings could leave the shop until the end of the month."

"That's correct. You can still purchase one, luv, but it will have to hang here a few more days."

Siobhán pointed to the empty space on the wall. "So where is this one?"

Molly stared at the spot, then held her finger up and

headed for the counter. She reached underneath and pulled out a notebook. She thumbed through it. "Number eleven. *Deadly Herbs*. It was a painting of Jane Delaney's garden." She gasped. "You don't think?"

"When is the last time you remember seeing it here?"

"I couldn't be sure. I'm so used to them, I don't look anymore."

"What about CCTV?"

"I believe I mentioned before that we don't bother with that here, luv. I think the ones on the street are aimed mostly at the bank and the betting shop. There's not much to steal here except the sugar."

"Was the painting sold?"

Molly ran her finger down the notebook. "No." She clenched her fists. "First that note, now this. I guess I haven't been paying enough attention." She sighed. "I hope Annabel won't hold me responsible."

Siobhán wanted to reassure her that Annabel wouldn't do that, but the more she learned about the folks in this village, the less she was sure of anything.

"Who painted it?"

Molly glanced at the notebook, then at Siobhán. "That's the other funny bit."

"Go on."

She turned the notebook facing outward. "It was the only one without a signature."

Siobhán pounded on the door to Annabel's studio. It took three more goes at it before Annabel came to the door, her blond hair sticking to her face with a drop of paint, a brush in her hand.

"Garda O'Sullivan," she said. "I'm sorry. I'm working."

"This is urgent. May I come in?"

Annabel looked as if she wanted anything but, yet she finally relented and allowed Siobhán to enter.

"There's a painting missing from Molly's Café."

"Missing?"

"Unless you took one back?"

"No. Sales aren't supposed to go to the owners until the exhibit is down."

"I need to know who painted it. The title was *Deadly Herbs.*"

Annabel scoffed. "That's the one they stole?"

"Who painted it?"

She hesitated. "I did."

"You?"

"Is there a problem?"

"You painted the wolfsbane in the Delaney garden?"

"Yes."

"That's the poison that killed Ellen Delaney."

Annabel gasped. "I had no idea."

"Why did you paint it?"

"It was Ellen's idea to paint her garden. I often took the group outside to paint. Nothing sinister about it."

"Did anyone from the group comment on it?"

"Not that I remember." She frowned. "We were interrupted that session."

"What do you mean?"

"Joe's children. He and the missus stopped by for Geraldine and they were running amuck. That was it. His wee one tried to pick the wolfsbane."

"The girl or the boy?"

"Lilly. The wee girl."

"Then what?"

"I lightly scolded her that she shouldn't pick them."

"Did you tell her they were poison?"

"I didn't. But Ellen did." Annabel covered her mouth. "She went into great detail. How the roots when ground up could kill you." The mean schoolteacher strikes again.

"Are you positive?"

"Yes, it was quite the scene. The poor ting started wailing at the top of her lungs. That's when Mary Madigan lit into her for scaring Lilly half to death."

"What's going on?" The voice was male, and came from behind Annabel. She stepped aside to reveal Danny MacGregor standing in the shadows. "Siobhán. What are you doing here?"

"One of her paintings was stolen from Molly's Café," Siobhán said. "I just wanted to let her know."

"Which one?" Danny asked.

"The murder weapon," Siobhán said. Just then, her mobile and Danny's went off at the same time.

"Uh-oh," Annabel said.

Hers was a text from Macdara. **Trouble at the inn.**

"The inn?" Danny asked, holding up his mobile. She nodded. "Come on. I'll give you a ride."

Siobhán's heart leapt in her throat as they pulled up to the inn and she took in the garda cars and folks gathered on the footpath. Where were her siblings? She started to run. It was then, as she drew closer, that she saw the main window of the inn had been smashed. Soon she saw her brood, huddled together. She headed for them. "What happened?"

"Someone threw a rock through the window."

"A rock?"

Gráinne pulled up her mobile, scrolled through, then turned the screen to Siobhán. On it was the photograph of a rock lying on the floor of the inn. Painted on the rock in red letters it said: "BELIEVE."

"You!" Siobhán turned to find the front desk clerk glaring at her. "This is all your fault," he announced, shaking his fist.

"Why do you say that?"

"It was that seanchaí. I caught him running away. He was shouting, 'Tell the redhead girl she's after me!'"

Siobhán pointed to herself. "I'm after him?"

The clerk frowned. "Why would he want me to tell you, that you're after him, like?"

"I'm just trying to clarify." *She's* after me. Who? Geraldine? Or had Danny started in on Eddie after their talk? Did Eddie think Siobhán was going after him?

"Calm down." The directive came from Macdara, who had snuck up behind them, putting Siobhán's heart in her crossways.

"Eddie Doolan did this?"

"He's mental," the clerk insisted. "Standing in front of me, shouting."

"What was he shouting?"

"I just told you twice. Do I need to make it tree times?" He was clearly incensed. "Then he throws a rock through me window!"

"Did he say anything else? Anything about where to find him?"

The clerk sighed. "Something about back where it all began."

Siobhán turned to Macdara. "I know where he's going."

"You're not going alone." He glanced at the guards. "Do you want to tell Danny?"

She shook her head. "Let's check it out first."

He nodded. "Let me get Mam and your ones sorted first."

"Ask James to stay with them."

"Why do you think he's out here?" Macdara asked as they traversed the meadow on their way to Ellen's campsite.

"Back where it all began," she said.

"You get his riddles."

"I'm working on it." Soon they were past the hawthorn tree again, and almost on the campsite. "Look." Ellen's tent was positioned where she'd first found it, standing tall as if it had been recently erected. Something didn't feel right.

Macdara shifted beside her as he eyed the tent. "The guards didn't remove it?"

"Or someone put one back up."

They stopped. "I don't have a good feeling about this," Macdara said.

Siobhán pulled two sets of gloves out of her pockets. "That's why I brought these."

They pulled the tent flap open together. Eddie Doolan lay on his back, eyes closed. A large knife protruded from his chest. Blood pooled in the middle. A piece of clothing was balled up next to him, a white lump covered in streaks of dirt. "Dear God," Siobhán said. "I think that's Ellen's top. The missing one." She crossed herself and said a little prayer. On the side of the tent, in blood, there were three tic marks and a single word:

III
RUN

"Run." Macdara's head snapped around. "What if that is meant for us?"

Goose bumps rose on Siobhán's arms. It looked like the same handwriting in the sink. Both done in blood, only this time, it was way more than the blood of a mouse. Was this a trap? Someone out there, waiting for them. Not just anyone. The killer.

Siobhán searched the rugged grounds in front of them, the bushes, the trees, the rocks. Too many places one could hide. The skies were dark and the clouds nearly on top of them. In the distance the gnarled hawthorn tree stood on the hill, as if reigning over the land. "It feels like someone is watching us," she said.

"They want us to run. So we stay still." He put his arm out protectively as he took out his mobile and dialed 999.

"I'll call Danny," Siobhán said as she removed hers. Thunder rumbled overhead and soon the rain was coming down.

"The blood," Siobhán said. "Don't let it wash away." She tried holding the flaps of the tent together, but the wind wrestled her for them, blowing rain into the tent.

"We can't stay here," Macdara said. "It could be a trap." He felt it too, and she had learned to trust that feeling. Maybe it was nature who was watching. These beings who kept coming and going throughout time while they remained.

"Geraldine's house is the closest," Siobhán said. She had to shout to be heard.

"What if she's our killer?"

"The cottage then." The cottage was the last place she

wanted to be trapped in a storm, but Macdara was right. Geraldine could have lured them here, knowing the storm was coming, hoping they'd make a run for her house. And although the two of them could certainly hold their own against the older woman, where there were two knives there was a set. If it was a trap, the killer was several steps ahead of them.

"Come on," Macdara said, grabbing her hand, as the rain pelted its unforgiving fury. "Let's make a run for the cottage."

"They've changed the locks."

Macdara shook his head. "I have the key. I was supposed to retrieve things for Jane."

Finally, a little luck. They ran.

Inside the cottage they locked the doors, pulled the curtains tight. They changed out of their wet clothes and found warm ones. Macdara put on a flannel shirt and work trousers of Ellen's that were actually loose on him, and Siobhán slipped on one of Jane's dresses. The rain continued to beat on the roof as Siobhán made a fire and put on the kettle. Macdara was staring into the sink. Siobhán followed. The sink was free of the dead mouse but the eerie words remained.

"Jane. Tree," he said. He turned to Siobhán, a pained look on his face. "Was I wrong? Is my cousin a killer?"

He had it wrong again. The order. Tree. Jane. Not Jane. Tree. There was a difference. This time she didn't correct him. She ruminated on the balled-up shirt in the tent next to poor Eddie's body. She'd seen it before. She was just about to go through it all again in her mind when Macdara interrupted her.

"Was this here before?"

Siobhán turned to find him staring at the wall of the living room above the sofa. On it hung a painting. The hooded purple flowers. Some called it friar's cap. Others wolfsbane. Or aconite. But its roots, by any name, were poisonous. She moved in closer. This one had been titled: *Dead Beautiful.*

Chapter 32

"That's insane." Siobhán stood in the garda station arguing with Danny. Jane was being released. They were holding Eddie Doolan responsible for the murder of Ellen Delaney and himself. "How many people stab themselves in the chest?"

"The writing of the blood on the tent flaps matches the writing in the sink. That puts him at both crime scenes. He had been stalking her for years, Siobhán. I thought you'd be happy. We've released Jane."

"Why did he kill her? Why now?"

"We found a gold coin on him. He stole her hoard and she caught him."

"This is too hasty. What about Geraldine's walking stick? Did you check it out?"

He sighed. "Even if it is a metal detector, that doesn't mean she's a killer."

"It gives you leverage to bring her in for questioning."

He shook his head. "You don't like it when a case is solved, is that it?"

Macdara stepped forward. "She has the best instincts of anyone I know. You said it yourself."

"Ellen's shirt. I know where I've seen it before. Lilly Madigan was wearing it the other day." Mary scolded her as if she'd taken it off the line, assuming it was dirty. But if it was Ellen's shirt, it was already dirty. And if she found it on her property, then a member of that household was a killer.

"If you have proof that someone else is our killer, I'd be happy to take it to the sergeant," Danny said. "Otherwise my hands are tied."

"What about the shoe print in the cottage?" Macdara asked.

Danny folded his arms across his muscular chest. "I don't know."

"Check on the results," Siobhán said. "We'll wait."

Danny's eyes flashed with annoyance, but he told them to wait as he headed back to his office. It felt like hours, but minutes later he returned with a folder.

"Let's go outside," he said to Siobhán and Macdara. Jane wasn't thrilled to be left waiting, but she acquiesced. Outside Danny lit a cigarette as he handed Macdara the folder. Macdara scanned it. "Aiden Cunningham."

"It was his shoe print?"

"Not just that. His fingerprints were also found in Ellen's truck."

"This is big," Siobhán said. "You have to bring him in."

"What else?" Macdara said. "What about my aunt's mobile phone and handbag from the truck?"

"Her money was still in the wallet, so it wasn't a robbery." He looked away, then back at them. "She made several calls to Aiden before her death."

"Are you joking me? And you're not reopening the case?"

"None of the calls were picked up. But he did try to call her back. Why would he do that if he killed her?"

"Because he doesn't want you to think that he killed her," Macdara said.

"We have a photograph of Eddie Doolan at the scene," Danny said.

"At Ellen's bedroom window," Siobhán interjected. "I believe he saw the killer."

"Based on what?" He was clearly miffed that Siobhán was onto something he wasn't.

"He told us twice."

"Are you on about the sink?" Danny was like a dog watching another dog steal his bone.

"Yes. And the writing on the walls of the tent."

"The only name he mentioned was Jane. You just pleaded her innocence, we released her, and now you're accusing her again?"

"That's the challenge with riddles," Siobhán said. "They're not literal. It's easy to misunderstand."

"Aiden?" Macdara asked. "Is that who Eddie saw?"

"No," Siobhán said. "I think Aiden Cunningham arrived next. He discovered his lover's body and panicked. In his terror he forgets Dylan's manuscript. Busted the window to make it look like a robbery gone wrong, and stole her handbag, mobile phone, and truck."

"I already have guards on the way to pick Aiden Cunningham up," Danny said. "But it's not going to do any good."

Macdara frowned. "Why is that?"

"If they were having a relationship, then that easily explains his presence in the cottage. Including his footprint and the manuscript, not to mention his fingerprints in the truck." He threw up his hands. "It's not against the law to have a secret relationship."

"This is outrageous," Macdara said. "The footprint and manuscript put him at the crime scene."

"Yes," Danny said. "But we can't prove *when* it was left there. I'm afraid this isn't going to be enough to get Sergeant Eegan to reopen the case."

"Not when he has a poor dead seanchaí to blame it on," Siobhán said.

"You're one to talk. It's obvious you think you know who the killer is. This isn't a parlor game, so why don't you just spit it out?"

"I have a request. It's going to sound strange."

He shook his head. "What is it?"

"The dead mouse," she said. "I'd like to see it. Not a picture. The mouse."

"What in heavens name do you want dat for?"

"I'll tell you only if I'm right."

"You think you'll be capable of running some sort of test we couldn't? Or do you think the killer left his fingerprints on the mouse?" He waited for a response, got none. "I can't do it. I *won't* do it."

"I just need proof."

"Then don't bother me until you have it."

"Not a bother," Siobhán said. "That's what I'll do, so."

Macdara grabbed Siobhán's hand and threw a glare at Danny that made her want to cheer. She hated that this case had eroded the bonds of friendship, but this was too important to worry about his ego.

* * *

Their bags were packed and in the car, but Siobhán couldn't bring herself to get in. "If we leave now, a killer is going to go free."

Macdara placed his hands on the steering wheel and pretended to bang his head into it several times. He glanced at her to see if she was smiling. She couldn't help but do just that. He soon turned serious. "I get why you didn't tell Danny, but why are you keeping your theories from me?" She hesitated. "Do you think it's Jane? Is that why you're all buttoned up?"

"I'd rather keep the element of surprise."

He exhaled, clearly frustrated. "How can I help?"

"We need all of our suspects in one place. Let everything come out. I want to hear from Aiden and Geraldine. I think both of them were at the cabin that evening. And not just them. Eddie Doolan was there as well, peering through the window. Geraldine digging—Aiden leaving the manuscript on the counter."

Macdara sighed and rubbed his face. "As far as Aiden Cunningham is concerned—as Danny pointed out—we don't know when he left it there."

"No," Siobhán said. "We can't *prove* when he left it there. But Ellen was a neat freak. Everything in its place. Apart from the one item she always kept on the counter— and she might still be alive if it wasn't her habit to leave her bottle of Powers out in the open."

Macdara bowed his head. "That something so simple could turn so deadly. We just never really know, do we?"

Siobhán grabbed his hand. "We have to cherish every single day. Lastly, we know that Eddie Doolan, sometime later, snuck back into the cottage leaving a dead mouse and a riddle in the sink."

"A riddle that accuses Jane."

"No. I don't think it does."

He sighed. "Jane. Tree. What else could it mean?"

Siobhán wanted the killer to be the first to hear it. It was the least she could do for poor Eddie Doolan. "We have to do something to get everyone in the same place. Most people who are telling a story will stick to some semblance of the truth. We need to root out the discrepancies. We need all the lies out in the open."

"They're never going to talk to us. Not when they think the killer has been caught. Who in their right mind would come forward now?" He stared at her. "What?" he said, waggling his finger at her. "You've got that look."

He got her there. The idea required several props and help from the Ballysiogdun guards, but it was a good one. "I can think of one thing that would bring everyone in this village together. One thing that every member could not resist coming out to see." And before that, she was going to bypass Danny, find the detective sergeant and tell him what she needed to see.

The bulldozer loomed in front of the cottage. As Siobhán had hoped, the news that the cottage was going to be razed brought all of their suspects out to watch. The killer was amongst them, Siobhán knew it in her bones. And now that Eddie Doolan had been blamed for it, he or she had no reason to suspect they were being set up. And of course the guards were present. They had to make sure the demolition went off smoothly.

"Before we begin," Siobhán said, "I'd like us all to gather inside the cottage to say a prayer in memory of Ellen Delaney."

There were glances between the participants. Geraldine stood with her son and daughter-in-law. Thankfully, the children were with Molly from the café. Annabel huddled near Danny. She'd been a good sport and brought the painting Siobhán requested without asking why. Dylan Kelly scratched notes and snapped photographs of the cottage, ready and eager to document his climactic ending. Aiden Cunningham was looking uneasy in his suit, large patches of sweat visible underneath his armpits. Danny had come through with one item—Geraldine's walking stick, the one with the round base. It hid in the cottage, waiting for story time, along with the other props. And boy, did Siobhán finally have a story to tell.

They filed into the cottage, standing nervously in the small living room. "Why haven't the furnishings been removed?" Geraldine asked.

"Because we're not really going to bulldoze it," Siobhán said. "Not today anyway."

Dylan Kelly stepped forward, jabbing his pen. "What kind of sick joke is this?"

"This is no joke," Siobhán said.

Geraldine let out a yelp as she noticed one of the props in the corner. "My walking stick."

Siobhán stepped forward. "Why don't you show the people what it really is?"

"What do you mean?" Geraldine sputtered.

Siobhán headed for the walking stick, removed scissors from her pocket, and began to snip at the strings.

"Stop!" Geraldine shrieked. But it was too late. As Siobhán snipped, the colorful yarn dropped to the floor, revealing the base of the metal detector.

Siobhán turned it on. The machine whirred and blinked. "This is what you'd been using to locate the buried treasure," she said.

"Treasure?" Annabel said. "What treasure?"

"Would have been a nice addition to your book," Siobhán said. She turned to Dylan Kelly. "Care to enlighten her?" He blinked and pushed the spectacles up from the bridge of his nose. "The truth will set you free," Siobhán said. "Unless, of course, you're the killer."

Dylan Kelly cleared his throat. "Alright, so. While researching my book I came across an article that hinted of a buried treasure in Ballysiogdun. It mentioned the treasure lay where the fairies dwelled." He cleared his throat. "I showed the article to Geraldine. After all, her family owned the land where the fairies dwelled."

All heads turned to Geraldine. "Fine. I've been looking for it. But I was too late."

"Ellen had already found it," Siobhán said. "When I first arrived I noticed a disturbed mound of dirt at the side of the cottage. At first glance I thought someone had been burying something. Instead, it's where Ellen had been digging." She turned to Geraldine. "And later, you. But Ellen Delaney beat you to the treasure."

Geraldine opened and closed her mouth but no words came out.

"That can't be," Macdara said. "Why would she borrow fifteen thousand euro from my mam if she'd already struck gold?"

"The gold couldn't be fenced right away. Legally she was supposed to hand it over to the Irish government. As far as the fifteen thousand euro, the facts show that she didn't succeed in buying the cottage. What we're missing is whether or not she *tried* to."

Heads swiveled to Aiden Cunningham. He wiped his brow. "She tried," he admitted. "When I insisted the sale couldn't go through she used the money to prepay the rent on the cottage. She was paranoid they were going to bulldoze it if she didn't."

Jane stepped forward. "If my mother had the gold coins, then where are they?"

"Let's rewind," Siobhán said, unwilling to let others take the narrative from her. She turned to Geraldine. "You were here the night of the murder." She pointed at Aiden. "And so were you."

"What is the meaning of this?" Aiden Cunningham said. "Eddie Doolan was the killer and the entire case is done and dusted."

"I agree. We don't have to listen to this." Geraldine turned to go.

"You do unless you'd rather answer questions at the station," Danny said, blocking the door. He nodded at Siobhán. "Continue."

Siobhán addressed Geraldine. "Lilly saw dancing lights and people dancing that night. The dancing lights were from the metal detector. And at first I thought the dancing was you struggling with Ellen."

"It wasn't!"

"I said 'at first.' Now, I realize, you were struggling with Eddie Doolan."

Geraldine stared at the floor. "He saw the body through the window. He told me she was dead. Said an evil fairy killed her. He wanted to go inside. I had to physically hold him back. I told him to go home."

"Which one of you broke the window?"

"It was Eddie. He grabbed my metal detector and smashed the base."

Siobhán turned to Danny. "You let me believe the window was smashed from the inside."

"I was just letting you figure it out for yourself, Sherlock," Danny said, his voice dripping with jealousy.

"I suppose Eddie thought he was a hero," Geraldine continued. "When I blocked the door, he was going to get in the window." She laid a hand over her throat. "I told him they were going to accuse him of the murder. Lock him away."

"You were worried about yourself," Siobhán said. "You didn't want the guards to know you were there digging, that you sent Ellen out on a fool's bet so you could be alone at the cottage, and that you'd hired Eddie Doolan to stalk her."

"He'd done it once before," Geraldine said. "But I never told him to hurt her. Never!"

"He didn't. But what if she'd hurt *him*? Or what if he'd frightened her so dearly she had a heart attack?" *Didn't these people play What If?*

"None of those things happened."

"You're right," Siobhán said. "Worse happened." She turned to Aiden Cunningham. "Tell us everything from when you arrived. And no more lies. Your footwear impressions were found, along with Dylan Kelly's manuscript and rejection letter on the counter, not to mention your fingerprints in the truck."

"You," Jane said, whirling on Aiden Cunningham. "I could smell your leather when I returned to the cottage that morning."

"We also have him on CCTV exiting the truck," Danny piped up.

Aiden had the look of a wild animal caught in a trap. He wiped his brow with a handkerchief. "Fine. I'll tell you everything. But I assure you, I'm no killer. Late in the evening, or should I say early morning, Ellen blew up my phone. It wasn't like her to call that late, or that often, for that matter. It was hard to understand what she was saying. Her words were garbled, and she wasn't making sense. But one thing was clear. She was in an absolute panic. But by the time I heard the messages and tried to ring her back, she wasn't answering. I was worried. When I hurried over . . ." He closed his eyes for a moment, then opened them. "She was already dead. I panicked."

"You panicked so much you took her handbag and mobile, drove off in her truck," Siobhán said.

He nodded. "Given the broken window, I thought a robbery was the most logical. I didn't realize I'd left Dylan Kelly's manuscript on the counter."

"This is unbelievable," Dylan said. "What a plot twist!"

"You also interrupted the killer," Siobhán added.

"Me?" Aiden pointed to himself. "I saw no one."

"The killer was hiding under the bed. Where he or she dropped the gold coin."

"How do you figure that?" Danny interjected.

"Ellen was taunting them with her stash. First with a painting. Then a tip to Molly. Then Eddie."

"Such an insufferable woman!" Geraldine cried out.

"One more comment like that and we'll have a third murder on our hands," Jane said. "And I don't care who locks me up!"

Joe Madigan stepped up. "If you think you know who it is, then just spit it out."

"It was your daughter who helped me solve the riddle," Siobhán said, turning to Mary and Joe.

"Lilly?" Joe said.

"She saw everything, she just didn't know everything she was seeing." Siobhán turned back to Joe. "You and Jane were having a secret affair. You two thought you were so good at keeping it a secret, but many people knew." She pivoted on Mary Madigan standing like a block of ice by the door. "Including your wife." Mary turned beet red. "At first I assumed you spent the weekend following your husband and Jane."

Joe turned to his wife, shame stamped on his face. "You knew?" He reached in his pocket and pulled out an envelope. "Is that why you didn't tell me about this?"

Danny stepped forward to grab the envelope. He opened it. "I don't understand." He turned to Mary Madigan. "You were accepted at Glasgow School of Art?"

"Yes," Mary said. "I leave in the fall with the children."

"No you don't," Joe said.

"Not with my grandchildren," Geraldine added.

"All your family drama aside," Aiden said, pushing through the Madigans and squaring off in front of Siobhán. "If you know who the killer is, I demand you tell us right this instant!"

Siobhán would not allow this bully to push her. Especially when he'd been running from their questions since the beginning. "When I first visited the Madigan farmhouse, Joe told us about an unexpected visitor in the barn that night. I think it was the killer."

Joe gasped. "I had no idea."

"There was also a bottle of Powers whiskey on your counter. Odd, given that you're all teetotalers."

"It was for a still-life painting," Mary Madigan cried.

She turned to Annabel. "The assignment was to paint something we feared. Tell them."

"Yes," Annabel said. "That's correct. Mary chose the bottle of whiskey, and Ellen did a series of paintings."

Siobhán approached the fireplace where she had propped all of Ellen's paintings. She began to line them up along the walls one by one. As the villagers exclaimed over them, once again she addressed Mary Madigan.

"You were the final person who was here that evening."

"Why would she be here?" Joe barked.

"She was waiting. Hoping Ellen would never return home."

"Waiting and hoping for what?" Joe sputtered.

"For the poison to take effect."

"That's absurd," Geraldine said. She started to laugh. She stopped when she saw the look on Mary Madigan's face. Pure defiance.

"I will consent that your pretext for having a bottle of Powers whiskey was Annabel's class assignment."

"Pretext?" Joe's face was a contortion of emotion.

"When I spoke to Molly, she mentioned that Mary Madigan paid Ellen a visit shortly before the murder. Under the pretext of trying yet again to convince Ellen to donate a painting." She turned to Mary Madigan. "Annabel, however, didn't remember this. And why would you come here to do that? Why not wait until you were in class with Ellen?"

"See?" Joe said. "It makes no sense."

"She came to switch Ellen's usual bottle of whiskey—the one she always kept on the counter—with the poisoned bottle. The one I saw in your kitchen must have been Ellen's original bottle."

Siobhán pointed to the wolfsbane painting hanging on the wall. "You overheard Ellen talking about how deadly the roots were, didn't you?" Mary didn't speak, or move. "Then you practiced. On mice."

"You?" Joe said. "You killed those mice?"

"Did she mutilate them too?" Danny asked. "Is that why there was blood in the sink?"

"Mary didn't put the mouse in the sink or use a knife on them," Siobhán explained. "Eddie did. After he found one of the poor critters poisoned. He cut the tail off."

"Why on earth would he do dat?" Danny was growing frustrated.

"Because it was part of his riddle. Remember, he'd seen the killer. He was looking through the window when he witnessed Mary Madigan suffocating Ellen Delaney with her own pillow."

Exclamations erupted. "What riddle?" Danny wanted answers.

Siobhán moved to the sink where the bloody words were starting to fade, taking on a ghostly quality. "Tree, Jane," Siobhán said. She looked at Macdara. "Not Jane. Tree."

"Who cares," Geraldine shouted. "He's saying Jane is the killer. That she sent her mother to die by the fairy tree!"

"No," Siobhán said. "He was writing phonetically."

"My God," Macdara said. "He didn't mind his *h*'s."

Siobhán knew he'd get it. "Correct. Tree is 'three.' I wasn't sure until he confirmed it in the tent, this time with three tic marks."

"Three?" Danny said. "Three what? Three Jane?"

"Blind," Jane answered, her voice filled with shock. "My name was code for 'blind.'"

"Yes," Siobhán answered. "Three blind."

"Mice," Macdara finished. "Three blind mice."

"They all ran after the farmer's wife," Jane sang, her soft voice wobbling.

"Who cut off their tale with a carving knife," Danny joined in. He whistled. "But there was only one mouse, like. Wouldn't that make it 'Three Blind Mouse?'"

"I'm sure he'd appreciate the grammar lesson if he was here to hear it," Siobhán snapped. "Can we focus on what matters. Or shall I say *who*."

En masse the group turned to Mary Madigan.

"A foolish riddle!" she sputtered. "It's hardly proof!"

Joe barreled up to his wife. "Tell the truth. You're a God-fearing woman. What did you do?"

Mary crumpled, tears gushing down her face. "How many times did we beg you to leave the cottage?" she said, whirling on Jane. "My poor boy got sick and even then you wouldn't go. When I tried to explain that to her—she—she was so *cruel*. She had the nerve to say that maybe a fairy had stolen William and that he was a changeling. That's why he was so clingy. I could have killed her right then and there." Mary turned to Geraldine. "She didn't just brag about the treasure. She was torturing us. Then she had the nerve to say that she'd purchased the cottage and it was never going to come down." She whirled on Aiden Cunningham. "How could you?"

Aiden bowed his head. "I told you the sale didn't happen. I had no idea she was spinning that lie."

Danny MacGregor stepped forward. "Mary Madigan. Are you admitting to the murder of Ellen Delaney?"

"And Eddie Doolan," Siobhán said quietly.

"Why on earth would she kill him?" Joe said.

"Because I'm not the only one who figured out that riddle. Mary did too. What a nice touch just now, acting surprised. But you already knew. That's why you left me a note at Molly's, hoping to distract me, and threw the rock into the window of the inn. You were hiding under the bed when Aiden came in. By the time you ran back to the farm, you were holding Ellen's shirt. You spent the night in your own barn."

"Why on earth would she do that?" Joe beseeched. "It's her house."

"Because she wasn't supposed to be home. She couldn't have Geraldine witnessing her return." She turned back to Mary Madigan. "Later I saw your daughter wearing Ellen's shirt. The one she wore camping. There were also strips of hay under the clothesline. You washed the clothes you wore that night, but after sleeping in the barn, you didn't get all the bits of hay. After killing Ellen, you heard Aiden arriving. You dove under the bed. Dropped a gold coin. Ellen must have dropped her shirt on the floor right where you were hiding. That's why you freaked out when you saw Lilly wearing it."

Joe's face was red. He turned to his wife. "Why would you bring that home?"

"I didn't even know I had it. Ellen dumped it on the floor. I guess I didn't realize I was clutching it until I reached the barn." Her voice was depleted. She knew the jig was up.

"Did you dress her?" Jane said.

"Her lovely red outfit was already hanging on the door. I was being respectful."

Siobhán had that piece of the puzzle slightly wrong. "You planted a teacup, hoping the guards wouldn't test for poison."

"Murderer!" Jane shrieked. She lunged in the direction of Mary's voice. Macdara held her back. "Was it you who nearly ran over us on the road?"

Danny cleared his throat. "That was one of the guards. Racing to get to the scene and passed up the entrance. Sorry about that."

Siobhán pivoted to Mary once again. "You didn't just break in to kill Ellen Delaney," she said. "Do you want to tell them about the gold?"

"Fools," Mary Madigan said. "Give me a head start and I'll tell you."

"No need," Siobhán said. She approached *Deadly Herbs* hanging on the wall. She took it off and turned it around. Taped to the back of the frame, filling every inch, were guineas.

The crowd moved closer as if the coins were magnets pulling them in against their will. "The hoard," Geraldine said. "I knew it was here. I knew it." The distraction worked in Mary Madigan's favor. She lunged for the door, threw it open and bolted. Danny and Macdara ran after her. Moments later, a loud roar rang out. The sounds of an engine firing up. Outside the open door, the yellow bulldozer roared, wheels churning up dirt as it began to move.

"Everybody out!" Siobhán shouted. "Now!"

Chapter 33

The bulldozer plowed forward, heading straight for the cottage. The paid operator, who had been smoking a cigarette on the grounds, had his hands on top of his hard hat and was shouting up at her to stop.

"How does she know how to drive that thing?" someone asked.

"She's been on tractors all her life," Joe said. "It's not that difficult."

Despite the guards screaming at her, Mary Madigan rammed the bulldozer into the building. "Seems she doesn't know how to work it completely," Macdara said as the impact shook the cottage and rattled the windows.

"It was just a prop," Siobhán said. "It would take a lot more than that yoke to bring the cottage down."

"You yelled at us to get out," Macdara said.

"Safety first," Siobhán said. "Plus, I really didn't want to miss this."

Mary backed the bulldozer up and rammed it into the cottage again. Dylan Kelly was filming it, encouraging her. On the third go, the bulldozer shut off, and after, all they could hear was the grunt and whine of the engine shutting down, and her sobs. A gust of wind came through, followed by a creak. All heads swiveled to the front of the cottage where the door still gaped open. Then heads swiveled to the back door, a mirror image.

"Looks like the fairies got their way," Geraldine said. "A free passage from front to back."

Naomi's Bistro comforted them with all the trappings of home. The kettle was on, the fire was crackling, and the pie was out of the cooler. "Thanks be to heaven we're away from the fairies," Gráinne said.

"I never got to see one," Ciarán said. "Can we get a fairy tree?"

"You've got your pocket full of stones," Siobhán said. "You can put them in a ring in the back garden." Ciarán skipped off to do just that, their pup Trigger barking at his heels. They had dropped Jane off with Macdara's mam. She would stay with her for a while before deciding her next move. Siobhán sat across from Macdara long after their pie was gone, enjoying a rare bout of silence.

"Want to set a date?" he asked her softly. "That is, if you'll still have me?"

"I was giving it a bit of thought myself," Siobhán said. "A ceremony at Saint Mary's and then a reception at the abbey sounds just about perfect. What do you think?"

"I think," he said, taking her hands in his, "I wouldn't want it any other way. Now about the date. Is next fall too soon?"

The bell on the front door jingled and a familiar voice filtered into the bistro. Macdara arched an eyebrow. "Is that?"

James flew into the room, holding hands with Elise.

"Guess what?" James said.

"We're getting married," Elise trilled.

James's grin spread ear to ear. "Next month."

Elise jumped up and down. "We're having the ceremony at Saint Mary's and then—get this—the reception at the abbey!" The proclamation was topped off with an ear-piercing squeal.

Macdara, to Siobhán's surprise, started to laugh. He tried covering his mouth, but that just made it worse. Soon, he was roaring with laughter. Siobhán didn't know whether to laugh or cry, or punch Elise in the face. "If you didn't believe in the curse of fairies before," Macdara said, "you might want to think twice about it now."

"What is he on about?" James asked.

"Nothing at all," Siobhán said, getting ahold of herself and stepping forward. "Congratulations, luv." She hugged her brother, as Elise chattered in the background, mouth running about her wedding plans. Siobhán glanced out the back windows to the garden, where Ciarán and Ann were standing over his ring of stones in the grass.

Evil. Vengeful. Fairies.

I hear ye, Siobhán thought. *I hear you loud and clear. Believe.*

The grand opening of a new bookstore in the County Cork Irish village of Kilbane becomes the closing chapter of an author's life—and a whodunit that tests even Garda Siobhán O'Sullivan's deductive reasoning . . .

Between training the new town garda and trying to set a wedding date with her fiancé, Macdara Flannery, Siobhán is feeling a bit overwhelmed. She's looking forward to visiting the new bookshop and curling up with an exciting novel—only to discover the shelves contain nothing but Literature with a capital L. The owner not only refuses to stock romances, mysteries, and science fiction, but won't even let customers enter his store unless they can quote James Joyce or Sean Hennessey.

Despite the owner deliberately limiting his clientele, he's hosting a reading and autographing event featuring up and coming Irish writers who will be taking up residency in Kilbane for a month. Among them is indie author Deirdre Walsh, who spends more time complaining about the unfairness of the publishing industry and megastar bestsellers instead of her own creative works, causing a heated debate among the writers. She seems to have a particular distaste for the novels of Nessa Lamb.

Then Deirdre's body is found the next day in the back of the store—with pages torn from Nessa's books stuffed in her mouth. Now, Siobhán must uncover which of Kilbane's literary guests took Deirdre's criticisms so personally they'd engage in foul play . . .

Please turn the page for an exciting sneak peek of Carlene O'Connor's next Irish Village mystery MURDER IN AN IRISH BOOKSHOP coming soon wherever print and e-books are sold!

Chapter 1

The Twins' Inn looked cheery in the orange glow of the morning light. Kilbane, County Cork, Ireland, had a back-in-time charm that often took visitors by surprise. Once befuddled that anyone, let alone Padraig and Oran McCarthy, would open a bookshop here, after spending some time in Kilbane and witnessing its charm, it made perfect sense now. Kilbane may not have held the same bustle as an Irish city, but there was no doubt it had character. Everyone was fast asleep—perhaps the argument that had broken out last night had taken its toll—and now residents were blissfully unaware of the trouble to come. It was a powerful feeling, knowing something they did not. The kind of power a writer well knows, playing God, crafting his or her stories. A tinge of red on the horizon foretold the approach of ominous weather. It was fitting; a storm was brewing in more ways than one. The pair of

gray wolfhounds who had perched last night like statues
by the office door, their regal bodies stiff, their eyes alert
to every sound, was nowhere to be seen. Asleep inside no
doubt. But not for long. *Good boys.*

Everything, in the space of twenty-four hours, had
changed. Human beings never had enough. They were
bottomless pits of need. *Insatiable.* The argument played
internally on an endless loop:

> *You can't do this.*
> *I am already doing it.*
> *I'll ruin you.*
> *I'd like to see you try.*
> *Don't push me. You. Are. No one. You. Are. Nothing.*

Words said in anger. Give it time. Give it a chance. Patience. The most powerful virtue of them all. And time
had gone by. There had been no more mention of this pre-
posterous idea, this act of outright betrayal. One could almost breathe again. Go to bed without worry pressing
down like an anvil. Wake up without the dread of a ringing phone. *Damage control.* One hoped it was all forgotten. Forgiveness was another matter. But then this. A
note. Five little words written on a piece of paper taped to
the door. Five little words. The proverbial cat was out of
the bag, and he was already screeching. The cat might
have nine lives, but humans did not.

One might argue that in the act of putting those five little words to paper, the writer was to blame for what was
to come. The valley of death. *Walk, my lovely, walk.*
There wasn't much time. Every detail must be considered. It would cause waves, of that there was no doubt,
and adjustments would have to be made. No choice, no

choice, no choice. Don't think. Do. Action was character. The method was there, in and out like a soft breath, no need to think twice. Poison. Who needed old lace when arsenic alone would do? Thank heavens the purchase had been made when this avoidable debacle first began. The regular Web now held the same opportunities as the Dark Web. What had been once unthinkable was now easy-peasy. Guided by gut instinct, and backed up by preparation. Preparation was always key. And everyone knows: *practice makes perfect.*

And now, the skies had come to play. Thunder and lightning, nature's stamp of approval. Ireland would see heavy thunderstorms over the next few days and warnings of power outages abounded. The ideal setting for a murder. Atmospheric. *You did this. Your death was brought on by your hands. I am but a messenger.* But first, the details. It was always in the details. The crime scene would tell a story, and a story needed to be shaped.

Connect with Us

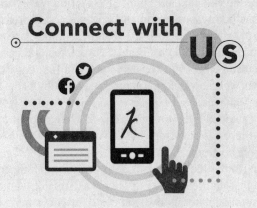

Visit us online at
KensingtonBooks.com
to read more from your favorite authors, see books
by series, view reading group guides, and more.

Join us on social media

for sneak peeks, chances to win books and prize packs,
and to share your thoughts with other readers.

facebook.com/kensingtonpublishing
twitter.com/kensingtonbooks

Tell us what you think!

To share your thoughts, submit a review,
or sign up for our eNewsletters, please visit:
KensingtonBooks.com/TellUs.